The Cr̶̶ Eternal

TRIPOLI
"Blank Check," by Diane Duane: A Templar's faith—and the Temple's future—will be tested by a mystery woman's improbable demand . . .

ACRE
"The Company of Three," by Deborah Turner Harris and Robert J. Harris: A young Knight must decide if a gruesome supernatural relic is the Templars' most sacred treasure—or the cause of their damnation . . .

AVIGNON
"Occam's Razor," by Robert Reginald: A famed Franciscan logician must discover whether Pope Clement and King Philip were murdered—or cursed . . .

THE NEW WORLD
"Stonish Men," by Andre Norton: Pursued by brigands, two settlers discover a gift from the past—and a link to Eternity . . .

POUGHKEEPSIE
"Selling the Devil," by Debra Doyle and James D. Macdonald: The "satanic ritual" was bogus—but now *something* is butchering the participants!

ON CRUSADE
MORE TALES OF THE
KNIGHTS TEMPLAR

EDITED BY
KATHERINE
KURTZ

ASPECT®

WARNER BOOKS

A Time Warner Company

Warner Books, Inc., 1271 Avenue of the Americas, New York, NY 10020
Visit our Web site at http://warnerbooks.com

A Time Warner Company

Printed in the United States of America
First Printing: May 1998
10 9 8 7 6 5 4 3 2 1

Library of Congress Cataloging-in-Publication Data

On crusade : more tales of the Knights Templar / edited by Katherine Kurtz.
    p.   cm.
   ISBN: 0-446-67339-0
     1. Templars—Fiction.   2. Military religious orders—Fiction.
3. Knights and knighthood—Fiction.   4. Historical fiction, American.   5. Middle Ages—Fiction.   6. Crusades—Fiction.
   I. Kurtz, Katherine.
PS648. T4505   1998
813'.0108382557913—dc21   97-34461
                                                                  CIP

Book design by H. Roberts
Cover design by Don Puckey
Cover illustration by Greg Call

Contents

Introduction

Nine centuries ago, in the aftermath of the First Crusade (1095–9), a French knight called Hugues de Payens and eight of his countrymen journeyed to Jerusalem to form a community of warrior-monks who came to be known as the Order of Poor Fellow-Soldiers of Christ and the Temple of Solomon, or, later, the Order of the Temple of Jerusalem: the Knights Templar. Making monastic vows of obedience, chastity, and poverty to the Patriarch of Jerusalem, and granted leave by the newly crowned King Baldwin II of Jerusalem to establish their headquarters near the site of King Solomon's Temple, they were charged with the duty to "maintain, as far as they could, the roads and highways against the ambushes of thieves and attackers, especially in regard to the safety of pilgrims."

From this apparently humble beginning, the Order of the Temple grew to be the single most powerful military presence in the Holy Land—an incomparable fighting machine whose warriors neither asked nor gave quarter, whose rule did not allow them to be ransomed if captured or to retreat from battle unless the numbers of the enemy were at least three times greater than their own—and even then, if ordered by their commander to stand and die, they must do so. Bearded and white-clad, bearing the red cross of martyrdom upon shoulder and breast, and fighting under the distinctive black and white battle standard, Beauceant, their very presence on the field was enough to inspire dread among their adversaries. Their motto proclaimed their devotion to their holy cause: *Non nobis, Domine, non nobis sed nomini tuo da gloriam*—"Not to us, Lord, not to us but to Thy Name give the glory."

Their zeal and single-minded focus on recovering Christianity's sacred places in the Holy Land inspired generous donations of lands and revenues by wealthy patrons eager to support their work and gain favor in the life to come. To manage the assets thus generated, and to facilitate transport of men and matériel for the military operation in the East, they developed a wide range of skills in what, today, we would call "diversified financial services": providing safe deposit facilities, transporting specie and credit for same, acting as agents for collection, administering trusts, arranging finance, holding mortgages, managing properties. The Order flourished for nearly two hundred years, answerable only to the pope, accruing a legacy of legend to augment their worldly success. Such success was bound to generate resentment and envy.

Their world came crashing to a halt on October 13, 1307—a day so infamous that, to this day, Friday the thirteenth conjures a frisson of superstitious dread in the minds of many. In a well-orchestrated operation nearly a year in the planning, officers of King Philip IV of France acted on sealed orders opened simultaneously at dawn and swooped in to arrest every Templar knight, sergeant, and chaplain they could find. By the end of the day, several thousand men lay in chains, on charges that included heresy, blasphemy, various obscenities, and homosexual practices. (For a more detailed account of the charges and subsequent trials, see *Tales of the Knights Templar,* 1995.)

No shred of evidence was ever produced to prove any

of the accusations, though torture and the threat of torture at the hands of the Holy Office of the Inquisition did elicit "confessions" from some of the men. Scores died under torture, a few took their own lives to escape further torture, and more than a hundred knights later recanted their confessions and paid the ultimate price—for relapsed heretics were condemned to burn at the stake. In May of 1310, just outside Paris, fifty-four Templars perished in one day, protesting their innocence to the last; in total, at least one hundred twenty were burned. The last Templars to suffer this fate—and the most famous—were Jacques de Molay, the last Grand Master, and his Preceptor for Normandy, Geoffroi de Charney. The curse pronounced by de Molay would claim the lives of both king and pope within the year.

But in 1118, a glorious future still lay ahead of the fledgling Order—and perhaps a hidden agenda. Though given the charge to protect the pilgrim routes, the founding nine seem to have exerted little military presence during their first decade in Jerusalem. Indeed, these proto-Templars rarely ventured forth from their base camp amid the foundations of King Solomon's Temple (whence they took their Templar name), clothing themselves in cast-off garments, subsisting on the charity of their patrons, keeping to themselves—and engaged in extensive excavations beneath the Temple Mount that have all the earmarks of a highly focused archaeological dig. Nor do they seem to have added to their numbers during this time.

Yet, by the time of the Council of Troyes in 1128–9, the Order burst into prominence with sudden wealth, papal patronage such that they answered only to the pontiff, a rule given them by the future St. Bernard of Clairvaux, and an influx of new recruits whose numbers rapidly multiplied by scores, then hundreds and even thousands. Speculation in recent years suggests that, since they conducted little or no military activity during those first ten years (and, in fact, seemed largely occupied with their excavations beneath the Temple foundations), perhaps their initial purpose in the Holy Land was not the protection of the pilgrim routes at all, but to search for some treasure buried there—and that they found it.

Certain it is that the Order grew rapidly in size, wealth, and influence, and their prowess in battle against the forces of Islam soon assumed the weight of legend. At the same time, they were building one of the finest fleets in the known world and breaking new ground in the field of financial services—and perhaps already well involved, at least at some level, in secret operations of a more mystical nature.

—Katherine Kurtz

Blank Check

Diane Duane

The room was white, as most things were around here. Under the sun that seemed to shine just about every day between March and October, there were few things that did not become blinding even if they were not whitewashed. This at least made writing indoors easy for nearly all one's waking hours, which was just as well, for writing was how de Burgh spent almost all his waking hours anyway.

He breathed out, and lifted his eyes to gaze out the square window at the spill of square houses and buildings and storehouses past the castle walls. Every one of them was white: the whole city of Tripoli was as white as so much spilled salt, scattered in big cubes and small, right down to the hot blue sea. After a long day's work, the hot white light, the glittering blue sea, together left you blinded. He would be glad to escape into the shadows, eventually, when the day drew to a close. But in this pitiless noon, de Burgh could do little but concentrate on his paperwork: it was the only way to make the time go by any faster.

Very little of it was paper, of course. Down here, that would have been even more of an expensive luxury than it was back home.

Home . . . some part of his brain said, thinking of green trees and shade that whispered, instead of the harsh rattling rustle of the palms.

De Burgh put the thought aside, with some annoyance, and bent his attention back to his work. A pile of old and much-recycled parchments lay on the table nearby, and one parchment that would not be recycled any time soon: the monthly report to the regional prior on the chapter's assets. *May 1180* . . . The pen and the inkhorn were well out of reach for the moment, though: de Burgh was doing his figuring on the third of a set of wax tablets that he was astonished were not melting, considering the hot wind coming in off the sea, strongly enough to occasionally lift the piled-up parchments.

The columns of Arabic digits on the wax tablet got longer and longer. The chapter's assets were considerable, this time of year. Since the late spring, repayments of loans, with the usual attached "gifts" from the grateful debtors, had been flowing in. Some of these repayments and gifts—never say "interest": usury was illegal—were due to profit from early crops, or speculations on the crops of the upcoming seasons. Futures trading had become very popular in the eastern Mediterranean when the countries interested in selling goods and services to the Crusaders realized that there were some things, like food, that would have to be purchased eventually, no matter how much the Crusaders brought with them in the way of supplies.

The other major source of funds was booty. It was a touch early in the season for that, but de Burgh expected he would see the first shipments coming in for assay within the next few weeks. The sword might be mighty, but when it came time for assessments, the pen had the final say: he had seen great lords watch his stylus working on the wax pad as fixedly as any man might watch the knife leveled at his throat.

De Burgh's assistant Jacquelin came in: a young knight wearing what his master wore in this weather, just a light, sleeveless pale tunic with the Order's cross over a lighter shirt of cotton, and cotton breeches. His arms were full of parchments, rolled up, and a few sewn together in informal flat reference codices. These he put carefully down at the far end of the table.

"Those are the redemption-in-kind records from last year?" said de Burgh.

"Yes, sir. They were misfiled."

De Burgh sighed. It was hard to keep staff around here long enough to teach them the filing system. Either they tended to be inept, so that he had them sent elsewhere, or else they were clever and quick but wanted to go off somewhere and fight, and pulled every string they could to make it happen. Usually de Burgh complied, since unwilling laborers in this particular vineyard could cost one of the bank's patrons vast sums if records were lost—and when your patrons were people like the King of France, their annoyance was not something you courted.

At least Jacquelin was careful about his work and seemed interested in finance. *If he lasts,* de Burgh thought, *he might be my replacement someday. And I can go home. . . .*

He put the thought aside again. "All right. What kind of appointments do we have this afternoon?"

"Nothing. The ship's captain who was coming in seems to have sailed without bothering."

De Burgh put his eyebrows up. "Without sending word? I wonder if something's going on out there that we ought to know about. . . ."

"When *isn't* there, sir?" said Jacquelin.

De Burgh breathed out once, as close as he got to a laugh in front of his juniors. "Well. My pitcher's empty."

"Yes, sir," Jacquelin said, picking up the red clay pitcher from the windowsill where it sat in hope of catching some cooling breeze.

Wan hope . . . de Burgh thought, as Jacquelin went out.

The sound of footsteps faded away down the stone stairs, and de Burgh allowed himself one more silent laugh. Jacquelin was, of course, right. This place was a war zone: you never dared forget it. Every twitch of a sail, the wind changing quarters, a man missing an appointment—or changing it—could make you sit up and wonder whether the next morning would dawn on an enemy fleet in the harbor.

War . . . years of it. They had been the cause, some thirty years ago now, of the Bishop of Tripoli coming to plead with the visiting Templar Commander of Acre to take his castle, please!

"I can't defend it," he had admitted, finally, after exhausting all the other good reasons, financial and otherwise, that the Templars should take it over.

And that reason, more than any other, had weighed heavy with the Commander. Almost all the great trading cities of the Mediterranean—the great *Christian* trading cities—had large and reliable garrisons to secure the castles that dominated them. That there should be one city lacking such a garrison . . . would attract unwelcome attention. The Templars in general, and de Burgh in particular, were all too aware of the interested eyes of the Berber tribes gazing at Tripoli from the desert, always on the lookout for a way to further their cause with the great sultanates to the east. The castle of Tortosa, dominating this great bay and harbor—and, past it, the whole coastal sea lane from Morocco to Egypt—could have tempted even the sultanates themselves to make a grab, had it fallen out of proper defensive posture . . .

. . . which, at that point, it already had, for the Bishop of Tripoli was prince of a very dwindling local church, indeed. Christians, except those passing through for trade or on their way to the wars, were thin on the ground here, and the Bishop—mostly thrown on his own resources by a Rome that had problems enough elsewhere—was very short of money.

And there was another problem: The Count of Tripoli had had a disagreement with the Knights Hospitallers. After giving *them* Tortosa and another Tripolitan castle in 1142, and the right to have their own military relations with the Turks, the Count had taken the donatives back again only nine years later. Some personal matter between him and Rome, de

Burgh had heard. There was nothing left to judge by but gossip, since the Count was long dead—at Acre, de Burgh thought. But Tortosa, which had so long been defended for free (from the Bishop's point of view), was empty . . . and the Bishop could hear the Berbers stirring in the desert, like mice rustling in the presses.

So the Templars had listened to the Bishop's desperate requests, and had moved into Tortosa a little after 1152, seeing to the castle's fortifications, and looked around to rejuvenate other matters as well. The Hospitallers had had a small banking facility here for some years, nothing fancy—just straightforward draft payments, no foreign exchange—but around 1150, as Christian merchants became fewer, they had withdrawn in advance of the Count's tantrum, leaving a vacuum in the local business community that the Templars had been only too glad to fill.

And de Burgh was kept busy enough filling it. He had seven other staff besides Jacquelin, mostly busy with accounting and filing, and sometimes he wondered if they were enough.

Footsteps on the stairs again. Unlikely that Jacquelin would have been all the way down to the well and back already.

The young knight put his head in the door. "Sir," he said, "there's a lady downstairs to see you."

He blinked. "We don't do private banking in the mornings, everybody knows that. Ask her to come back this afternoon."

"She says she can't stay that long, sir. I think she may be sailing shortly. But she has a sealed draft."

De Burgh put his eyebrows up. "Where's she from?"

Jacquelin shook his head. "Her clothes are local . . . but that could mean anything. Her accent—" He shrugged a little. "She might be from Jerusalem, or she might have stayed there awhile."

De Burgh sat back in the chair, tossed the stylus to the table; he was sick of looking at the wax pads, as it was. "All right," he said, "ask her to come up. Is she attended?"

"No, sir, she came alone."

Interesting: women of quality rarely went unattended in this part of the world. Yet if she wasn't a woman of quality, what was she doing with a sealed draft . . . ? "Send her up, then," de Burgh said, "and leave her with me."

He waited while the footsteps dwindled away down the stairs, then came up again. De Burgh listened for the second set of feet on the stairs . . . and couldn't hear a thing.

She was in the room before he thought she would be: a dark form, very discreet, completely robed in black, and veiled in the same, though in a material just sheer enough to see through, while very effectively hiding the face. The robes and veil were well made, and expensive: de Burgh knew very well what that particularly fine-woven muslin went for in the markets.

He rose to greet her, slightly nettled that he had not been on his feet when she came in, but she moved so quietly . . .

"Sir," she said in lingua franca that did, indeed, have a touch of that Jerusalem drawl about it, "thank you for seeing me."

"A pleasure to be of service, madam. Will you sit?"

She sat down gracefully in the chair across from his. De Burgh turned to Jacquelin, and said, "I won't need you for a while."

"Yes, sir," said Jacquelin, as casually as if the phrase had not really meant, *Stay within earshot.* He went off down the stairs again.

"My assistant tells me that you have a sealed draft to be handled."

"Yes," she said. A slender hand, graceful and lined, emerged from under the dark robes and handed him a parchment, a foot long and half a foot wide folded, bound around with linen strings and two seals, one of wax, one of lead. His attention at the moment, though, was less on the seals than on the hand. It had seen hard work, in its time: the back of it was netted with tiny wrinkles, and old calluses had left their ghosts between thumb and forefinger; she had done her share of spinning. But the hand had not done much of that kind of work lately. Some great lady's servant, perhaps once a slave and now freed? But not a young woman at all. Maybe as old as fifty . . . ?

He looked at the seals. "I take it," said de Burgh, testing his conclusion, "that you are acting for another."

A pause. Odd how you could get the feeling that you were being smiled at, without actually being able to see the expression. The smile was not mocking: de Burgh had a feeling that she found something about her business amusing. "Yes," she said.

The seals were those of the Commandatory of the Land of Jerusalem, the administrative headquarters of the Templar treasury. The leaden seal showed, on the obverse, the horse with its two knights mounted up, symbol of the Order's vow of individual poverty; the reverse showed the cross patée and, surrounding it, the inscription D•G•COM•TERR•IERUSALEM. The presence of this seal confirmed that the document had been through the Commander's office and had been seen, either by him or his personal secretary. It was useful as an authentifier—the serrations at the outside of the seal had a few "teeth" missing in a way that might look accidental, due to wear, but was not.

The wax seal, though, was where more important coding might lie, and de Burgh looked at it with more care. It was red wax, still smelling faintly of the bitter tincture of myrrh that was always mixed with it. He scratched it with a thumbnail: it resisted, as it was meant to, and flaked slightly at the spot. This wax was purposely made too friable to carve, to prevent alterations after it had hardened. Embedded in it were the proper black and brown specks: not just sand left over from drying ink on the parchment, as might have been assumed by someone who didn't know better, but sand without a single white grain in it. The design was identical to that on the lead seal, except that the missing serrations were slightly different. Their order held a code that identified the date on which the document had been sent out, as a further check on the contents: if the inside and outside dates were mismatched by more than three days, the draft was invalid, since all drafts written at a given Templar banking house had to be issued and dispatched within that period. De Burgh noted the date—the eleventh of April—and opened the draft.

It was written in the small, fine hand of one of the secretaries at the Preceptory there. *Pay to the bearer, regardless of person . . .*

He stopped.

. . . an amount without limit, to be designated by the bearer.

He had never seen a draft like *that* before.

Impossible. If drafts like this were allowed, anyone could walk in and simply empty *the place. . . .*

Yet here it lay before him. In growing nervousness, he lifted the parchment right to his eyes and peered at it. Coded seals were one thing, but there was one aspect of their bearer drafts that the Templars knew no one had yet managed to counterfeit—though there had been some interesting attempts.

Parchment, after all, had been part of a living thing at one time. There were cattle farms in the South of France where, about two months before a given group of cows was scheduled to be slaughtered, they were quietly taken off separately into a shed. There, a wooden implement was used numerous times on their flanks. The implement was a handle with a block of wood at the far end: embedded in the block of wood were long slim needles in a specific pattern. The piercings would quickly heal up, but when the cows were later slaughtered and their hides processed for vellum, the fine scars of the needle-marks, now healed, would show in the finished parchment. Each month's markings were different, and each Templar banking establishment received notification, every month, of which pattern was valid for the month in question. There was no faking this "watermarking" of the parchment.

The draft now lying before de Burgh had the correct watermarking for April.

He sat back in his chair.

I can't honor this draft—

—but I can't not honor it—

De Burgh swallowed. The only test remaining to him would be to compare the document against its counterfoil, which would be kept at the issuing Preceptory. If the counterfoil, or "check" as some called it, matched the original document, there would be no problem: the transaction was authorized. If not . . .

Blank bearer drafts had occasionally been stolen from Templar banking facilities before and forged, and *very* occasionally cashed. But not often. This kind of transaction—"buying" a piece of, in itself, worthless parchment in one place, and then redeeming it for its face value in another—was a very new development in the way money was handled. Its practitioners tended to be very cautious about the redemptions; if one went wrong, the knight handling the transaction was held responsible and dealt with accordingly—that is, as if he had been complicit in a fraud. No one working at the banking end would soon forget what had happened to the Preceptor of the Irish Preceptory, Walter le Bacheler, who had been caught embezzling Order funds, and at his trial had been sentenced to be locked up in the London Preceptory, in a cell so small he could neither sit nor lie down. It took him eight weeks to die.

De Burgh had no desire to see the inside of that room under any circumstances. Yet, if he honored the draft in front of him, he was certain that he would see it, and sooner rather than later.

He very much wanted some way out of this situation. He turned to the lady and said, "You cannot possibly expect me to— What do you want this *for*? Whom do you represent?"

"Sir knight, you astonish me. That is not your business to ask. Anonymity for the redeemer is the whole purpose of this kind of bearer draft." Once again he got a sense of that slight smile behind the veil.

She was, unfortunately, right. He tried again. "The amount—the way it is written is completely irregular. Unheard-of. I cannot honor it without first checking with the Treasurer in Jerusalem—"

"You must honor it," she said. "It is not counterfeit . . . as you know."

"But—"

"If you do not honor it, I will first go to the Bishop," the lady said. "I will tell him that you have refused to pay a bearer draft. He will not care very much about the circumstances. He will, properly, be very concerned. So will all the businessmen and merchants in this city when they hear about it—in a matter of hours, I should think: the Bishop is not as restrained as he might be in whom he talks to—and many others all up and down these coasts will become just as concerned. It would be only a very short time before word got back to Europe, for messages of this urgency certainly travel by more means than just the sea roads. Should confidence in Templar banking be undermined in *Europe* because of your actions . . . then you, personally, sir knight, would have much more serious concerns than the state of the treasury of Tortosa. And I doubt you would have those other concerns for very long."

De Burgh thought of that little cell in London, and swallowed.

"What then, lady, is the amount you are seeking?"

"I would hope to have your advice on that matter," she said. "I need a quotation for the cost of about four hundred thousand cubic ells of stone—*removed*."

His mind was already doing calculations, which started and then had to stop again as she pronounced the last word. "An excavation—"

"Several of them."

"But, for what purposes—"

"Well," she said, "I suppose you must know that in a general way, for the sake of the calculation. I am acting for a man who is about to be in a position of some influence in Ethiopia. He is building . . . a fortress, a place of protection."

"By excavation."

"There are valleys in his domains suitable for such use. The total amount of stone to be removed is as I have quoted it. More must be carved and fashioned after that work is done. My principal estimates that several thousand workmen and artisans will be needed for at least five years."

He shook his head, dazed. "A fortress," he said. "In the middle of nowhere. For protection against *what?*" Ethiopia was a vast desert, hiding nothing of value—not since the ancient kings and queens of the place had stripped it bare and then vanished themselves. Nomadic tribes roamed there, tending their few lean cattle . . .

. . . or so de Burgh had heard. Was there possibly more that could be said about the place?

Or was he being colossally tricked?

"Who is this man?" he said.

"He is a King," she said. "Or is about to be."

Oh Lord in heaven, de Burgh thought, *I am going to give her*—he went over the figures in his head again, for that kind of labor, for that kind of time, and found the answer not at all improved—*just about all the money in our treasury! For what? Some obscure dynastic war, most likely. This isn't about any building, any fortress, this is insane. . . .*

Her eyes rested on him, serene.

And there lay the draft . . . genuine.

Apparently.

He stared at it. He knew it was real, by every test he knew how to apply to such a document. The only thing wrong with it was the amount. No one had ever drawn up a draft in such a way.

But that doesn't mean they couldn't, he thought.

De Burgh looked at the draft.

What do I do now?

Should he trust to his professional assessment . . . even though it flew in the face of everything he knew? Or should he deny his own judgment . . . and possibly bring his world crashing down around his ears as a result?

No one would think it unreasonable, the thought came suddenly to de Burgh, *if you held this woman in Tortosa, just for the few days until confirmation came through. The situation is so irregular, and the—*

"If you are thinking of keeping me here," said the woman, "I would advise against it. There are people waiting for me, and they know where I have gone, and on what business. News that the Order was interfering with a legitimate business customer—no matter how odd *you* may find the circumstances— would spread as quickly as the news that you had failed to cash a draft. With similar results. The whole success of the Order's financial side lies in the fact that they can be trusted not to sell the passengers their ships carry, into slavery . . . that they can be safely entrusted with things of great worth . . . that they can be *trusted.* Hold just one poor woman against her will while you reassure your own fears for yourself and your position . . . and who knows if the King of England will ever deposit the Crown Jewels with you again?"

He looked at her.

I am good at my job, de Burgh thought. *That's why I was placed here. What if this draft is genuine, and I don't cash it?*

But if it's not . . .

He took a long breath.

"I must ask you to unveil," he said. "Should this— I mean—"

"You must, of course, be able to describe me to your superiors," she said. "I understand."

She reached down and lifted the veil. She was dark, very dark indeed. The face was a little sharp, the high cheekbones perfectly setting off the long, elegant, aristocratic nose. Her looks were eloquent of good blood; perhaps even Ethiopian, though it was hard to tell. Her eyes rested on him, serene.

"Well," she said, "will you have faith in me?"

He breathed in, breathed out. "It is one of the commodities," de Burgh said, "in which bankers do not commonly deal without security."

She simply sat and looked at him.

Lord, he thought, perfectly poised between terror and indecision, *send me a sign! What should I do??*

Nothing happened.

Trust. Do you trust your instincts . . . enough to bet your life on them?

He breathed in, breathed out . . .

. . . then reached across to the draft, pulled his pen close, and his inkwell, and inked the pen, and signed the draft. His hand shook: he had rarely had so much trouble writing the word "Executed."

De Burgh turned toward the door, and said, loudly enough for it to carry, "Jacquelin?"

Footsteps on the stair. Jacquelin came in, waited. He looked rather pale.

De Burgh entirely understood why. He swallowed. "First, go down to the gates and let the warders know that no one is to be admitted to or let out of the fortress until this lady leaves. Then you will take care of her needs. She will require armed escort to her ship, and a small pack train. Have the grooms get five mules ready—no, six. Tell Gironde and Malplaquet to go to the main treasury and pack all the high-denomination coin, and approximately forty pounds of plate gold in addition. Pack it all up securely and try not to be too obvious about it; and be quick— if the gates are closed too long, people will start talking."

"Sir. *All* the high-denomination gold?"

"All of it. Go swiftly."

*   *   *

And swiftly it was done. When word was brought that the mules were ready, de Burgh got up, and said, "You will pardon me, lady, but if I go down to see you off, that will attract attention. Otherwise, you might be carrying any sort of trade goods in those coffers: we get a certain amount of redemption in kind, and I shall see that Jacquelin has given you a few bolts of silk to make up the final tally, and confuse the unwary."

"So I see. I thank you for your thoughtfulness."

"And if you will now kindly sign this receipt."

She signed it in a long flow of characters that de Burgh recognized as a Hebraic cursive; then she stood up, and bowed slightly to him as she let her veil fall once more. "Until we meet again," she said. "Though that will not be here."

"No?"

She shook her head. "You will not be here that much longer," she said, calm-voiced, as if reporting yesterday's news rather than tomorrow's. "Time brings its changes. . . ."

She went out of the room, after Jacquelin. A while later, the gates boomed closed, and the sound of them made de Burgh shudder.

He saw no one else all that afternoon. With his tiniest and most delicate pen, a mere sliver of metal, de Burgh spent the afternoon copying out the document on a sheet of the very thinnest of paper, almost exactly as the original had been written, except for the size. It was tedious work, but he was good at it: in his training, to teach him how to recognize counterfeits, he had been well trained in making them himself. He carefully noted the codings and marks that appeared on the seals. He noted, and copied in small, the coding in the pattern tattooed into the parchment. And when that copy was made, he made another one. At the bottom of each of them he made a record of the transaction, and a copy of the woman's signature on the receipt.

He sat gazing at his work for a long while, and finally had to stop, since the sun was starting to get low.

"Jacquelin?" he said, and the young man came in with a pigeon in a cage, one of their trained carriers.

"Jerusalem, sir?" said Jacquelin.

"That's right," said de Burgh.

They folded the delicate paper small and packed it into the capsule that would be fastened to the bird's foot. While Jacquelin was making it fast, de Burgh held the bird, stroking it, and then looked it in the eye.

"Don't get killed," he whispered.

"She won't," Jacquelin said. "She's our fastest."

"Not half fast enough for me," de Burgh said, and threw her out the window. The bird found her wings, circled once, and then shot off eastward, quickly lost in the still-blinding day.

De Burgh spent three awful nights during which he did not sleep, and three days during which he avoided his paperwork. He had never done such a thing before. But if he finished his paperwork now, he would have to write down the fatal total at the bottom of that parchment.

Coward, coward, part of his brain railed at him, as he paced around the table, unable to sit at it and write down that one last string of figures. *Where are your oaths, to serve your Order faithfully?* But he simply could not do it.

On the third day, as he paced, staggering, in the thin light of dawn, de Burgh saw the flutter out over the water: not a gull. He leaned on the windowsill and watched the brown-and-white bird come. It flew straight to the accustomed window, farther down in the fortress. As it ruffled its feathers back into place, and bobbed and cooed on the sill for a moment before a hand came out and snatched it in, de Burgh felt his tongue cleave, dry, to the roof of his dry mouth, as if he saw the sword coming toward him and was unable to stop it, the way he had seen it come when he had been fighting in Egypt under Amalric so long ago.

He stood there by the window and trembled: it was all the response that was left in him. Some few minutes later, young

Jacquelin, looking nearly as haggard as he did, came pounding up the stairs and lurched into the room. He handed de Burgh the capsule.

His hands shaking, de Burgh cracked it open, extracted the small piece of paper, unfolded it, stared at it.

Authorized, said the first word.

He stuck there for a long time, unable to read past that word, lost in a welter of conflicting emotions: relief, shame at his own fear, astonishment. Eventually he made his way to the next sentence.

Counterfoil matches. Transshipment of funds to support pending transactions is being arranged: expect first shipments early next month.

Jacquelin was shifting from foot to foot. "Sir?" he said. "*Sir?*"

"Approved," de Burgh whispered. "Oh, my God, approved . . ."

And he passed out.

There were a thousand questions he wanted to ask about the transaction, as he finally finished up his paperwork for May. When a ship came in with documents from Jerusalem three weeks later, de Burgh looked all through them for any mention of the draft. There was none.

De Burgh was not a foolish man. The funds he had been promised arrived two weeks after that; and even in the documents accompanying them, there was no mention of the draft. From this he gathered that those high up thought the matter was better not mentioned again . . . so he did not mention it, or the lady, to anyone.

For a while he thought of her often; then, as a year passed, two years, less often; then, hardly at all. Then 1188 rolled around, and the dust clouds on the horizon and the lateen-rigged sails in the harbor suddenly told the world that change was coming again. The occupants of Tortosa had had some warning, but even advance warning did not make it any more pleasant when Saladin and his armies stood at your gates and began banging on them.

Tripoli was shattered in the assault, though Tortosa stood, too well defended and well built, with its back against the sheer sea-cliffs, to fall. Young Jacquelin went out to fight, along with many another Templar who used the pen more frequently than the sword. He did not come back. De Burgh did, though with another wound that laid him up for months; finally they sent him back to Jerusalem, where the doctors, supposedly, were better.

He was not so sure of that himself. The fever associated with the wound kept recurring for months more, no matter how they bled him, and he would lie for days and rave, and waken feeble and confused, to lie that way for days more. The dreams were very strange.

She walked into one of them, one still and baking-hot night, when no breeze came in through his sickroom window from the sea. But it was not his sickroom: it was the old room where he did his figuring in Tortosa, the room that had had the wall knocked out of it by a stone-cast during the siege. It was unhurt now, though, and his old table stood where it had before, and his chair. He sat in the chair, and across from it, she sat again, veiled, and under the veil, smiling.

"Tell me now," he said. "Tell me who you are."

"I am a guardian," she said. "One of many."

"What do you guard?"

The answer to the question was there on the table before him; staggered by the blazing brilliance of it, he turned his face away, closed his eyes, covered his eyes. It did no good. He could still see the cup. The ferocious light of it, as if it were carved out of lightning instead of olivewood, struck as relentlessly through his flesh as if through air or water—

—and was gone. He would have slid out of his chair and to his knees, but was too weak to move.

"And it will be kept . . . in the place that money built, in that 'fortress' you spoke of?" he whispered, when he could find the strength.

"I would not say 'kept.' But it will always be there. Even when it seems not to be . . . or when it seems to be somewhere else."

He shook his head, bewildered.

She laughed. "Omnipresence," she said, "is an attribute of godhead, so they say. And how can something that God has touched, not become God? How can the making fail to be part of the maker?"

She lifted the veil again, shaking her head a little as if the heat bothered her, and she was glad to be rid of it. "There may sometimes seem to be more than one of what we guard," she said. "There's purpose in that: a wise guardian knows how to misdirect the search for his charge when the wicked come hunting it for their own ends. Counterfeits . . ." She smiled at him, a slightly wicked look. "Yet it would be cruel to toy with those who truly seek. The true searchers *do* find what they seek . . . no matter which one they stumble across at last."

"But that one . . . surely *that* one was real—"

She laughed, looked out the window at the hot white sun and the stark blue shadows, the unforgiving, concrete landscape, all hard edges and blinding color. "In *this* world," she said, her voice amused, "what makes you think the word 'real' applies at all?"

He was bewildered, but the Order had its own mysteries, which had often bewildered him just as badly, and he had learned over time not to waste time trying to unravel the subtleties of philosophers. The riddles would come undone in their own time, or not: this dark sibyl was plainly not going to sit down and undo the knots for him.

"Still," she said, "you had faith. And it lives, now, in what you built . . ."

. . . which towered, or rather yawned, before him.

Fortresses, indeed, he thought in the dream, amused; for though they could have been held as such, in case of attack, that was hardly their purpose. They were churches. In this desolate and seemingly uninhabitable place, a great empty plain of red stone all cracked with great fissures, massive churches had been cut out of the ground. First the red volcanic rock had been excavated, in great trenches, from the fissures, leaving, in each one, a huge central block of stone untouched. Then the blocks themselves had been hollowed out for apses and chapels, halls and hermits' cells and colonnades and cloisters: all delicately ornamented, graved and carven and painted with countless holy images. Again and again de Burgh saw the cross patée, in paintings on ceilings and walls, carven into the stone of the floors, embedded in massive columns. Not just decoration: acknowledgment. Among the columns, robed figures moved, chanting never-ending prayer to the Maker of something that was housed there . . . or seemed to be . . . and, there, would always have a safe place to which to retire.

The dream passed. De Burgh woke weak again, but it seemed that the worst of the fever had passed with that last bout of madness. He improved enough to be able to travel, and the doctors thought it would be best if he went home to France. When he was recovered enough, he made his way to Acre to take ship for home. There, since the party with whom he traveled had a couple of days to spare before the ship sailed, he went with them to see the celebrated ebony image in the church there.

He had not realized that ebony is not usually black unless treated in certain ways. This image, surrounded by an elaborate gilded reredos to protect it from the smoke of the church, had kept ebony's true color, that deep rich brown with the hint of the equatorial sun in it. The color struck him instantly as familiar. But what astonished him—struck him silent for many minutes, so that his host thought he had become lost in artistic appreciation—was the image's face: a little sharp, the high cheekbones perfectly setting off the long, elegant, aristocratic nose; the face eloquent of good blood, very good blood, in the recent past . . . and, as he now recognized, in the distant past as well. Very good blood indeed: the woman was crowned with the stars, and the crescent moon peered out somewhat apprehensively from under her long, plain gown, and under her heel, a serpent's head was crushed.

He sank to his knees, very belatedly, half expecting the image's face to move and show him what he was sure the woman's face would have showed: just the faintest annoyance, tempered by a mother's understanding of her children's tendency to overreact. Well enough he knew the images of this woman that had been sent into the world as hints of what was yet to come—moon-goddesses, goddesses of fruitfulness, dark-faced powers that hinted at present or future rule over the heavens and the earth. Now, though, rather belatedly, he understood the slight amusement at his statement: "I take it that you are acting for another."

His companions were slightly surprised by his reaction. He let them be. The next day he went back to France, where the shade whispered rather than rattled, and settled into the routine at the Paris Preceptory, where he spent his last days.

Even there, though, they noticed how old de Burgh never drank from any cup without looking at it for a surprisingly long time, and smiling a slow, strange smile. . . .

INTERLUDE ONE

There can be little doubt that the Templars played a significant role in developing the foundations of Western banking practices. Less certain is any obvious connection with Ethiopia. Yet the excavation described to de Burgh in the previous story could well refer to a spectacular series of eleven rock-hewn churches mysteriously carved out of the red volcanic tuff at Roha, near Axun, in Ethiopia. The structures were commissioned around 1190 by one Lalibela, an exiled Ethiop prince recently returned, after a twenty-five-year sojourn in Jerusalem, to take back his throne—and perhaps should be ranked among the wonders of the ancient world, in terms of workmanship and aesthetics.

The technology by which they were created remains a mystery. The legends speak of them being made by "red-and-white men," perhaps an allusion to the Templars' white mantles bearing the red cross. These legends connect, in turn, with stories of a fabulous treasure being brought out of Jerusalem to Ethiopia: the lost Ark of the Covenant—which, perhaps, is what the Templars had been looking for under the Temple in those early years. Built as a resting place to house the Ark, the Temple was destroyed by the Babylonians in 587 B.C. But Ethiopian Orthodox Christians claim that the Ark was carried away just ahead of the destroyers; that it was hidden away for many hundreds of years, until it eventually came to rest in a church very like those carved from the red volcanic rock; and that it rests there to this day, in a church dedicated to St. Mary of Zion, the Mother of Jesus, secreted within a Holy of Holies and tended by an Orthodox priest whose only function is to guard and serve it. A British television crew tried to investigate the claim several years ago, but, as expected, they were not allowed access to the inside of the church. Is it the current resting place of the Ark? No one knows.

This may seem an odd diversion, but the Ethiopian connection with the Templars is important, whether or not the Ark now rests in that far land. The sudden appearance of the technology necessary to build the churches cannot be explained by modern architects and engineers; Ethiopian legend ascribes it to the handiwork of angels. Nor can the "experts" explain the slightly earlier explosion of new technology that was expressed in the sudden blossoming of Gothic architecture in France in the 1130s, immediately after the Council of Troyes gave the Temple official status. The north porch of the Cathedral of Chartres, perhaps the crown jewel of all Gothic cathedrals, depicts the Queen of Sheba, who was Ethiopian, whose son by King Solomon was the ancestor of that same King Lalibela who built the red churches. (It should be noted here that Chartres was in the domain of the Count of Champagne, who was kin to Hugues de Payens, the founder of the Templars, and who himself joined the Order as its eleventh member in 1124–5. Furthermore, most of the other founding members had connections with the counts of Champagne or a few other interrelated ruling families of the area.) Close by can be seen a Grail containing a Stone and a depiction of the Ark of the Covenant being moved. Like many a Gothic cathedral built at that time, Chartres is dedicated to the Virgin Mary; and though the Madonna of Chartres is not a Black Virgin, many others are, perhaps in reflection of the Woman glimpsed by our Templar de Burgh.

The building of Chartres also coincides with the first mention of the Grail in literature, in an unfinished narrative poem written in 1182 by Chrétien de Troyes, whose principal patron was the Countess of Champagne. His theme was then picked up by Wolfram von Eschenbach, who in 1195–1200 began writing *Parzival,* building on the work of Chrétien and transforming the Grail into a Stone, and incorporating many Ethiopian elements, and Prester John, and the Templars as guardians of the Grail. The ripples extending outward from these connections and "coincidences" are many and varied, and begin to elaborate upon the hints of something mystical about the Knights Templar, something to account for their unprecedented success.

Indeed, resentment of the Templars' rapid accumulation of wealth and their success in general in the two centuries that followed were contributory to their eventual downfall—and perhaps fueled later speculation that the vast treasure amassed by the Temple not only was of a physical nature, but also included more esoteric treasures: mystical and even magical knowledge and/or powers. The persistence of interest in this particular Order, long after its abolition and far out of proportion to the other great crusading Orders, and ongoing speculation about the nature of the "Templar secrets" do suggest that, whether or not it was true, at least people *believed* that the Templars had knowledge of this sort—and it was part of what led to their downfall.

The presumed connection of the Temple with the Holy Grail persisted through the centuries. Whether or not they ever possessed it, or even were instrumental in providing it a safe haven, we probably shall never know. But it is historical fact that the Templars did, indeed, accumulate a variety of religious relics of various sorts and various faiths, in addition to their vast wealth of a more conventional nature. Some were sublimely beautiful or supremely important as objects inspiring faith, such as fragments of the True Cross, perhaps the Shroud, perhaps various Hebrew artifacts possibly recovered whilst carrying out their excavations beneath Temple Mount. Some, without doubt, would have been very dangerous, as we shall see.

The Company of Three

Deborah Turner Harris
and Robert J. Harris

Armageddon had come to Acre.

Christ's Kingdom was dying before his eyes, and for the first time in his life, Armand Breville found that his prayers were stillborn on his lips. For months, the armies of the Prophet had pressed against the walls of the city with the determined ferocity of a man who sees final victory only inches from his grasp, and now those walls were crumbling like a thin line of sand giving way before the incoming tide. Surveying the enemy from his post on the city's north rampart, the young Templar knight grasped the hilt of his cruciform sword tightly in both hands, as though that symbol of his faith could supply him with the strength he knew he would need to sustain him through this ultimate trial.

Six weeks ago the besieging armies of Sultan Al-Ashraf Khalil had arrived outside the walls of the city of Acre, last remaining bastion of the crusader Kingdom of Jerusalem. Overwhelming in their numbers, the Mamelukes had come equipped with a daunting array of catapults and mangonels. That night, the enemy watch-fires dotted the surrounding plain for as far as the eye could see. With the coming of the dawn, a deafening blare of trumpets and kettledrums signaled the first attack.

During the days that followed, the skies over Acre rained down a continuous storm of arrows and mangonel-shot. The city's defenders, for their part, stood firm, fortified by the knowledge that their walls and bastions were as formidable as human ingenuity could make them.

Repeated appeals to the rest of Christendom for military support had failed to elicit more than a token response. Pope Nicholas IV had sent a small army of peasant levies from Italy, but these had proved more trouble than they were worth. The monarchs of the Christian West, their minds set on their con- flicting feudal interests and struggles for succession, had turned their backs on Outremer, leaving the citizens of Acre to fend for themselves.

Now, after weeks of unceasing bombardment and fanatical assault, the final battle was upon them, but no angels filled the skies and no legion of saints marched to the aid of the belea- guered Christians, to save this last remnant of their hard-won kingdom from being swept into the sea. If it had been God's will that Christ's armies should have captured Jerusalem from the Unbelievers and established a kingdom there in His name, how, Armand wondered, could He turn His back now, in this most desperate hour, leaving them to flee for their lives or die where they stood beneath the swords of their foes? The question hung over him like a shadow, even as he watched the enemy swarm- ing among the broken ruins of the outer fortifications.

It was two years since Armand had taken his final vows as a knight of the Order of the Temple. When he closed his eyes, he could still see, as if in a dream, the preceptory chapel in his native Brittany, where he had been received under the spon- sorship of his mother's brother, Sir Geoffrey de St. Brieuc. He had given his word with a whole heart, dedicating himself and his fighting arm in good faith to the service of God. Now it seemed as if God held that service in so small esteem that He was prepared to fling their lives away in pointless martyrdom.

There were outbreaks of skirmishing all up and down the length of the inner battlements, sudden and bloody clashes of steel and the clamor of rival battle cries. On the north rampart a warning trumpet sounded the call to arms as a large company of white-clad desert warriors broke away from the main battle line and hurled themselves at the Templar Ward. The response from the citadel was a hiss of arrows and crossbow bolts. Many of the attackers dropped in their tracks, but the rest surged on, screaming imprecations to Allah as they came.

The vanguard reached the base of the tower. Urged on by their officers, the rank and file began flinging up siege ladders. Within moments, the walls were swarming with white-clad shapes. There was an answering flash of steel from the battlements above as the Templar defenders drew their swords and charged forward to meet the attackers.

Within seconds the enemy were swarming over the parapet. Yelling encouragement to the men flanking him, Armand felled one adversary with a scything sweep of his longsword. Before another could take his place, the young knight gripped the top of the nearest ladder and dislodged it with a forceful shove. The ladder toppled backward and crashed to the ground, taking four of the attackers with it.

With a fierce whoop of satisfaction, Armand sidestepped to meet another rank of intruders head-on. One man went down with his skull split. A second fell back disarmed and was promptly dispatched by one of the Frankish bowmen. Heedless of his own safety, Armand hacked his way through a thicket of enemy blades until something heavy fetched him a ringing blow to the back of the head.

His helmet took the brunt of the stroke, but the impact half stunned him. As he staggered to his knees, his assailant kicked the sword from his hand. He tumbled backward and found himself gazing up into the snarling face of a white-turbaned officer. Poised in the air between them was a razor-sharp scimitar.

Glaring defiantly up at his assailant, Armand braced himself for the killing stroke. In the same instant, from somewhere off to his left, came a lightning flash of movement. The

Mameluke gave a mortal cry and toppled aside, his innards spilling from the wide gash that had been opened in his belly. Standing over him, with bloodied blade in hand, was Vicente Ibanez, Armand's battle-hardened commander.

The lean, hawk-nosed face beneath the Spaniard's helm was as dark as that of any Saracen. It was a face that might have looked forbidding to anyone who had not seen him smile and speak a kind word of encouragement to a young brother newly arrived in this strange land. Armand knew little of Vicente's past, other than the fact that he had previously distinguished himself as a soldier and scholar at the court of Alphonso the Wise, King of Castile. Vicente's exotic appearance, combined with his command of the Eastern languages, had allowed him to travel in disguise far beyond the narrow borders of the Christian kingdom, returning with vital intelligence for the Grand Master.

Before Armand could summon a word of thanks, the older knight reached down and hauled him unceremoniously to his feet. "Pick up your sword," he ordered brusquely, "and come with me."

The fighting had receded toward the other side of the roof-gallery. The clash of weaponry was subsiding, indicating that the enemy had been driven into retreat for the time being. Armand hastily retrieved his weapon.

"Where are we going?" he demanded breathlessly.

Vicente's face was tight. "The preceptory," he said shortly. "Now step lively. We may not have much time."

"But the battle . . ." Armand objected, even as he followed.

Vicente turned, visibly checking his own impatience as he laid a hand upon the younger knight's shoulder. "There is a greater war at stake than the one you see there," he said, gesturing toward the battlements. "The city cannot be saved, but the battle for our souls and the fate of our Order must yet be fought."

Armand could scarcely imagine what the Spaniard was

talking about, and in his bafflement the only question he found himself able to utter was, "Why choose me?"

"Because this day, a pure heart will serve us better than a sharp sword," Vicente replied grimly. "There are so few I can be sure are untouched by the corruption I seek to end that I must take what allies I can and expect them to act on faith. Will you trust me and follow my commands?"

"You are my commander," Armand answered lamely, for he knew it was more than his knightly obedience the Spanish master sought. "Yes, where you go I will follow," he added with firm resolve, "even if it should take me to the gates of hell."

"Let us pray it does not come to that," said Vicente with only half a smile.

Guy de Tours, a senior knight of the treasury, was on hand to greet them when they arrived at their destination. He had three horses standing ready in the courtyard. "God be praised! I was beginning to think you'd never get here!" he exclaimed.

"Have you got what we came for?" asked Vicente.

"It's already strapped to your saddle," said Guy. "The sooner we get it clear of here, the better. As long as the battle hangs in the balance, everyone has better things to do than to pay any attention to our actions. I was able to arrange for trusted men to be guarding the treasury vault, and they will speak of this to no one."

Armand could bear the mystery no longer. "I don't understand," he faltered, as they mounted up. "Are we leaving the city?"

"That's right," said Vicente.

"But, what of our duty to our brethren?"

"The Order, believe me, is better served by our departure."

With these cryptic words, the Spaniard turned his horse around and made for the exit, Guy following.

Crowding through the gate behind them, Armand craned his neck for a look at the casket they were escorting. It was made of wood, bound with brass and steel on which were engraved markings he did not recognize and could not interpret. He was aware that a number of sacred relics had come into the hands of the Order and that they were stored here at the preceptory. It had been his assumption that they would be shipped to Cyprus, along with the Order's other treasure, if and when the decision was made to abandon the stronghold. What, he wondered, could be so special about this particular relic that it should be singled out from the others? And where were they taking it?

Spurring his horse forward, he hoped that he would live long enough to learn the answers to his questions.

By this time, fear of the city's imminent fall had infected the population like a fever. As the three Templars approached the waterfront, they found the intervening streets clogged with people struggling to make their way down to the docks. Many were clutching bundles to their chests. The air was loud with a growing clamor of panic.

The enemy bombardment had resumed. Each fresh burst of explosions brought more frightened townsfolk hurrying out of their houses to swell the gathering throng. The press was so tight that the horses were eventually brought to a standstill.

"This is no use," said Guy to Vicente. "Let's see if we can find another way around."

They retraced their route and began exploring the neighboring backstreets, but every lane and alleyway was similarly blocked.

"What do we do now?" asked Armand. "Try and force our way through?"

"I wouldn't advise it," said Vicente. "It wouldn't take much to start a riot."

"What, then?" said Guy. "If we can't leave by sea, what other choice have we got?"

"There is always the land route," said Vicente.

Guy stared at him. "Aren't you forgetting the sultan's army? Or have you perhaps discovered some way to render us invisible?"

"No," said Vicente with a hint of a smile. "But for what I have in mind, the effect is much the same."

At his instigation, they abandoned all further attempts to reach the harbor and set out northward along one of the city's main thoroughfares. The sun was going down, and the skyline of the city to the east of them was luridly backlit by explosive flares. Leaving the city's inner ward behind, they reentered the devastated area that formerly had been the suburb of Montmusard, now a wasteland of derelict buildings.

Vicente led them toward the north rampart. During their brief absence, the line of the wall had been altered by further bombardment. Fresh gaps were visible all up and down the battlements where the enemy's mangonel-fire had taken its toll. Two of the auxiliary guard turrets had been leveled, leaving behind only broken stumps of masonry. Even as Armand paused to survey them, a new barrage of catapult stones came hurtling toward them from the enemy entrenchments.

Those that failed to strike the parapet crashed down among the ruins beyond. The horses shied and whinnied as a stray hundredweight ball smashed through the roof of a nearby building. Even as the three knights struggled to control their startled mounts, there came another volley of enemy fire. A shrill, long-drawn whistle pierced the air as another rain of incendiary missiles came plummeting out of the sky like thunderbolts.

A wave of explosions swept through the ruins. A shell exploded inside an adjoining house and brought an entire wall crashing down. Armand and Vicente wheeled around in shock to see Guy and his horse disappear under a collapsing avalanche of stones. When the dust parted, they saw that the steed was utterly crushed, leaving only the upper half of the knight's unconscious body exposed amid the rubble.

Armand's immediate impulse was to rush to the treasurer's aid, but he looked to his commander as his monastic discipline demanded that he should. Vicente was staring intently at their injured counterpart, one hand resting upon the mysterious chest, conflict vivid in the lines of his dark face as his concern for his fellow knight warred with the compulsion laid upon him by his mysterious and vital duty. Armand swallowed hard, uncertain of what to say. In that same moment, a figure appeared out of the surrounding ruins as if from nowhere.

The man was a tall Easterner with flashing dark eyes. Armand assumed he must be one of the city's native inhabitants, though he was surprised that one should have remained here in the midst of such danger, when all others were fleeing toward the harbor. The newcomer was richly dressed in robes of emerald and azure brocade. His silken headdress was surmounted by a diamond-studded brooch that was fashioned in the shape of a star.

The Easterner knelt beside Guy's slumped form and waved at Vicente to continue on his way. The Spaniard gave a terse nod of acknowledgment and spurred his horse onward. Baffled by Vicente's apparent confidence in this stranger, Armand reluctantly fell in behind his commander. When he looked back, the Saracen had set about tending their wounded companion, and Armand could only hope that his own actions were for the best.

Vicente guided his young companion swiftly through a tangled maze of rubble to the gutted ruin of what had once been a small tavern. Here he dismounted, motioning Armand to do the same.

"This is where we leave the horses," he said, lifting the casket from his saddle-bow. "From here on out, we'll be traveling in close quarters."

The tavern lay within a stone's throw of the city's massive curtain wall. Armand marveled that any of the building was still standing as he ducked under the sagging doorframe and followed the older knight through to the remains of a kitchen.

Embedded in the floor to the rear of the kitchen was a square block of stone out of which protruded a stout iron ring.

Vicente took hold of the ring and heaved. The stone shifted with grinding protest. Armand peered over the Spaniard's shoulder as he hefted it to one side to expose a dark cavity below.

"An underground passage!" he exclaimed.

"An old smugglers' tunnel," Vicente explained as he lowered himself into the opening. "My scouts have been using it to slip in and out of the city ever since the siege began. It will take us well beyond the city walls."

The tunnel was black as pitch, and cramped as a coffin. Armand had to keep his head bent to avoid scraping the roof as he inched his way along behind Vicente. Overhead, they could hear the ongoing thunder of further explosions. With the earth quaking and trembling around them, Armand found himself praying that the passageway wouldn't collapse on them before they reached the end.

He had no idea how far the tunnel was taking them. It came as a sharp relief when he arrived suddenly at a widening point. A sinewy hand gripped his shoulder, and Vicente's voice spoke in his ear.

"Come over here, Armand. I need the benefit of your strong arm."

He drew the younger knight forward three paces and guided his hands toward the roof. Exploring by touch, Armand realized that he was standing directly underneath another opening blocked by a stone.

"One man alone can shift that, but it takes two to do it quietly," Vicente informed him. "When I give the signal, I want you to lift—but do it carefully! We don't want to make any more noise than we have to."

When the way was clear, the Spanish knight eased himself out of the tunnel and motioned his younger counterpart to join him. Emerging into the open air, Armand saw that Vicente was crouched behind a large rock, peering over its top to what lay beyond. He edged forward and pulled himself up beside his commander. A single glance revealed that the underground passage had brought them out amid a nest of boulders a few hundred yards beyond the northern perimeter of the enemy's encampment.

The ground to the southwest of them was dotted with tents, banners, and campfires. Farther off, they could see plumes of smoke rising over the shattered walls of Acre. The noise of the ongoing bombardment was reduced to a distant drumroll. The clatter from the enemy camp was little more than a rumor riding on the breeze.

"Where do we go now?" breathed Armand, unnerved in spite of himself by the knowledge that they were now separated from their own forces by the whole Mameluke army.

Vicente displayed no such uneasiness. It was clear that this sort of scouting work was commonplace for him.

"Our destination is a village on the coast, about nine miles to the northeast," he informed his young companion. "We will make better time if we do not attempt the journey on foot."

He gestured toward the horse lines, dimly discernible at the outer edge of the Mameluke encampment. "The ground between here and there is pitted with rocks and gullies," Vicente explained, pointing. "There is cover enough to let me approach without being seen. The rest must be stealth and swiftness."

They both slipped back into the concealment of the boulders.

"You go alone?" Armand inquired.

The Spaniard nodded. "You must remain here and guard this."

He handed the casket to the younger knight. Armand accepted it in both hands, conscious of a shrinking reluctance he was at a loss to explain.

"Stay out of sight," Vicente warned. "I will not be long."

With an easy grace, he disappeared into the rocks and began his noiseless progress toward the enemy camp.

Armand set the casket down on a small rock and examined it more closely. The markings on the metalwork were certainly oriental in origin, but he had scarcely mastered more than the rudiments of the local language, and could make nothing of them. He wondered what he was supposed to do if Vicente failed to return. He had only the vaguest notion of where it was the Spaniard intended to deliver his burden, and he had not the remotest idea of what it was they were transporting. He did not even know if Vicente had the key to the casket with him, or whether it had been left behind in Acre.

He touched the metal of the keyhole with a tentative forefinger. Instantly his fighting instincts caused him to whirl swiftly around, his right hand leaping the hilt of his sword. When he scanned his surroundings, he could see nothing but empty shadows, and yet he could have sworn that he had heard a voice whispering among the rocks just as he made contact with the casket.

Cautiously he approached the box again. Again the ghostly suggestion of a murmuring voice caused him to draw back. He drew his sword from its sheath and listened, but the murmuring ceased before he could pin down its location.

Armand drew a long breath and muttered a prayer, as much to steady his nerves as anything else. He sheathed his blade and hunkered back down in the shadows among the sheltering boulders. The impulse to find a vantage point and look out for some sign of Vicente was almost irresistible, but he knew that if the other Templar's theft of the horses had not gone unnoticed, the Saracens might already be searching for intruders.

The thought came to him unbidden that his fellow Templar might be, at this moment, betraying him to the enemy; that this whole business was, in fact, a trap set by a man who was as much Saracen as Christian. Armand tried to shake such thoughts from his mind, but there remained a canker of doubt eating away at his heart. Separated as he was from the rest of his Order, how could he know who to trust?

His own unwelcome suspicions kept him on the alert for any sound of an approaching enemy. Even so, Vicente almost took him by surprise when he materialized suddenly in the gap between two nearby rocks. Disregarding Armand's startled recoil, he flashed the younger knight a grin of satisfaction.

"We are spared a long walk," he told Armand, gesturing over his shoulder to the pair of riding mounts he had secured. "Even so, we had best make our ride a speedy one, before our enemies make a count of their horses."

The Spaniard had also obtained a pair of Saracen robes, one of which he was already wearing over his Templar raiment. He tossed the other at the younger knight and moved toward the casket. He checked sharply when Armand drew his sword and used the blade to bar his path.

"Not so speedily," the young Frank declared with as much resolve as he could muster. "We go no farther until you explain to me what we are doing here. My vow of obedience has been stretched to the limit, and matters must be settled now, while we still have the means to return safely to the city and replace whatever relic this is that we have taken. I will not carry it deeper into enemy territory simply because you say we must do so."

The Spanish knight's right hand moved to the hilt of his own sword. "We have not the time for this," he warned.

"You have had many dealings with the Saracens," Armand said, "walking among them, dressed in their clothing and speaking their tongue. I heard it said once that you had even supped in the secret fortress of the Assassins. Have you given yourself over to them, I wonder, and will you now surrender our treasure to them, to gain some advantage for yourself?"

Before Armand could press him further, the Spaniard's sword seemed to leap from its sheath of its own accord. Blade met blade with a shuddering clang that sent Armand staggering backward. He recovered himself with a bound and lashed out in his turn. Vicente deflected the stroke with a powerful two-handed beat of his own weapon that dashed the sword from Armand's grasp.

It struck the ground with a dull clatter. An instant later, Armand found himself pinned back against a boulder with Vicente's blade-point at his throat. The Spanish knight's dark eyes were blazing with chill intensity. Then, abruptly, the older man's expression softened, and he lowered his weapon to the dry earth at his feet.

"It is your honor that prompts you to challenge me, Armand, and it was that very quality that made me choose you as my companion," he said on a subsiding breath. "Yes, it is true that we are heading into the midst of those who would drive us from this land. But think on this: Who is the greater enemy? The foe arrayed outside our walls? Or the traitor who stands at our side, ready to betray us, not into the hands of a besieging army, but into the very pit of perdition?"

He stooped to pick up Armand's sword and handed it back to him before sheathing his own weapon. Armand's heart was still hammering as he slid his blade back into its scabbard.

"What has this to do with a sacred relic from the Order's treasury?" he asked.

Vicente gestured toward the casket with a bleak grimace. "This box contains no hallowed bones, no fragment of the True Cross. What it holds is damnation—damnation for our Order and the lands we hold dear."

He reached inside his tunic and pulled out a small iron key with a length of black ribbon tied to it. He tossed the key to the younger knight and stepped back, leaving him free to approach the casket. "Open it if you will," he instructed grimly, "but pray that your faith will be the shield of your soul."

Armand felt an involuntary tremor run through his hand as he placed the key in the lock and gave it a grinding turn. Reaching in from arm's length, he gripped the edge of the lid and lifted it up.

Spectral voices broke out in a sibilant chorus. The chorus

spilled into the desert night, filling the surrounding air like a shower of dust from a newly opened tomb. The voices spoke in a myriad of different tongues, but Armand understood in his heart that each was offering him unspeakable temptations and forbidden delights, all of it tinged with withering fear and the promise of fire. Vicente's sinewy hand came firmly to rest on his shoulder, and at once the horrid susurration subsided into a haunted silence.

Armand drew a deep breath. Only then did he venture to look down into the box. What he saw paralyzed him with a horror greater than any he had ever experienced, even among the atrocities of the battlefield. It was a severed head, the skin yellow and dry, the black hair matted and disheveled.

Before he could wrench his gaze away, the sunken eyes suddenly burst open and fixed him with a fathomless glare. The desiccated lips twitched into life, giving vent to a voice that was like sand scraping over stone and parchment turning to ashes at the center of a fire.

Armand's eyes dimmed and he saw, as though in a waking dream, the head resting upon an unholy altar in a desecrated church, with knightly figures kneeling down before it. Naked bodies were fixed to the bloodstained walls with iron spikes driven through their hearts, and all around, black candles burned with a sickly light, their smoke scented with the stench of carrion flesh.

Armand choked, and his knees began to buckle under him. Then the lid of the casket abruptly slammed shut, and Vicente's strong arm came to his aid, bearing him up and turning him away from the ghastly reliquary. As the awful vision faded away, Armand wiped the sweat from his brow and looked at his commander with new understanding.

"W-what is it?" he asked falteringly.

"It is the head of the Baptist," Vicente answered flatly, "preserved by a lost sect of heretics and given an unnatural semblance of animation by the sorcerous arts. It was brought out of the desert more than a century and a half ago, while we still held Jerusalem, and ever since, it has worked its baleful influence. Now do you understand why we must get it away, and not allow its taint to follow the Order back to Europe, there to wreak ruination on our homelands as it has brought us to destruction here?"

"I understand better than I would have wished," Armand agreed with a deep-seated shudder. "How can something so terrible have remained so long in our midst?"

"Only a few within the Order are aware of its existence," Vicente explained. "Of those few, some have fallen under the thrall of diabolic influences. The others have had their hearts so poisoned by despair that they have come to believe that they can save the Order and recover the Holy Land only by utilizing the powers that the head may grant. They do not see that it is this very thing they have embraced so blindly that is destroying them."

"But, who are you taking it to?"

"There are believers living in and beyond the lands of the Prophet," Vicente replied. "I have been in contact with them for many years, and some among them have the means to remove this desecrated relic of the Baptist to a hidden sanctuary where it can be cleansed of the evil influence that has been worked upon it. They will meet us at the village I told you of— but only if we get there before we are overtaken by the soldiers of the sultan."

Armand drew himself up and raised his eyes to meet those of his commander. "Forgive my earlier doubts," he said contritely. "Henceforth I will do everything I can to assist you, even at the cost of my own life."

Vicente's response was a flicker of a smile, as warm as it was brief. With a nod, he locked the casket and took it under his arm before leading the way down through the rocks to the spot where he had tethered the horses to a dry stump.

They mounted up bareback and headed northeast, keeping to the cover of rocks and trees for as long as they could before taking to a hard-packed trail where haste was their best protection. They passed only a few scattered dwellings along the way, the meager homes of poor peasant-folk whose sole allegiance was to the land they clung to while armies and empires passed them by.

The trail, in time, brought them back to the coast. The sea lay calm beneath the westering moon, and Armand could only marvel at the silence here, after the tumult and fire they had left behind them. By the time they came within sight of the village, it was nearly dawn. On Vicente's instructions, they left their horses tethered among the trees in a fruit orchard, and set out on foot along a path that led from the outskirts of the village into the surrounding hills.

"There is a ruined chapel not far from here," Vicente said. "It is there we shall rid ourselves of our burden."

Armand had never before been in the midst of a region that was under the control of his enemies. He was grateful for the predawn darkness that made him feel less naked and exposed. The desert robes he and Vicente were wearing seemed a thin disguise, should they encounter any of the sultan's troops. Pushing that thought to the back of his mind, he squared his tired shoulders and trudged on up the rocky trail.

Vicente led the way to a sheltered valley deep among the rocks. The ruined chapel of which he had spoken stood at the head of a dry watercourse. Tumbled fragments of stone and plaster lay scattered about on the ground where rain and wind had widened the holes in the damaged walls. The shattered dome of the roof was surmounted by a broken cross, whose one remaining arm pointed back toward the sea, as though directing travelers away from the valley itself.

As he and Vicente drew nearer, three shadowy figures emerged from the chapel's interior. At first glance, Armand assumed they must be the three mysterious friends the Spanish knight had spoken of. Vicente started forward, one hand half-raised in greeting. Then abruptly he stopped short as another figure left the shadows by the chapel door and stepped forward into the chilly gray dawnlight.

Armand fetched up short behind him. To his astonishment, he saw that the three men in front were arrayed in the livery of the Knights Templar. Taking a closer look, he thought he recognized their faces from the garrison at Acre, though he could not recall ever speaking with them. It was the fourth, unknown member of the party, however, who commanded Armand's attention with a dark force of presence that made the hairs at the nape of his neck begin unaccountably to bristle.

The stranger was swathed head to foot in black desert robes, his face wholly invisible within the shadowy folds of his hood. Cold menace seemed to emanate from him in palpable waves.

Vicente tightened his grip on the casket and swept his sword from its sheath with the air of a man preparing to stand his ground at all cost. His attention was riveted on the dark figure lurking in the background, but he addressed himself first to the three Templar knights who were advancing silently toward him.

"Cortoni, de Vessois, Grandjean," he said in a steely voice, "stand clear and leave me be, if you value your faith and your lives."

The three knights halted. One of them gestured toward the casket. "Give us the relic, Ibanez, and you may go in peace. Do not persist in your treason."

Vicente took a firmer grip on the hilt of his sword as the other Templars drew their weapons. Armand took up a flanking position on his commander's left, his own blade gleaming at the ready.

"Whoever it is you think you serve," Vicente appealed to the other knights, "open your eyes and see the truth. We have been carrying a poison in our midst, taking it with us from place to place, so that defeat and destruction follow wherever we go. Soon we will leave this land forever, and we must not take this blight with us to work its evil in our home-lands."

There was a moment's breathless pause. Then the dark fig-ure hovering in the background took a sudden stride forward. A skeletal hand, like the talons of a mummified vulture, reached up and loosened the folds of the enveloping hood. Then the hood itself fell back to expose a pale, skull-like face, with the skin pulled tight over sharply jutting bones, and eyes that burned like embers in their hollowed-out sockets.

"Your speech is wasted, Vicente Ibanez," the ancient hissed in a dry, croaking voice. "They are entirely persuaded to my cause, and I have promised them rewards that would make your soul shrivel."

The Spanish knight's dark eyes were hard and bright as diamonds. "I should have known you would come to gloat over your handiwork."

"You know me, then?"

"I have heard men speak your name," Vicente retorted, "but only to curse it, Thierry de Challon. It was you who brought this unholy prize with you out of the desert where it should have been left."

The name was lost on Armand, but he could see for him-self that this hideous, aged creature was nothing if not the very soul of evil.

"How did you know to find us here?" he demanded hotly, his revulsion at the ancient traitor overcoming his fear.

Thierry's head swiveled on its thin neck, and he regarded Armand with a quizzical expression, as though he were sur-prised to hear the younger knight speak.

"Time itself can be bent by the mystic arts, and a day is but a curtain to be drawn aside, to see what lies beyond," he replied with a casual gesture of one bony hand. "I have been granted many gifts in payment for my services."

"Amongst them, longevity, it appears," Vicente observed.

The sorcerer laughed, a sound unpleasantly akin to the dry-throated rattle of a carrion bird. "That is the merest trinket among the jewels I wear in my crown. And it is one you will not share," he added, beckoning his men to attack.

The three renegade Templars darted forward like dogs loosed from their master's leash. Vicente tossed the casket aside and met the attack head-on. A whirling slash of his blade dealt the first of the renegades a fatal slash across the face and neck. As the man staggered back in a welter of blood, the Spanish knight spun around on his heel and caught his second opponent's blade on a ringing upstroke.

Armand sidestepped a scything blow from his own opponent and made a thrust with his own sword. His point glanced obliquely off the other man's mail shirt and he almost lost his footing. His adversary's weapon slashed through the air a hairsbreadth from his flank. Recovering, he jumped back and raised his blade in time to block a second attempted stroke that would have cloven his skull.

Steel rang on steel amid showering sparks. The shock jolted Armand's forearm, but, instead of retreating, he placed his free hand against the flat of his blade and drove forward, forcing his enemy's sword arm up and throwing him off balance. Twisting about, he kicked one leg out from under the other knight and sent him sprawling to the ground. Before the man could recover, Armand gripped the hilt with both hands and drove the weapon point-downward, straight through his opponent's throat.

Blood fountained up from the mortal wound, spraying the surrounding scrub. Wrenching his blade clear, Armand turned to help his commander. Vicente, however, had already laid open a deep gash down his opponent's sword arm. As Armand looked on, he rammed his point home through the wounded man's breast with a thrust that pierced his heart.

As the older knight wrenched at his blade to free it, a flicker of movement off to his right caused Armand to spin around. To his horror, he saw Thierry de Challon bending low over the fallen casket with a predatory grin twisting his withered lips.

Crying out a warning to Vicente, Armand bounded forward. A violent sweep of his sword knocked the chest clear of the grasping yellowed fingers. The force of the blow smashed the lock, and the lid of the casket gaped open. The hideous head rolled out and landed with its eyes gazing upward at the dark sky, its lips parted in a silent cry.

The sorcerer drew back with a snarl, his taloned hands upraised in a gesture of warding. Breathing hard, Armand pointed his sword at him, and a righteous rage lent force to his words.

"Once you were of our number. Now you are a thing accursed. It is time your unnatural span of life was cut short."

Thierry's response was a chilling laugh. "What do you know of life—or death, you poor fool?" he rasped. "Mortals are but the playthings of death!"

With a deft gesture of command, he barked out a single guttural syllable in a tongue that raked the ears. As Armand flinched and covered his ears, the three dead knights lurched up off the ground with their swords gripped fast in their hands.

Vicente decapitated one with a desperate executioner's sweep of his sword. Before he could recover, the second animated corpse dealt him an impaling blow that drove between the ribs in a mortal effusion of blood.

Armand could do nothing but cry out in horror, for the other corpse bore down on him swinging its sword viciously. It beat upon his blade with inhuman force, each blow jarring his body like a hammer striking an anvil.

Out of the corner of his eye he saw Thierry stoop down and seize the Baptist's head by the hair. In desperation, he did what he had been trained never to do, and turned his back on his opponent. Naked steel sliced through the air behind him as he hurled himself at the robed figure who stood brandishing his trophy and cackling in grisly triumph, unaware that vengeance was coming for him.

With a vaulting leap, Armand swung his blade in a vicious overhand downstroke. There was a gristly crack as the blade's descending edge sheared clean through the other man's wrist. Thierry reeled back with a howl of anguish and frustration, his incredulous gaze following the flight of his severed hand as it hit the ground alongside the head.

The animated corpses of the traitorous knights screamed in shrill unison with their master, sharing the pain of the one who had imparted to them a share of his own diabolic life force. They seemed to shrivel before Armand's appalled gaze, their skin blackening and peeling from their bones. Like plants withered by a scorching sun, they crumpled to the ground, leaving the sorcerer alone in his agony.

Thierry buried the bleeding stump of his arm in his robes and shrieked hatred at the young knight. His malice took on the form of a blast of pitchy flame that erupted from his eyes and mouth and slammed into Armand with the force of a mountain torrent. The sorcerous eruption simultaneously scorched his flesh and seemed to freeze the blood in his veins. The burning chill blasted him with an agony that took his breath away and knocked him onto his back.

His sword went flying from his grasp. Thierry continued to shriek. Gasping a prayer for relief from his suffering, Armand rolled onto his belly and dragged himself painfully to where the Baptist's head continued to stare mutely up at the fading stars. With one trembling hand, he groped for the dagger at his belt. Dragging it loose, he heaved himself up onto his knees and brought the dagger-point to bear mere inches above the Baptist's brow.

It was a stoutly forged implement. All he had to do was drive it downward with all his weight, and the point would shatter the skull, cleaving the brain in two. He had no certainty that this would end the sorcerous life of the thing, but the threat obviously had given Thierry pause.

"Stay your hand!" the sorcerer barked in a voice that was accustomed to obedience. "It is the life of your Order you are striking at, you fool. Have you not reasoned it out? You cannot escape the taint that has come upon you, nor the suspicions and hatred that have already been brought down on your Order. Only by using the power the head offers to protect yourselves can you oppose the forces which are mustering against you in the very heart of Christendom. Your choice is a simple one: to use the power and conquer, or to abandon it and die."

The words struck deep into the young knight, and he hesitated. Thierry took a tentative step nearer.

"A boat waits beyond the headland to carry the casket to Cyprus," he pressed softly. "There it will be restored to its proper place among the hard-won treasures of Christendom. The glory of saving the relic will be yours, young knight, and your name will be revered for centuries."

The sorcerer's voice was calm and reasonable, but still it bristled with a bestial quality that he could not quite disguise. Armand looked to where Vicente's body lay still beneath the shining stars, and he knew that whatever else he might doubt, he owed it to this noble knight to fulfill the mission for which he had been chosen as a companion.

"No!" he gasped, casting his defiance in Thierry's face like a gauntlet.

He raised his arm to strike, only to have his wrist caught and held by the sorcerer's thin yellow fingers. Gasping, he tried to pull away, but Thierry's grip was infused with a demonic strength. The seemingly frail fingers tightened like a vise, bruising his flesh to the bone. Armand groaned aloud as he felt his remaining strength being leeched out of him, leaving him weak and defenseless.

Thierry bent closer, his hot breath foul on the younger man's cheek. "I'll have no more of you, little knight!" the sorcerer promised, a glowering flame gathering in his deep-set eyes.

Meeting his gaze, Armand stared his own destruction in the face. Even as he framed a mute prayer for the salvation of his soul, there came another voice, breaking in upon the terror of the moment like a sudden burst of light.

Armand's heart gave a sudden leap. It seemed to him that the voice was speaking from someplace far, far away and yet intimately close at hand. It was a voice that had rung out over the deserts of Palestine centuries before, bringing fear and joy in equal measure. The words were foreign to Armand, yet the sense of them was being whispered in his ears by other lesser voices that hung in the air about him.

The Baptist was speaking as he had done so long ago, of blazing fire and of judgment to come—but Thierry de Challon no longer had to wait for his judgment.

Each of the Baptist's words was like a dagger striking out at the sorcerer. Each syllable slashed deep, opening gashes like razor cuts all up and down his emaciated arms. Thierry's knotted fingers slackened and slipped loose of Armand's wrist. As the prophet's voice continued to rise and fall, the sorcerer uttered a rending shriek and turned as if to flee.

The voice of the Baptist rolled like thunder. Sonorous and inexorable, his words echoed off the surrounding rocks. Howling, Thierry tried vainly to shield himself with his gashed arms, but cuts were now breaking out all over his body. In place of blood, thin tendrils of angry red smoke rose hissing from the wounds.

In the midst of his agony, the sorcerer's gaping eyes were fixed on a point behind Armand's prostrate form. Turning, the young knight was amazed to see three bearded Eastern sages standing there with hands upraised in a gesture of invocation. Their lips were moving silently in unison, and he realized with a shock that they were the ones who had summoned up the Baptist's damning words.

Thierry's jaws worked as he struggled to hurl a final curse at those who were destroying him, but he had been sliced almost to ribbons, and no vestige remained of his power. At last, with a final choked screech, he crumpled to the ground in a dissipating cloud of crimson dust.

The Baptist's lips fell still, and the accompanying voices faded into a silence that made Armand shiver as he edged fearfully away from the crumbling corpse. Averting his gaze from the three newcomers for the moment, he dragged himself upright and hurried to where Vicente lay. Kneeling over the body of his commander, he murmured a prayer for the repose of the Templar's soul and signed his forehead with the Cross. Only then did he venture to rise and face the three strangers.

One of them was dressed in green and blue brocade and wore a star-shaped brooch in his turban. Armand's eyes widened as he recognized the man who had come to the aid of Guy de Tours and urged Vicente on his way. His two companions were both dark-eyed and dark of skin like himself. They also wore colorful robes, and, in place of a star, their respective turbans bore the emblems of the sun and the moon.

Armand retrieved his sword and wiped it clean before returning it to its sheath. He felt no sense of danger in the presence of these three sage strangers who approached with no visible weapons. The man Armand recognized looked down at Vicente's fallen form with a mixture of sadness and resignation on his face.

"Vicente Ibanez was right to choose you for this task," he said in a lilting accent that Armand could not place. "He foresaw all too clearly the probability of his own death, for such is the fate of those who come into contact with this relic of the Baptist without submitting to the infernal powers that have claimed it."

Armand licked his lips and forced words out of his dry throat. "Are you the men he came here to meet?"

The Easterner nodded. "He sought us out years past, having heard legends of our existence. He agreed to help us end the curse that had infected your Order and was now threatening to follow it to the lands of the West, there to spread its contagion without check."

One of the other Easterners had picked up the head and was carefully enfolding it in a length of crimson silk. The third had recovered the empty casket, and now brought it to the one who bore the sign of the star. There was something about these three strangers that made Armand confident of their goodwill.

"Who are you?" he asked wonderingly.

"You have heard of us, even if you do not know it," said the Easterner who bore the star. "We belong to a brotherhood that existed centuries before your Order was formed, even before your Savior's birth. From time immemorial, Darkness and Light have opposed each other in a battle beside which your wars with the followers of the Prophet are little more than a squabble, and through all this we have traveled far and wide to oppose the bringers of Darkness."

"Now that you have what you came for, what of me?" Armand asked. "Shall I return to Acre?"

The Easterner shook his head. "No, the city is doomed, though now the doom will stop there. There is another task for you to perform. A ship is waiting, as the accursed one said, to take the casket to Cyprus, there to be reunited with other sacred relics salvaged from your crusade."

"Is this all that is left for me," Armand demanded with a sudden flare of indignation, "to carry an empty box across the sea?"

"Not empty," the Easterner corrected him. "It is not enough for the source of the sickness to be removed. A remedy must be provided, lest the harm persists. Have you not read in your own scriptures of the unclean spirit that was driven out of a man, only to return with seven others more wicked than itself? When an evil has been removed, a good must be set in its place."

He turned to his companion, who was holding the open casket in his outstretched arms. The man with the star reached under his robes and produced a folded length of plain cloth, which he placed inside the box. There were markings on the cloth, barely visible in the gloom, but to Armand's eyes they resembled a face.

"What is this?" Armand asked, staring curiously at it.

"A relic we have guarded these twelve centuries past," the Easterner replied. "It is a burial shroud, a source of faith and inspiration that will undo much of the harm that has been done. Guard it well and deliver it safely, for there is much danger ahead that it may yet help to avert."

He lowered the lid of the box, hiding the shroud from Armand's awed gaze, then handed the precious charge over to him. The young Templar nodded his acceptance of the burden that had been entrusted to him, grasping it firmly in his dirt-stained hands.

He had no doubt of what this burden was, nor of the identity of the men to whom he had been speaking. As they turned eastward to vanish into the night, he recalled that they traveled always in a company of three, and that they were famed above all else for their gifts.

INTERLUDE TWO

The decade after the fall of Acre saw a decided shift in the fortunes of the Temple. Given that the loss of the Crusader Kingdom had hardly been sudden or unexpected, the Temple had had ample time to transport their Outremer-based wealth and treasures to other safe havens. The retreat to Cyprus, first intended as an interim arrangement, a base from which to launch harrying missions against Saracen shipping and to drum up support for yet another crusade, began to acquire the earmarks of a much longer-term arrangement. In the next decade, though the next (and last) Grand Master, Jacques de Molay, began an active campaign for a Fifth Crusade, he was, perhaps, one of the few men of power not to realize, or at least to admit, that the Holy Land was, indeed, lost.

Meanwhile, back in the land whence the Order had sprung, the King of France was eyeing the wealth of the Temple with ever more acquisitive eyes. Himself beholden to the Temple several times over, for both financial and physical rescue, and no doubt humiliated by the rejection of his efforts to be admitted to the Order as a secular knight, Philip le Bel had begun plotting a redress of grievances. If he could not access the Order's wealth by joining it, perhaps he could gain control in another way. With the military situation collapsed in the Holy Land, and the great crusading orders expelled, perhaps an amalgamation of those orders—with Philip as Rex

Bellator, or War King—could reestablish a Western presence and gain access to the Temple's wealth.

The king's chancellor was a man called Guillaume de Nogaret, already proven ruthless and ingenious in his services to the crown—the bane of two popes and several lesser prelates. Easing Philip's financial embarrassment was hardly a new assignment, nor was the Temple the only potential source of wealth to be tapped. On July 22, 1306, in what may have been a dry run for his attack on the Order little more than a year later—and to ease the king's financial embarrassment of the moment—Nogaret masterminded the roundup and expulsion of the Jews from France, with the concurrent seizure of all their assets.

Or, *were* all the assets seized?

Borne on a River of Tears

David M. Honigsberg
and Alexandra Elizabeth Honigsberg

28 Tamuz 5066. Yom Sheini

Surely G-d—*haShem,* blessed be His name forever—must weep as I weep for our people. The pavements are wet and the time is yet days away. But my city, my dear Paris, is already shrouded in mourning. The mists from the Seine wind their way through the streets as if in procession, bringing the sad news to all, though they do not yet know it. Maybe it is better this way. Let them sleep a few days more. Time enough for sorrow there has always been.

But I wander.

I, Samuel, have been given the foreknowledge of our impending doom. I keep this chronicle so that the *mitzvot* might be fulfilled, the *yizkor* kept. Never forget. Never.

It is just sixteen years since our brethren across the Channel were given but three months in which to vacate their country. Now we Jews here in France face a similar edict. Who knows whether our Philip the Fair will live up to his name or even be as kind to us as Edward was to our people in England?

Only this morning it was when, into my shop, came Monsieur and Madame Bijoux, two with whom I have been friends for nearly forty years. They sometimes come to buy my garments. At other times, they stop by to chat or to bring me a little extra food from their table. On rare occasions, they ask me a question about the *Torah* or some other bit of the Law. I'm no rabbi, though a *kohain* of the ancient line of priests, but I am well versed enough in our traditions to answer them fairly and be of service. And there are certain areas of the Law with which, I admit with pride, I am very familiar. Unfortunately, those have little to do with daily, practical things. Still, it is all of *haShem,* blessed be His name, and thus important.

This visit was different from all others. The pair seemed greatly agitated. I could see Jacob's big hands trembling as he sampled a bolt of cloth whilst Miriam continuously glanced at the door. We exchanged the usual pleasantries, but I knew there was something they needed to say to me.

"What is troubling you, my friends?" I finally asked.

Jacob's gaze wandered around the room as he absent-mindedly set aside the cloth and stroked his beard. His burden seemed great, blanketed the room in silence.

I made haste to find three chairs so that we could be more comfortable. For a man of sixty-four, I can move very quickly when I need to. I retrieved the chairs and a bottle of wine as well.

"Jacob," I said, as I poured for each of us, "you look as though you've heard from the dead."

Miriam spoke first, tears in her eyes. "We have heard from Ephraim," she said.

My eyes widened. A voice from the dead, indeed. "What can he possibly want from you?"

"He wants nothing from us, Samuel," Jacob answered. "He came to warn us. And we thought it best to warn you, too, old friend."

"Warn me? Of what should I be warned?"

Miriam buried her face in her hands and began to sob. Jacob gently touched her shoulder as her body trembled.

"It is over, Samuel," he whispered. "Finished."

I shivered, though the air was hot and sticky. "Not an eviction?"

Jacob shook his head. "That and worse. Arrest and confiscation, too. Good King Philip needs to replenish his coffers, it seems. The Jews of France are to fill them."

"And Ephraim knew?" I didn't want to believe this, but I knew it had to be true.

Miriam sat up, her eyes red. "We have nowhere to go, Samuel. And no family, now that Ephraim is dead to us. You were the first person we thought to come to. You have always been so kind, especially when Ephraim—"

"—*Sha*, Miriam. We have spoken his name too many times already," Jacob snarled. He turned to me, sorrow etched upon his face. "Samuel, I know that we cannot warn the entire country. Perhaps we cannot even warn all the Jews in our own city. And I know that you don't have fortunes to protect, either. But, as Talmud teaches, if one is saved, it is as if you have saved the whole of the world."

"And you choose to save me, Jacob?" I rose from my chair and clasped his hands in mine. "Thank-you, my friend. You have no idea of how much you have done. Yet I need to ask of you one favor, which you must not refuse me. You must carry a message to Ephraim. I must speak with him."

The room was quiet, save for Miriam's sniffling.

"Samuel, I cannot—" Jacob began.

"No!" Miram snapped. "It will be done!" Jacob spun to face her, but the look of determination on her face made him bite back his words. He nodded.

"It will be done," he repeated. The tension drained out of him as he helped his wife to her feet. I inked a note on a parchment scrap, the back of a bill, folded it, sealed it, and handed it to Jacob. They said their farewells and walked out of the shop.

I poured myself another goblet of wine and drank it down quickly. There was much to be done in the next few days. And everything depended upon my meeting with Ephraim. For while it was true that Jacob had saved me, he had also done much to save the soul of all *Yisrael*.

21 July 1306. Wednesday
This journal I keep unto myself, but truly unto the glory of

God, through Jesus Christ, His only Son, our Lord. It is the only bit of privacy allowed me in our community.

I stood outside of Samuel's shop for what seemed like hours but was, in reality, no more than a few minutes, I am sure. The clouds hung heavy, grey. A mist clung to everything. Though I had called this part of Paris my home, now it felt strange to me, stifling. My once-neighbors crossed the street to avoid me, nearly stumbling into its malodorous slop-trough in the center, and ducked under porches and into shops. Doubts assailed me. Sinfulness! They had been my people. How could they not see what I see? Yet I cannot save them from themselves or the coming storm. We are all in God's hands—may my sword stay strong in His service!

I took a deep breath and entered the shop, a prayer for protection to the Blessed Virgin upon my lips. It was hotter inside than in the streets, and the blast of warmer air made me stop a moment. The dark wood walls, irregular with age, and shelves piled with all manner of cloth and trim, closed in around me. The familiar smells of the place—all dust, wool, and linen—made my head swim with memories, unbidden.

There he sat, Samuel, my old mentor, Papa's friend. He studied a chessboard with its polished wooden pieces, his old form hunched over, the *kipah* upon his head covering the bald spot that had always been there. How odd it was when the old words came back to me. It never happened in the fortress. And that old Samuel should have been the first one to teach me what I have, as of late, come to know as a warrior's game. God truly works in mysterious ways.

I heard the bell on the shop door as it opened and I spun around, alert, hand on the hilt of my blade. Before my eyes could adjust from the shop's dim light to the glare of the street coming through the doorway, I heard a woman's stifled cry. "Ephraim!"

A dark form shadowed her and spoke. "Come, Miriam. We must go." It could almost have been my own voice. The thought chilled me despite the heat, and I remained frozen there, suspended in time, the two ghosts from my past long gone.

I heard a cough behind me and turned.

Samuel studied me, his eyes narrowing. His gaze wandered to my surcote, its bold red cross upon a field of pure white. He walked to the door and locked it.

"How did they know I'd be here?" I said. "Did you tell them, old man? Is that what this is all about? A family reunion?"

He answered, a queer glint in his eye. "Of a sort. Of a sort, Ephraim ben Yaakov. And it is good to see you again, too, boy. You can hardly be missed in those clothes. Why don't you let me make you a nice cote? Ah, but I forget, we haven't the time now for that, have we?"

"Ephraim is dead, old man. I am reborn and now called Peter."

"Peter, is it now, boy? He was the one who denied his lord and people three times, was he not?"

His insolence sorely tried my patience. "I am well past my majority and an agent of the King and God. You would do well to mind your manners with me and my brethren. Since you already seem to know so much, you must also know that we'll have your lives in our hands."

"Only the Lord our God, may His name be praised, holds the power of life and death. You hold nothing but a sword." He shrugged. "We have faced swords before."

His eyes never left mine. Brave and foolish man. Are they all like him? I didn't recall them so, but that was through the eyes of a child. I am a man, now.

It is hard to argue The Word with one who knows but parts of it and has twisted views. But Samuel was always a sly one, a crafty one, always with his head in the books, the ancient tomes. I should have known that he had read the Gospels as well. Good strategy. Know thine enemies.

Samuel disappeared behind the counter to reappear with

two goblets and a decanter. He smiled. "But where are my manners? Sit, sit. Relax. It is such a hot day." He filled the goblets, handing one to me. I declined the offer with a wave of my hand, but took a seat.

"You have turned your back on the fruit of the vine, as well as your heritage, Peter?"

"Not at all," I answered. "I drink at the table of our Lord. He is my heritage, my portion."

Samuel shook his head. "Your lord, not mine." He continued. "I hope that you don't mind if I have a sip or two." He pronounced the appropriate blessing, raised the goblet to his lips, and drank deeply. For a time, his attention was drawn back to the chessboard, then returned to me. I'd forgotten how disconcerting his gaze could be. It had always given me the impression that he knew secrets, forbidden things. Now it also made me remember how my fellows had stared at me when I entered the Order, how they whispered behind my back, and how, even now, five years later, they did not yet fully trust me.

"You are well?" he asked, as he set down the wine.

"Yes, thank-you."

Another prolonged silence.

"Ephraim." Samuel caught himself. "I'm sorry. Peter. Thank-you for coming to see me. When your parents told me of what was to happen to us—well . . . Did I ever tell you that my father was at the disputation in 5000?"

This man could chatter, and my mind had begun to wander, but that last question captured my attention.

"The one in which Nicholas Donin proved the blasphemy of the Talmud?" I said. Donin, one of my heroes, was a great French Jew who had come to know our Savior.

Samuel spit on the floor. "Donin couldn't have proven anything, if the inquiry had been a fair one. Rabbi Jehiel was a great man. He wasn't given a proper chance to disprove Donin's case. A travesty! My own father's copy of the Talmud was burned in the aftermath. Our lot has not been an easy one since that time. But some things they could not destroy. Father saw to that, as I do now!"

I leaned forward, eager to explain to Samuel that Nicholas Donin was a true believer, that he had accepted Christ, as all Jews would do, ultimately. But I saw, before I began, that his heart was closed, that he would only see me as an apostate, as all in this part of the city saw me. I changed the subject.

"You did not call me here just to cast aspersions upon the blessed memory of Donin," I said. "Have out with it, man. What is it that you want?"

"I need that you should do something for me, Peter."

"Samuel, just because I know of the edict does not mean that I can do anything to help you or any other Jew in Paris," I said. "I sent word to my parents so they might have a few days to prepare—not so they could warn everybody in town. Were I to be caught aiding Jews, it would surely not go well with me."

"You misunderstand me," he replied. "And you misunderstand your mother and father, as well. I believe that I am the only one they spoke to. I think it is because I have known them for so many years. But it is lucky for both of us that I was told."

It was my turn to watch him carefully, study him. His calmness in the face of the upcoming disaster was impressive. If I had been told that in two or three days I would be arrested and all of my property confiscated to our King's treasury, I do not think I could have been so placid.

"How so?" I asked.

Samuel took a deep breath. His manner became yet more serious, reverent. "There is something I have in my possession that I do not want falling into Philip's hands, Peter. I have decided to entrust it to you. You are the only man in Christendom who can truly understand and appreciate its importance."

I laughed out loud. "Samuel, I can grant no such favors! Our fair King's soldiers, along with my fellow Templars, have their orders. No exceptions."

Samuel's eyes smoldered with anger.

The discussion was ended. I stood and turned to the door. "I am sorry that you've wasted our time, old man. Whatever it is that you're hiding will, I am sure, make a fine addition to His Majesty's treasury."

"I ask again, Peter." Samuel's words came out clipped. "I ask you to make one exception."

I reached the door and moved to unlock it. "No exceptions," I repeated.

"Not even for the *aron kodesh*?" His voice was a mere whisper, but the words struck me as no blows in the lists ever had.

I stopped. My heart pounded in my chest. I spun around, sure that I had heard wrong. "What did you say?"

"I said, 'Not even for the *aron kodesh*?'"

"Surely you don't expect me to believe that you, of all people—a Jewish tailor!—are the keeper of the Holy Ark?" Sweat trickled down my spine beneath my undertunic, and I praised God that I had not donned my mail shirt.

He shrugged. "And who else should have it? Certainly not the *goyim*—at least not till now. If you don't believe me, then King Philip's men will no doubt find it. With the Ark at his side, the nations will tremble before him, as it is written." He lowered his voice and whispered conspiratorially, "But if you, Peter, find it and return it to its rightful place in *Yerushalayim,* both your name and the name of the Knights Templar will be praised in all the Earth, *l'dor va dor,* from generation to generation. For this, you can make an exception. You must."

I did not know what to say. A man I had known all my life, one who had been the epitome of humbleness, who had helped my parents when he had but little and they less—a man who, when I was a boy, had spun stories of the great Biblical heroes while I sat at his feet—wanted me to believe that he was the guardian of the Ark of the Covenant.

A thought then came to me. Perhaps he was *just* the kind of person who would be given this sacred duty. Perhaps it was his humbleness and love for tradition that allowed him to keep the Ark without boasting of it to others.

Perhaps.

"I will be back tomorrow morning, Samuel. You had best be ready to prove yourself. If not, I can promise you that you will wish that you had never mentioned this to me." I strode to the door and unlocked it.

"You will see for yourself, Ephraim. You might think about four men you can trust. Swear them to secrecy. I know how important vows are to your people."

I barely responded to my old name. And vows? What did he know of vows? Everyone knows that Jews gather on *Yom Kippur* to renounce even the vows they have not yet made.

I opened the door and stepped out into the hazy, muted sunlight. The streets were preternaturally empty, but I could feel their eyes upon me, all around me, especially Samuel's.

2 Av 5066. Morning, Yom Chamishi

After Ephraim left the store, I finished my wine and climbed the creaky stairs that led to my rooms above the shop. I was greeted by the indignant and insistent vocalizations of my orange mouser, Samson. Must have locked the poor boy up here all day in my absentmindedness. I gave him a bowl of milk, and he seemed to forgive me. Good. I needed to keep my friends, especially now.

Try as I might, I could not think of the man I had been speaking to as Peter, no matter how much he eschewed his birth name. Ephraim was an honorable name—"fruitful" in the holy tongue—and one that his parents had chosen carefully for him, their first son. I shook my head in dismay and made my dinner. He whom I had known as Ephraim wasn't the good Jewish boy I had once bounced upon my knee.

I sighed, realizing that I didn't have much of an appetite. I was sick to my soul with the news of the edict. Even so, I had to chuckle. Our King obviously hadn't consulted a proper calendar in order to make his plans. Had he done so, he would have waited just a few days more, until the ninth of the month, when the entire community would be in mourning for the destruction of the Temples in *Yerushalayim*. What would have been one more national tragedy on such an auspicious day as that?

I pushed these musings from my mind. There was work to be done. I ate just enough to keep from becoming faint as the evening wore on. Then I latched the shutters and closed out the sounds of the street below. Curtains drawn, I lit my two best beeswax candles in their heavy *Shabbat* candlesticks, being careful to concentrate upon the words of the blessing as I did so, blessing *haShem*—the Name—for the creation of fire.

"*Baruch atah Adonai, Elohaynu melech haolam, boray moray ha'aysh. . . .*"

I removed a piece of parchment—rolled and sealed— from its hiding place and tucked it beneath my undertunic, the unlocking ritual long since committed to memory.

After the candles were lit, I removed my shoes and sat upon the floor—my precious little carpet from the East, worn, but soft to the touch—facing a large trunk that sat in the corner of the room. Taking deep breaths, I cleared my mind of all extraneous thoughts—something that I found very difficult to do, as I could not help but return to the day's events, over and over again.

Finally, I succeeded, and began the evening's work. I closed my eyes and intoned the first letter of the alphabet, *aleph,* followed by the second, *bet.* I pronounced the combination, *ah-beh,* then spoke the third letter, *gimmel,* combining the first with the third—*ah-gih.* I continued in this fashion until I had combined *aleph* with each other letter in proper sequence.

As I finished I felt the energy in the room shift, rise to a higher level, a greater intensity. I then combined *bet* with *gimmel,* then with *dalet* and on and on, just as the mystic, Abulafia, had written should be done. Each letter I combined with each other letter until, nearly exhausted from my labors, I softly spoke the last combination. I took a deep breath as I finished, knowing what I would see when I opened my eyes.

Where the trunk had been, there now stood the most magnificent artifact ever wrought by human hands, more exquisite than the finest piece of jewelry, more breathtaking than Solomon's Temple must have been. Before me, in all its golden glory, lay the Ark of the Covenant, the *aron kodesh,* the final resting place of the tablets of the Law that Moshe received at Sinai. Seeing again the two cherubim upon the lid, their wings outstretched toward each other, brought tears to my eyes. It was the last night I would spend in the presence of this holy creation.

I sang the psalms of praise until dawn, Samson curled up at my side, purring in blissful ignorance.

22 July 1306. Thursday

I emerged from the barracks before sunrise and joined the others for *Lauds*. There was scant light from outside, even as the sun struggled to make its reluctant way above the horizon—the weather still on the verge of a downpour, it seemed—to set the stained glass of the chapel ablaze. But it still awed me, even in muted glory. The flickering candlelight and smoke from the incense transported me to God's realm as our voices rose in song. I was in this world, but not of it. I prayed that I didn't seem anxious about anything. This was the day that Philip had decreed for the arrest of the Jews. This might be the most important day of my life, my chance to prove my loyalty before all, and cast a mighty blow against their doubts.

Though too tense to eat, I took a light meal in the refectory—some bread and cheese, only. I did not want to arouse any suspicions, as my prodigious appetite was legendary and of some concern to my superiors. I then set about my work.

I left the compound to patrol the streets for a while, a short shift before the real task of the day was to begin. My steps took me along the *Île de la Cité,* in the shadow of *Nôtre Dame,* the heart of the city, on its island in the Seine, to the Jewish quarter. Samuel came to mind as I walked, and I wondered if the old Jew really was the guardian of the Ark.

I picked up my pace, my soul trembling with the possibility. If only it were true! I could not imagine in my wildest dreams what it would mean to us, to the Templars, if the very heart of the Temple of Solomon were in our possession. Surely the *Mamelukes* and their heathen hordes would fall before us as we marched triumphantly into Jerusalem behind God's might!

With such thoughts of glory racing through my mind, I almost strode past the entrance to Samuel's apartment. Ignoring the stares of the passersby, I knocked upon the door. Within moments Samuel answered, his eyes red and puffy, followed by that grouchy old cat of his. I realized that the old man had been weeping and wondered, were his tears for his people or himself? He said not a word to me, but turned around and began to walk back up the stairs. I followed him, the door closing behind me. Each step sank and sang a bit beneath my weight.

We entered the foyer and I immediately felt a change in the air. It was not warmer, nor colder, nor anything that I can describe other than to say that it was *different.* My eyes searched the area for danger, for enemies, for anything that I could make sense of. Even as I did so, I knew that I was safer with Samuel than I had ever been during my entire life—and in grave danger. We turned the corner into his living room, and I gasped.

Before me, just as I had seen it in my dreams, was the Ark of the Covenant. It gleamed brighter than the sun, and from its surface radiated the most profound sense of holiness that I have ever felt. I rushed in front of Samuel, careful not to touch it, and fell to one knee, thrice crossing myself.

"Lord Jesus Christ," I whispered. I heard Samuel spit on the floor behind me as I spoke His name. "I thank Thee for giving me this glimpse of Thy glory, Thy might, Thy holiness. May I be worthy to guard Thy sacred Ark from harm for as long as it is within my keeping. In the name of the Father, and of the Son, and of the Holy Spirit, amen." I turned to Samuel but could not, would not, allow the image before my eyes to fade.

"It is so beautiful," I stammered.

He nodded. "I have been up all night. I have prayed and I have cried. I have prayed that what I am doing is the right thing to do. And I have cried at the injustice of this world, which forces me to give up one of the true joys of my life, the joy of knowing that I am a faithful guardian, as was my father before me and his before him, and so on, back to the beginning." He sighed. "The world is full of injustices, though. This is but one more. What can we do? We can flee again, as we have in the past, or we can become apostates." He glared at me as he said that. "Or we can die. But it is not time yet to die, I don't think. Plenty of time for that, someday. But not now. Not just yet."

Samuel walked to a chair and sat down, leaden.

"How will I ever bring it out into the streets?" I asked.

"Do not be concerned," he answered. "The Holy One, blessed be He, provides. You will be able to take it with you without revealing its true nature."

I began to voice my doubts, but Samuel held up a hand to stop me. "It shall be taken care of," he assured me. "Now go. Go and let me do what I must. For your part, you must be sure that you find a way to bring the *aron kodesh* to the Holy Land. It belongs there. The presence of *haShem*, which still dwells between the wings of the cherubim, cries out for Her people." The old Jew's eyes were bright as he spoke. "You must do this—not for me, not for yourself, but for your people. For though you deny it, your soul is still that of *Yisrael*, Ephraim. Your blood is still our blood. Never forget that, because *they* never will, either."

I knew that what Samuel said was not true. My soul was as Christian as my heart, and had been so even before my baptism. My blood had been cleansed by His blood. The old man's words were just the fevered ravings of a frightened Jew.

"I will be back later," I informed him, "with others. You had best prepare yourself."

I left the apartment and walked down the stairs. As I reached the door, I heard Samuel mumbling to himself. It sounded as though he were reciting the Hebrew alphabet backward, combining the last letter with the next to last and so on, voicing nonsense syllables.

I shook my head in bemusement. Perhaps heat and fear had gotten to the old man. I left the Jewish quarter and felt so buoyed by my vision of the Ark that I purchased a rich pastry from a street merchant and nibbled it as I walked back to my barracks.

2 Av 5066. *Yom Chamishi*

As the morning wore on, I began to wonder if Ephraim had been given false information regarding our King's edict. Outwardly, I remained unconcerned, and did my best to help my customers whilst constantly thinking about what lay ahead for me—for Ephraim, for his parents, for all the Jews of France. Most of all, I wondered what lay ahead for the *aron* itself. Would Ephraim do what he could to bring it to Palestine, or would he and his Templars try to use it for war? What, I wondered, would King Philip say if he knew that such a precious item were sitting a short distance from his palace? I smiled to myself at the thought of the King, livid with rage and powerless.

The morning turned into afternoon. My night-long vigil began to catch up with me, and, more than once, I almost fell asleep standing up. In the middle of the afternoon, I heard voices in the streets—men and women alike, pleading, begging others not to take them away.

So it begins, I thought to myself. *So it begins.*

The few who were in my shop at that moment stopped to listen. One, a gentleman close to my age, reached for the door to see what was happening. As he touched the latch, the door flew open, knocking him backward and onto the floor. Four men entered, two wearing our King's livery, two in the white surcote with red cross of the Templars. Ephraim was at their head, mail glinting at his throat. He moved like a cat, and, for the first time, I felt fear in his presence. I rushed to the side of my fallen customer.

But I never reached him. Ephraim grabbed me by the arm to stop me and proclaimed, "By order of Philip, King of France, it is decreed that all Jews on these premises are to be arrested and detained. All their possessions are to be forfeit to the Crown. It is further decreed that in no more than one month's time, all Jews currently in France will leave. Those who do not do so on their own will be forcibly evicted from her borders."

He smiled sidelong at his companions. "Come, let us see what riches this Jew has kept hidden from our good King."

Ephraim glared at me as he left the store. I heard the sound of footsteps on the stairs leading up to my apartment and ran after the knights as best I could, leaving those in the store to fend for themselves. I snatched Samson before he could bolt from the windowsill and looked down. Men, women, and children hurried through the streets hoping, per- haps, that they would be able to salvage something of their belongings before our King's knights arrived at their homes.

Knowing that this day was drawing near, I had taken the liberty of hiding some jewelry under the floorboards of my bedroom, sure that the rooms would be ransacked, but not destroyed. I hoped that these were the men Ephraim had chosen and not three others who had been assigned to accompany him upon his rounds. I rushed into my living room, breathless, just in time to see Ephraim stopping one of the knights from opening the trunk.

"I rather fancy that piece," he said to the man. "I think I'll claim it for myself." He noticed that I was there. "I hope that you don't object to that, Jew," he sneered.

I shook my head and said, "Take it and whatever else you want and get out of my home."

I sank into my chair and watched as the few trinkets I had left about were stuffed into a bag. Ephraim ordered Philip's knights to take the trunk. Although I knew it weighed more than even ten men should be able to lift, the two picked it up as if it were weightless. I whispered a prayer of thanks that the *aron* would be in good hands with Ephraim and hoped that it might safely be delivered to *Yerushalayim.*

But before Peter-Ephraim—whoever he was—vanished from my sight, he turned to me. I felt a weight against my heart—and a connection.

"Are you sure there's nothing else, old man?" he asked.

I made to shake my head "no" but bowed it instead, dejected. "There is one more thing. It goes with that trunk of my father's that you so fancy."

I reached into my garments, removed the parchment, and tossed it at him. He snatched it from the air with great ease. A warrior like Judas Maccabeus he had become.

A prayer of protection I spoke, for all of us, and nearly smiled.

"Let's get on with it, men. A rich harvest awaits." He stormed out.

The other Templar helped me to my feet and escorted me down the stairs. I kept Samson wrapped in my surcote, though he struggled mightily, and went next door, intending to lock up my shop, then realized that it was futile. All I owned now belonged to Philip.

I stood in front of my store, tears streaming down my face, and watched as my people were marched off to jail. A cart laden with precious artifacts from our *yeshiva* passed by, and I prayed that our rabbi and his sons had saved one of our sacred *Torah* scrolls, G-d's word to His people. Another soldier pushed me into line. I did not look back.

10 October 1307. Tuesday

Today, I again stood in the shadow of *Nôtre Dame,* staring up at the Portal of Judgment. I almost spoke aloud to the faces there, and wondered what they would say if I told them about the treasure I have been guarding for over a year.

I sometimes wish that Samuel were still here in Paris. There is so much that I would like to have asked him—about the Ark, about the scroll he gave me before he was taken away. Alas, within two weeks of his arrest, he was gone from France. I did not see him before he left, nor do I know where he journeyed. Perhaps this is the way that it should be. I am sure that it was destined by the Father that the Ark become a possession of the Templars.

I have offered up fervent prayers of thanks and petitions that I might be worthy of such an honor as the guardianship of the *aron kodesh*. Since that fateful day in July, I feel that my prayers have been answered, proving once again the power of our Lord. For I have dreamt of a time when even my kind will be gone. I have seen the signs: Philip's own knights are keeping their distance from us, as though our presence is no longer welcome. I wonder what is being discussed behind the closed doors of the Palace. It seems Philip's appetites know no bounds, and his vows to us are of the moment only.

Against that day, which I am sure is upon us, I have been granted, by the grace of our Lord, Jesus Christ, the opportunity to leave this city with my most precious cargo. Even now, a simple wooden trunk—with its glorious secret—is being loaded onto the ship that will take me to far Ethiopia and, perhaps, from there to the Holy City itself. If I am not destined to take it there, I know that it shall be delivered to its rightful place one day—one day when the heathens have left the city. This must be done, for the glory of our Lord.

Am I worthy of such an honor? In truth, I do not know. Yet I trust in the Lord. He would not ask of me something that I could not do. I will be ready for the task. I will succeed. I must, for the sake of all that is Holy.

In the name of the Father, and of the Son, and of the Holy Spirit.

Amen.

INTERLUDE THREE

The wealth acquired by the expulsion of the Jews from France was significant—and, in Philip's mind, was justifiably seized, not only as a means of easing his financial situation, but also in response to his belief that he was cleansing France of a presence bent on undermining its Christian ethos, for Philip believed that the Jews regularly desecrated the Host. The charges soon to be brought against the Templars would reflect similar allegations of heresy, blasphemy, and other depravities—and would also lead to actions that would replenish the coffers of the king.

But in the summer of 1306, while the Jews were being arrested and their goods confiscated, the Temple's officers seemed not to be aware that plans were under way to move against the Order in a similar fashion. When the Grand Master returned from Cyprus early in 1307, in response to a summons from the pope, he brought with him an escort of sixty mounted knights and their sergeants and squires and servants and a baggage train of twelve pack horses laden with plate and jewels, which riches he deposited in the Paris treasury—hardly the act of a man who felt himself or his Order to be vulnerable. Yet, after conferring with his Paris officers, he did order that certain documents and copies of the Order's rule be gathered up and burned, and members of the Order were cautioned not to speak to outsiders regarding the Temple's internal business. This suggests that someone, at least, was exercising caution, but rank-and-file members of the Order probably were not aware that time was running out. De Molay and his principal officers did not escape the arrests of October 13, but many high-ranking officers did. And most of the Temple's treasuries everywhere had already been emptied by the time the king's agents came to collect their ill-gotten loot.

Until that fateful day, however, recruits were added daily to the Temple's ranks—and perhaps even afterward. The latter possibility attracted young Robert of Troyes, whose encounter in 1311 with the fugitive Saxon Templar, Friedrich von Hochheim, led him to abandon his studies at the University of Paris to fulfill his childhood dream of becoming a Poor Knight of Christ.

Friedrich himself, like many of his now outlawed companions-in-arms, had refused to forswear his fidelity to the Order now under papal as well as royal ban. Despite the possibility of transferring to another military order—or confessing to some minor crime among the unholy litany ascribed to the Templars, accepting his penance, and perhaps even seeking release from his vows—Friedrich von Hochheim defied both king and pope. But thousands of his brethren had accepted the relatively generous provisions offered by the monarchs who had jointly crushed the rich and powerful Order in order to seize its lands and wealth.

In that regard, however, King Philip had failed conspicuously. To protect church property from royal confiscation, Pope Clement had transferred Templar holdings to the Knights of the Hospital. Worse, the Temple treasury had vanished from Paris, as had the eighteen ships, both cogs and galleys, harbored at La Rochelle.

Royal baillies and seneschals scoured the Kingdom of France for impenitent Templars who might possess part or all of the key to the mystery. And in their Paris dungeons, the Master and chief stewards of the Order awaited final judgment. In July of 1311, Friedrich von Hochheim and young Robert had other plans.

The Treasure of the Temple

Richard Woods

To Robert of Troyes, former student of the Sorbonne, it became embarrassingly evident only after the walls of Paris had disappeared behind the thickening forest under the hot July sun that he lacked any knowledge of their destination.

"Sir Friedrich," he ventured after an hour of growing discomfort, "where are we headed?"

The Saxon giant behind whom he sat astride a huge bay palfrey said nothing, nor gave any sign that he had even heard the question.

An hour later, Robert ventured another query with similar results. After a third hour, when the ache in his back and buttocks had become almost unbearable, he sighed with relief when the knight reined to a halt in the shade of a grove of beech and lime trees. A rivulet sparkled through the bushes a few paces off the road, and the grass nearby was invitingly fresh.

Robert slid to the ground and nearly collapsed from the fatigue in his legs. Still silent, the Saxon dismounted and led his big horse to the stream. Robert followed, struggling to remain upright.

"His name is Näscher."

"Sire?"

"My palfrey. He is called Näscher. It means 'sweet-tooth.' He likes apples."

"Er, so do I."

"Then eat." Friedrich produced some small, pink apples from his wallet and tossed one to the famished student. "But do not eat too much. You will be ill."

After Näscher had been allowed to drink and was treated to an apple, Friedrich led him to the small, lush pasture, where the dense shrubs along the road provided a natural corral as well as a measure of seclusion. Then he and Robert cupped their hands to the chill and, Robert thought, heaven-sent stream, drank, and refilled their water bottles.

"May I ask where we are going, sire?"

"Rampillon."

"Why, sire?"

"You are full of questions, Robert of Troyes. It should be enough to know that we go to Rampillon. However, since you will continue to ask, I will tell you. There we will meet with other members of the Order who are gathering to make plans."

"Plans, sire?"

"Plans."

Laying his sword beside him, Friedrich leaned back against a tree, and shut his eyes. Or eye: an ancient scar traversed his face from hairline to jaw across the pit of his left eye, now ridged by hardened flesh. Robert did the same, only to be rudely awakened moments later, it seemed, by the stamping of the palfrey.

Friedrich was already mounted. He extended his hand and hoisted Robert painfully to the pillion seat.

"There is a Templar commandery at Rampillon. A gathering of knights has been summoned there tomorrow to determine our next steps. Not all have accepted the vile decree of the French pope."

Robert tried not to groan as the palfrey set out at a canter. The horse, he was now convinced, was an animal never intended by God to seat even one, much less two riders.

"Sire, how far is Rampillon?"

"We will spend the night at Mormont, which is not far from here. No more than four hours."

"And Rampillon?"

"Five hours farther. No more."

And no less, Robert realized. Seditiously, the thought crept into his reflections that students at the Sorbonne were forbidden to own horses.

Sweating, itching, and increasingly sore, Robert suffered silently through the village of Brie-Comte-Robert into the rich plateau beyond. He occasionally prayed for numbness, paying little mind to the well-tended hamlets nestled among the grassy meadows and fields teeming with fat cattle.

Evening was drawing on when the knight and his saddle-sore companion passed through the scattering of well-kept houses called Mormont. Just beyond, Friedrich headed Näscher along a short, walled lane into the bustling yard of a prosperous fortified farm. A stable-boy ran up to take the palfrey's reins.

"Dismount," the Saxon said.

Too weary to reply, Robert stifled a groan as he slid from the back of the big horse and Friedrich likewise swung down. Again Robert almost toppled to the ground when his legs, trembling from fatigue, folded under him.

"You will get used to horseback soon," Friedrich said, propping him up as the young ostler led Näscher to the stables. "You will need to."

"Have you rescued another refugee, Sir Friedrich?"

The grinning inquiry came from a bearded, dark-skinned figure who had appeared silently at the Saxon's elbow. He gestured elegantly in the direction of the wobbly kneed scholar.

"God's grace to you, Joseph al-Kalim." Friedrich clasped the other's hand. "This is Robert of Troyes, recently of the Sorbonne. He wishes to join the Knights of the Temple."

The bearded man bowed slightly, and Robert gaped. The

man was slender and tall, though still a hand shorter than Friedrich. His skin was olive-toned, his eyes large and dark. By contrast, his teeth seemed unnaturally white. Even more surprisingly, he seemed to have preserved most of them. Although slightly grizzled, his close-cropped hair, like his short, well-trimmed beard, was the color of old ebony. His drab work tunic seemed longer than most, and his wine-hued breeches were loose and ungartered.

"But sire," Robert said quietly, "he is—he is—"

"A Turcopole. Or as you Franks say, *un poulain.* His father was a Christian soldier, his mother a Saracen. There are many such in our ranks and those of the Hospital. They are brave and devoted. Joseph has accompanied me as groom and retainer for over ten years."

"It is a great pleasure to meet you, young sire. You have chosen a difficult time to enter our company, but you are welcome."

"Joseph will educate you with respect to the care of the horses, tack, and equipment and, with God's help, train you in the use of sword and knife. We will *both* train you."

"Yes, sire," Robert agreed quickly, eyeing the curved dagger and falchion sheathed at Joseph's side.

"You will begin now with the horses. We leave for Rampillon at first light."

Joseph not only handled the horses but, as Robert soon learned, possessed skill in writing, hunting, and cooking. Adept with sword, dagger, lance, and arbalest, he also knew much of the art of healing. He led Robert to the stables, where he procured leather aprons and horn combs.

"This farm belonged to the Order," he explained as they rubbed down the palfrey. "Fortunately, it was made over to a trustworthy patron some weeks before the seizure of the Temple's properties by the King."

"Then, it was known that the King planned to arrest all the members of the Order at once?" Robert asked.

"It was so feared. The arrest of all the Jews of France the

previous year showed how efficiently the royal minions could strike."

"But nothing was done to ward it off!"

"We could not know the exact day or the hour, my young friend. And while there was little we could do to stave off the blow, we prepared for it as we might without alerting the King to our foreknowledge. Much in fact was done. But it is better that you do not ask further about these matters. Such knowledge could cause you sore distress, should you become suspect of having information of value to the King."

Robert sensed a sudden chill. He had heard tales of the refinements of torture developed in the royal dungeons to loosen Templar tongues. All the world must have heard by now, he thought. To suffer and die horribly at the hands of infidels for the Cross of Christ was a noble intent—one he had nurtured as a boy and still prayed for the courage to endure as a man. But to be tortured and executed by fellow Christians as an enemy of the Faith was not an end to which he aspired.

Even with regard to the Saracens and Turks, he increasingly found himself adding a small proviso to his prayer that he had adapted from the great Augustine: "Give me the courage to die for you, Lord—but, if you don't mind, not just yet." Life, he was discovering, was all too short as it was. He had also come to prefer a martyrdom that did not hurt unnecessarily.

The next morning, Robert rode pillion behind Joseph on a spirited gray rouncy called Amir. The Turcopole had donned a leather cuirass but was otherwise free of armor, although a light domed helmet hung from the cantle. Wahgemut, Friedrich's big chestnut destrier, was led behind Amir, carrying only the knight's war shield and great sword. The retinue was completed by a sturdy dappled pack horse laden with an arbalest, pieces of mail, bolts for the arbalest, an extra sword, cooking equipment, wine and water skins, and two panniers containing clothing, food items, and a host of miscellany whose nature Robert could only guess at.

Despite the heat, Friedrich was wearing a hauberk under his surcoat, along with a mesh-mail coif, which, by midday, he had unlaced and pulled back. Slung behind his saddle were a war-ax, a buckler, and his war helmet.

At Nangis, they turned south, and soon came to Rampillon, another small but prosperous village of Brie. The Templar church there had been larger than many. Like many of their properties, Friedrich explained, it had been made over to the Knights Hospitaller, but so far had not been possessed. Nor would it for some time, he predicted.

Robert saw horses everywhere he looked—tethered in the woods, pastured in the fields nearby, even in the graveyard. Inside the church, several dozen knights stood in groups, talking quietly. Their surcoats were of varied hues and for the most part devoid of insignia. Some were confrere knights, Joseph explained, now released from their temporary pledges, others fugitive monk-warriors like Friedrich, vowed for life.

But Robert sensed the general apprehension in their low, tense voices and the quick glances that darted through the gathering with each new entry. All were armored, swords hanging from their belts even in the church. Squires and retainers swelled the assembly, which must have numbered a hundred or more.

Almost at once Friedrich was approached by a burly knight with great, shaggy brows and a close-cropped beard streaked white. His surcoat, white and frayed like Friedrich's, also displayed a faded crusader's cross. In mail and chausses even in the heat of July, his neck and shoulders were protected by a massive collière. Sweat glistened on his forehead.

"Bogo de Montferrand," Joseph whispered into Robert's ear. "Friedrich fought under him at Acre, and they rode with the others to the Council of Vienne. I have heard among his men that he had hoped to join the Teutonic Knights and liberate the Lithuanians, but was denied because of his age."

"How is it that they were not killed at Acre?" Robert whispered back. "I thought that most of the Knights of the Temple died rather than surrender."

"When the city walls were breached, the Grand Master ordered Bogo to evacuate the women and children to Atlit and Cyprus. He, in turn, assigned Friedrich to command one of the ships. Afterward, we accompanied him to Venice and Königsburg. We entered France only when Grand Master Jacques was betrayed and arrested."

"You are well come, Friedrich," the commander said. "What is this?" He jerked his head curtly in Robert's direction.

"This," said Friedrich, "is Robert of Troyes, late of the Sorbonne, who would be a Poor Knight of Christ. He joined us in Paris as my valet."

"The greater fool for that. You are too late, Robert of Troyes. The Order no longer exists. Or did Sir Friedrich not tell you that?"

"The Order exists, Brother Bogo," Friedrich said, lowering his voice. "For we exist. It will continue to exist."

"Only in your dreams, I fear," came the reply, as de Montferrand turned back to Robert. "How old are you?"

"Sixteen years, sire," Robert said, exaggerating only slightly.

"Do with him as you please," the older knight muttered to Friedrich.

With a glance at Robert that conveyed more pity than contempt, the commander would have passed on, but Friedrich arrested him by the arm. The commander turned, ill-disposed to banter.

"In Outremer we fought with steel," Friedrich said, raising his voice for the others to hear. "But here we were conquered with quills and parchment rolls. In time to come, our battles will likely be waged as much with cunning words as with sword and ax. We have need for men such as Robert, skilled in writing and philosophy."

The Frankish knight snorted. "You are no doubt right. The balance of the world has shifted badly. I want no more of it."

With that, he shook off Friedrich's restraining hand, turned on his heel, and strode away.

"Perhaps the Lithuanians have cause to be grateful," Robert said under his breath.

Several more knights, most with squires and valets, arrived within the next half hour. When the church bell tolled for Nones, de Montferrand called the gathering to order. The knights formed a large half circle around him, including a young knight Robert had not noticed previously, who wore a blue and white surcoat, quartered. Clean-shaven and square-faced, his auburn hair was long and styled in the fashion of the court. Clearly not a Templar, then.

The squires and serving men, Joseph and Robert among them, fanned out to the perimeter of the church, some reclining against the cool stone walls, others standing to see and hear the discussion beginning in the center of the nave. Several retainers stood watch at the doors.

Suddenly, a familiar voice boomed over the others. Robert stood on tiptoe and craned to see.

". . . to Saxony," Friedrich was saying, "where the Poor Knights of Christ were never betrayed."

"You cannot return to Germany, either," came de Montferrand's reply. "Not as a Templar. Everywhere the Order has been suppressed."

"There is one place in Christendom where it remains possible," said the young knight in blue and white. "One realm where the ban has had but little effect, a kingdom where you will be welcome. Where you are needed."

"Where is that?" Friedrich retorted. "The Isle of the Blessed?"

The young knight smiled. "That's as may be. But I speak of Scotland."

"Scotland!" laughed a raven-haired knight in a patched green surcoat. "Might as well be the Kingdom of Prester John!"

"How are we needed there?" Friedrich said. "And who would make us welcome?"

"The King, Robert Bruce. His need lies in the great host being mustered by Edward of England to relieve the siege of Stirling. Before this time next year, the freedom of all Scotland will be decided. But he can rely no longer for support on Philip of France, who has compromised himself by marrying his daughter off to the English King. For your service, you will receive pay and pardon—and, so long as God allows, freedom to continue your life as Knights of the Temple."

"Even if we were willing," someone demanded, "how would we get to Scotland?"

"My name is Antony of Ross," the Scottish knight said. "Acting in my King's name, I can secure passage for as many knights as I can muster. With their horses and men."

A murmur of interest rippled through the throng of fighting men.

"Edward Plantagenet is still touring the Artois with his Queen," the young Scot continued. "He will no doubt return to England soon, but it would still be folly to attempt any northern ports. Only La Rochelle is safely accessible."

"But La Rochelle is now a royal port," one of the knights objected. "And the Templar fleet was harbored there. Surely . . ."

"That is why it provides the greatest security for impenitent Templars just now. The fleet has long since vanished and will never return. No, it is settled. The first Genoese ship is already under sail from Marseilles. Up to forty of you who wish to join me must be at La Rochelle no later than the ides of July."

"Two weeks!"

"It is time enough. But you will need to be cautious. Philip and Edward have spies everywhere."

Friedrich grunted agreement, if not approval. "They have galleys everywhere, too."

*   *   *

The discussion continued for more than an hour. Despite his efforts to remain alert, Robert's eyelids grew progressively heavier as he leaned against the rood screen next to Joseph. The Turcopole seemed to be listening intently, although his eyes were half-shut. Sitting like a cobbler, his back was nevertheless straight, not bent like one of his father's apprentices. Occasionally Joseph's lips moved.

Suddenly, Robert was jolted awake by a rough shake from the retainer, who had silently risen to his feet. The church was almost deserted. Friedrich was still locked in conversation with Bogo de Montferrand and Antony of Ross, but the meeting was clearly over.

The Saxon knight abruptly bowed and broke off from the others.

"Come," he said as he approached. "We must leave. Word of the assembly will soon spread, and it would not be wise for renegade Templars to be found so near to Paris."

"But where are we going, sire?"

"Going? To Scotland. But first, to Chartres. Sir Antony must first return to Paris, but will join us there."

Six days later the bell for Nones had just finished ringing when Friedrich, Joseph, and Robert rode wearily past the shadows cast by the unequal spires of the Cathedral of Our Lady of Chartres. A half hour later, they headed their mounts into the yard of the Inn of the Three Pigeons, less than a league south of the town—a ramshackle nest of thatched buildings surrounded by a few fields and some half-dead poplars. The shutters were dangling from rusted hinges, and mud and manure seemed to lie everywhere, but Antony had assured them that the stables were adequate and the innkeeper could be discreet—if appropriately bribed.

But the Scot was nowhere to be seen, nor had the innkeeper seen or heard anything of him.

"We will wait," Friedrich said, looming in the doorway of

the inn's cavernous taproom. "But we will also require lodging for the night."

The innkeeper scrutinized the grizzled, scarred knight, nodded, and left.

Glancing around the smoky room and eyeing its sparse clientele, Friedrich spied a table in the inglenook, where he could command a view of the entrance and the kitchen door. Robert and Joseph followed him across the room, acutely aware of the several pairs of eyes following their passage. Some of the patrons looked like men who might slit their mothers' throats for a candle. Friedrich appeared unconcerned, but Robert noticed that Joseph's hand frequently strayed to the hilt of his dagger.

Not long after welcome cups of watered wine were brought, the doorway was darkened by several figures clad in white robes and black mantles.

"Friar Nicholas!" Robert shouted, bounding from his bench. "Both of you!"

"Three of us, I fear," one of the friars laughed, clapping Robert affectionately on the shoulder. He glanced at Friedrich and Joseph, who had risen from their benches. "I see we are well met."

The speaker was more than middle-aged, as was one of his confreres, who was also taller and leaner than this stout, affable friar. The third was much younger and more robust than his companions. As if alerted by a silent signal, the three friars parted.

Behind them stood two women, each wearing a gray pilgrim's cloak. One was taller and younger than her companion. In one hand she held a small wooden casket banded with thin iron straps, in the other a pilgrim staff. Her hair was pulled back under a white coif and wimple, but Robert could see that she was plain rather than pretty, and only a few years older than himself.

Their eyes met briefly, and he found himself instantly attracted by the kindness and good humor he found in those blue-gray depths. Her companion, dressed alike, was even plainer, as well as heavy-set and more than a decade older.

By then Friedrich had joined them, followed a few paces behind by Joseph. The knight greeted the younger Nicholas warmly, and bowed courteously to the other friars and their companions, without looking directly at the women.

"It pleases me to see you again, Nicholas von Strassburg," the Saxon said. "I remain much in your debt."

"You are keeping well enough, Sir Friedrich," the young friar said. "Eckhart said you have a powerful guardian angel."

Robert was surprised when the big knight broke into laughter. "A busy one, by all accounts! But who are these holy companions of yours?"

"You may remember Friar Nicholas Trevet, from England," Nicholas of Strassburg said, placing one hand on the shoulder of the more portly of the two.

Recognition lit in Friedrich's good eye. "I do. You, too, were with Eckhart at the Gate of Paris when last we met," he recalled.

"Nicholas Major!" Robert interjected, pleased to see his friend once more.

"And this is Friar Nicholas Stretton, also of England," Trevet said, identifying the third man. "He is even more major than I. Robert will, no doubt, christen him appropriately."

"Maximus!" Robert offered triumphantly.

With a thin smile, the third friar scanned the little band with an air of curiosity and what could have been a flicker of amusement in his light blue eyes.

"Many Preaching Friars seem to be named Nicholas," Friedrich said. "Is that because he is the patron of travelers?"

"Or of thieves?"

The voice was Antony's. He had entered unobserved behind the others, flanked by two attendants: a thick-set, sandy-haired fellow with blue eyes, freckles, and a ready smile, and his opposite, an older, wiry man, dark of hair and eye, with

the look of a wolfhound to him. Trevet parried the Scot's irrev-
erent intrusion with an arched eyebrow.

"Friar Nicholas Stretton was provincial of England until last
year," Antony informed them. "The good friars travel with us
on their way to Avignon."

Friedrich stepped back sharply. "You seek the pope?"

"I seek a manuscript," Trevet assured him. "A far more difficult task, I might add. My brethren have other business, there
and in Italy. But allow me to present our fair companions."

With a gentle wave of his hand, he ushered the women forward.

"Yvette of Châtillon, of the Royal Beguinage in Paris,"
Trevet said. The beguine inclined her head slightly, keeping
her eyes modestly cast down. In turn, Friedrich, Joseph, and
Robert named themselves. She looked up when Robert spoke
and again met his glance. He blushed to his fingertips.

"Her maid is called Mathilde," Trevet said. The stocky,
square-faced peasant woman dipped and tried to disappear
behind Yvette. "You will know Sir Antony of Ross," the friar
said. "He is accompanied by his squire, Niall MacAndrew, and
his liege man, Alisdair."

Each bowed deeply.

"Now, come, let us sit together." Trevet herded the company toward the benches. "Walking these hot French roads has
given me an uncommon thirst."

As Antony passed, Friedrich placed a hand on his arm to
stop him.

"Knights of the Temple are not permitted to consort with
women," he said quietly. "Not even with beguines."

"A sensible precaution for soldier-monks, my friend,"
Antony said. "But the charge for which I returned to Paris was
to convey this lady and her maid to Scotland."

It seemed to Robert that Friedrich's face paled.

"Attend, sir knight," Trevet said, guiding the big Saxon to
the table as if he were a schoolboy.

To Robert's amazement, Friedrich made no protest. Seating him at his side, the portly friar raised a finger.

"First, since both Templars and beguines were condemned at the Council of Vienne last year, you now have more in common than you might care to admit. But, secondly," and another finger came up, "let me hasten to add that since Yvette and Mathilde are from the Royal Beguinage in Paris, they do not fall under the ban. And, third, they require your assistance as your even-Christians. Next," and the fourth finger, "at all times you will be in the company of your fellow pilgrims. Finally," and he displayed his hand fully, then slapped it conclusively on the table, "Eckhart sent her."

"Eckhart?"

"Eckhart."

Friedrich still looked none too pleased, but the cumulative force of Antony's announcement and Trevet's logic left him no easy way out.

"Have no fear, Sir Friedrich," Yvette said in a voice low and yet, Robert thought, firm and assuring. "My vows are as sacred to me as your own. Friar Eckhart told me you were a man of great honor."

Despite the dim light, it seemed to Robert that the knight turned crimson.

"With your permission, good sires, Mathilde and I will withdraw to attend our orisons. . . ."

Friedrich scrambled to his feet and bowed, while Trevet inclined his head and smiled. The others parted to allow the women passage, then crowded onto the benches.

"Now," Friedrich said, with sufficient finality that all eyes turned to him. "Explain how these women came into our midst. Eckhart said nothing to me of this."

"He could not," Nicholas Minor said. "For you had gone to earth."

Trevet beamed as additional cups were brought by the potboy. "The way of it is this," he said after slaking his thirst.

"On the last day of June, once our unlamented Brother Imbert was laid to rest and we bade farewell to Eckhart at the Porte Saint-Antoine, the prior was summoned by the Mistress of the Beguinage. Yvette had been found unconscious in the church, bleeding from the hands, side, and feet."

Instinctively, Alisdair, Niall, and Robert crossed themselves.

"Not to worry," Trevet reassured them. "She recovered fully. But when she awoke, she would say only that she had been ordered to Scotland, to carry the treasure of the Temple. She mentioned two names. The first was that of Sir Antony, who was then still lodged in Paris, and was previously known to her."

"That is true," Antony added quickly. "She had certain connections with the house of Baliol, and had been to court. I had met her there."

"The other was Friedrich of Hochheim," the old friar said.

"I know no beguines," Friedrich objected. "In Paris or elsewhere!"

"Nor did she know you," Trevet said with an amused glance around the table. "But she knew your name. And that you were to accompany her to Scotland. Or, perhaps, that she was to accompany you."

"By the Virgin's veil," Friedrich muttered. "This smells of witchery."

"Not so, my large friend," Trevet insisted. "Yvette of Châtillon is known to be a virtuous woman. The Mistress of the Beguinage and the prior have assured me of that. There is no scent of hellfire here."

"What, then, prophecy?"

Trevet shrugged. "Possibly so. In whatever case, her message has sufficient warrant for Sir Antony to consent to escort her to his homeland, even though the journey will be arduous."

"But you said she was sent by Eckhart," Friedrich reminded the friar.

"Eckhart had been her confessor for a time," Trevet said.

"From what I gather, he saw her before his departure from Paris and had foretold that a mission of importance was to be entrusted to her."

"I do not like it," Friedrich protested. "Eckhart told me nothing!"

"It was deemed wise to conceal our movements from the eyes of the English and also from King Philip," Antony said. "Both Scots and the Poor Knights of Christ labor under a common cloud of suspicion."

"But for different reasons," Friedrich pointed out.

"Nonetheless, it was not difficult to arrange licenses for pilgrims traveling to Tours and Santiago de Compostella," Antony continued, ignoring the remark. "Just beyond Poitiers, when the friars leave us for the south, the rest of us will turn west toward Niort and La Rochelle. You must attach these—" He set out several leaden scallops, badges of the great Spanish shrine. "Yvette and I will become pilgrims returning to Scotland with our retinue, should there be any challenge. Here are the licenses."

The following morning, rested but hardly refreshed by their stay in the noisome inn, the party set out for Châteaudun and the Touraine. Friedrich and Antony rode in front on their palfreys, the Scot's a spirited ash-gray named Stoirmeil, which he said meant "Stormy." The women walked behind them, followed by the friars and Robert. Next came Joseph and Niall, on their rouncies, with Alisdair bringing up the rear on foot, leading both burdened sumpters.

"I call my mount Gargail, because he thinks he is fierce," the Scottish squire explained as he mounted, loudly enough for Robert and the friars to hear. "And the pack mule is Speachean, for he kicks. So beware."

Joseph again led Wahgemut, Friedrich's destrier, and Niall had care of Antony's warhorse, a heavy dun stallion called Confadh.

"His name means 'Fury' in our language," Niall said.

"In the Saxon tongue, Wahgemut means 'Gallant,' " Joseph said. "If names were horses, they would travel well together."

"Speaking of traveling together," Robert said to Trevet as they walked, "have the Preaching Friars become partisans of the Scottish cause?"

"The Blackfriars in England are close-bound to young King Edward, lad," Trevet said, gravely enough to suggest that, again, Robert had asked the wrong question.

"In Paris," Stretton said, "we dined with him at Pentecost when he came with his young queen to visit her august father."

"He no longer grieves so deeply for his murdered friend, Gaveston," Trevet continued, "but his spirit is still bitter toward the barons."

"Sir Antony says he permitted the Templars to be tortured."

"He was so ordered by the pope," Trevet said. "And to please King Philip. But it was not to his liking. Very few so suffered."

"What became of them . . . after?"

"Some have become Hospitallers or Austin Canons," Trevet said. "Others have accepted pensions and returned to the world. A few have even fled north to join the Bruce pretender."

"So we have heard," Joseph said cautiously from Amir's back. "Is it to be wondered at?"

The friar sighed. "Not as this world reckons."

"It is said that Edward and his Gaveston pillaged the Temple treasury in London," Joseph added.

"Kings are sometimes constrained to act against particular interests," Trevet replied quietly. "For the common good."

"Philip and Edward seem to do that quite a lot, I think," Joseph said. But the Turcopole's tone was also mild. He seemed to scent the esteem in which Trevet held his king, and his own regard for the elderly friar was no less evident.

"Yet you accompany Sir Antony and Friedrich," Robert objected. "Does this not conflict with your allegiance to Edward?"

"Out of obedience, we agreed to accompany Sister Yvette and her maid as far as Chartres," Trevet replied smoothly. "The rest is in the hands—"

"Ambush!"

Friedrich's alarm shattered the tranquility of the green-arched forest road. Näscher trumpeted in protest, half rearing, but the knight threw himself forward to prevent toppling both of them to the ground. Recovering, Friedrich unslung his war-ax as a ragged line of men charged screaming out of the cover of the trees.

"Bandits!" Joseph shouted, at the same time spurring forward, forcing Robert and the friars to the side of the road.

Wearing scant armor, but brandishing swords, gisarms, and billhooks, the bandits seemed primarily intent on capturing the knights, although several made for the sumpters and their precious baggage. Antony's fine apparel meant a profitable ransom, and even capturing Friedrich, despite his plainer attire, might have been worth the effort had he not been a Templar, and an outlaw at that. But this at least one brigand would never know, as the Saxon's ax swept down in a sweeping arc, almost severing the man's head.

Antony had wheeled Stoirmeil around. Roaring his battle cry, he charged with his sword, followed by Niall on his rouncy. Alisdair released the two sumpter animals and also drew his sword, shouting as he ran behind them.

Robert guessed there might be as many as ten or twelve attackers. Some, he was sure, had been at the inn the night before. The friars were unarmed, of course, save for their staves. Even with himself and Joseph, the company seemed dangerously outnumbered.

He ran to their sumpter horse and wrenched at a sword tied to the pack saddle. Whipping it from its scabbard, he turned to engage, breathing a prayer to the Virgin in the sure knowledge that he would likely be dead within moments. Joseph, he saw, had dismounted and already had the arbalest to his shoulder. A bolt quickly found its mark in the chest of one of Friedrich's assailants.

A scream from behind told of Antony's work. Then Robert saw Yvette, standing motionless at the roadside, clasping the casket. Her eyes were shut, as if in prayer. Mathilde stood at her side, arms crossed, as if daring anyone to approach.

He had no time even to attempt reaching them as the two big destriers, now loose and inflamed by the sounds and sight of battle, charged riderless between them into the affray, kicking and biting at their masters' opponents.

Evading the billhooks, Friedrich slashed ferociously at his would-be captors, shouting at them in German. One, Robert saw, was crouching low, wielding a broad-bladed spear. Skillfully, he dodged Näscher's hooves and flailing head, attempting to get within range to cripple or kill the animal and, with that, to bring down his rider as well.

Yelling as fiercely as he could, Robert sprang forward, swinging his sword with all his strength. Alerted, the cutthroat brought up the butt of his spear and parried with a slashing sidestroke, knocking Robert to the ground. But as he raised his spear for a killing thrust, he froze and teetered backward, a spray of blood filling the air where a second before his head had been.

"Move!" Friedrich bellowed, wheeling to fend off yet another gisarmier.

As Robert staggered to his feet, a bolt from Joseph's arbalest hissed over his head, followed by a scream of agony somewhere behind him. For an instant, he caught sight of Yvette, still motionless by the side of the road, her eyes still lightly shut. But she was now flanked protectively by the two older friars as well as Mathilde. Nicholas Minor had taken a stand by the sumpter horse, holding his pilgrim's stick before him like a quarterstaff.

"Break off! Break off!" someone shouted hoarsely.

Robert glimpsed a form hurtling at him from the side and, without turning to see whether friend or foe, scythed his sword in a backhanded stroke with all his remaining strength. It connected with a shock that tore the weapon from his hand as it brought down his target, screaming in pain.

Running figures crisscrossed Robert's wavering vision as he staggered for balance, shouts and cries giving way to an eerie silence. Turning, he saw the surviving bandits scattering into the forest, an unlucky straggler falling to another of Joseph's well-aimed arbalest bolts.

An anguished cry brought him reeling around to see one of the bandits cringing on his knees, moaning as he pressed a bloodied hand to the side of his head. Bright blood pumped between the fingers. In the next instant, Alisdair had leaped astride the man and seized him by the hair, yanking back his head to slash his throat from ear to ear.

Robert gasped in horror as the man's body arched and collapsed. Alisdair regained his feet just in time to catch Robert as he, too, collapsed. The last thing he saw before sinking into a dizzying black void was Yvette, hurrying toward them across the blood-drenched road.

He awoke slowly, wondering at the delicate tracery of leafy branches against the pale blue sky. He also wondered why he was lying on his back in the grass.

Recalling the fight and its aftermath, Robert bolted upright, retched, then turned and vomited violently. Trembling, he struggled to his feet. Through the trees, he saw a quiet knot of figures huddled at the side of the road.

He spat and wiped a hand across his face, shocked to see the hand come away dark with half-dried blood. Frantically, he probed his face and head, but could find no pain or damage. With sickening but grateful insight, he realized that the gore on his face and tunic was not his own.

Unsteadily, he approached his companions. Antony was on one knee by the side of the road. Alisdair stood ready a few paces away, holding the horses' reins, his eyes scanning the edges of the forest. Niall sat on the ground nearby, his knees buckled, supporting his bandaged head in his hands. Nicholas Major stood behind him. The other friars were dragging corpses into a row among the trees on the nether side of the road. Yvette and Mathilde stood back a little ways, their eyes fixed on the group around Antony.

"Where is Sir Friedrich?" Robert demanded, suddenly fearful.

Pressing into the circle, he found Joseph bent over the Saxon, who lay on his back in a small grassy area. Protruding from the knight's left shoulder, piercing surcoat and hauberk, a crossbow bolt had buried itself almost to the parchment fletching. As the Turcopole examined the wound, Friedrich's dazed gaze roved from face to face, his jaws clenched against the pain.

"He was struck, I think, as the attack began," Antony said quietly. "From the angle of the shaft, the bowman would have shot from a tree. He may have aimed for the palfrey."

"But, how did he continue to fight, so wounded?"

"Because he was trained to," the Scot said, as if that should be obvious.

"I fear the head may be barbed," Joseph said.

"We can contrive a litter," Antony said. "There will be a farmhouse or monastery close by."

Joseph shook his head. "He must not be moved. The quarrel has sunk deep. It may kill him yet."

Going to one of the panniers, the Turcopole fished out a parcel wrapped in black silk. Returning, he knelt again beside Friedrich and untied the parcel, unrolling it on the grass. Robert could see an array of knives of different lengths and shapes and other instruments of surgery.

"What is he doing?" Robert cried, and started forward.

Hands seized his shoulders from behind and drew him back.

"He, too, is doing what he is trained to do," Nicholas Trevet whispered in his ear. "Be still."

After a moment's reflection, Joseph removed a short, thick-bladed knife with a curved blade. "Bring fire," he said.

"Get a priest!" Friedrich wheezed. "I will not die in sin."

"Rest easy, Friedrich," Antony said. "Friar Nicholas is here."

The others withdrew a few paces as Trevet knelt beside the supine figure.

"Confess me! I have killed in anger."

"Whom did you kill in anger?"

"Your brother, Imbert, the Inquisitor of Paris. It was I who made him eat poison. I brought the figs."

Trevet was silent for a moment, his eyes closed. Then, "Do you repent?"

"Not of his death, priest, but that my hand was raised against a Christian in vengeance. By my soul, I acted in God's own justice. But there was hatred in my heart for what he did to the Poor Knights of Christ."

"God alone judges the heart, Friedrich. And He alone forgives. May the merciful God pardon you and give you peace. What else?"

"Nothing else, priest. I have kept my vows."

"Ego te absolvo," Trevet murmured, tracing the cross of redemption over the wounded knight. "Go in the peace of Christ and his Church."

"Tell Eckhart. Say I confessed my guilt."

"I will. Rest easy."

"Then give me a penance, priest."

"I do not need to," Trevet said, nodding for Joseph to approach.

Following behind Joseph, Alisdair had a tin cannikin and a skin of wine. Joseph withdrew a small vial from his wallet, unstoppered it, and poured the contents into the cannikin, then nodded for Alisdair to add wine from the skin.

"Poppy," he said quietly, as he knelt and handed the cup to Friedrich.

The Saxon nodded grimly and drank off the potion. Then he lay back, closed his eyes, and surrendered his soul to God and his body to the Turcopole.

Robert watched, his head light and his stomach fluttering as Joseph cut off the end of a leather strap and placed it between Friedrich's teeth. At his signal, Antony and Alisdair knelt on either side of the Saxon, pinning his arms and legs to the ground. As Joseph began cutting away the fletching from the shaft of the quarrel, Yvette knelt at the Templar's head, placed her casket on the grass beside him, and cupped his face in her hands. Joseph looked up, apprehensive, but she cautioned him with a nod to say nothing. Friedrich could not see her.

Joseph nodded in reply and put aside his knife. He then gently eased the surcoat over the shaft, unlaced the hauberk, and eased that off as well. He next cut through Friedrich's bloodstained gambeson and undertunic, exposing the embedded shaft. The knight's loss of blood had not been great, but the skin around the wound was darkening. With a nod to Antony and Alisdair to tighten their hold, Joseph picked up another knife.

Not long after, the bolt lay bloody in the grass next to the semiconscious Saxon, whose barely suppressed cries of agony had at last ended. The smell of seared flesh hung in the still air. Fortunately, the head of the quarrel had not been barbed, and the removal had been less difficult than Joseph had feared.

"But he has lost much blood," the Turcopole said. "Still, he has the body of an ox, else he could not have fought on after such a wound."

"We cannot stay here," Antony said. "Night will fall soon enough, and the bandits may return. Is it safe to move him now?"

"I think he can be taken by litter to a place of healing, if there is one near at hand. But not far, lest the wound reopen and he bleed again to his death. Cautery is not enough."

While Alisdair and Robert set about constructing a litter from saplings, spare tack, and their cloaks, Joseph and Antony assessed their other needs.

"Is Niall able to ride?" Antony asked.

"The pain will be great," Joseph said, "but he can ride."

"Then gather any arms and whatever of value you can find on the bodies," the Scottish knight said. "We can at least deprive their comrades of that comfort."

Without means at hand or time to bury the dead, they covered the bodies with brush. Left by the side of the road, they would be found easily enough. A few coins would prompt the sexton at the next village to see to the disposal before the carrion crows and wild dogs did.

Soon they had lifted Friedrich onto the litter and set out. They traveled slowly, careful to prevent jostling the wounded man. As they passed travelers coming toward Chartres, the friars inquired as to a monastery or hospice.

Finally, they were told of an abbey a league north of Bonneval, only two hours ahead. Joseph nodded. But from his expression, Robert understood that traveling even that distance would severely tax Friedrich's remaining strength.

The black-robed monks extended the hospitality for which they were rightly revered. Both Niall and Friedrich were housed in a lodge adjoining the infirmary, the others provided with refreshment and the means to wash off the grime of battle. The squire was only lightly wounded, but needed rest. Friedrich's injury was pronounced grave. An ancient, half-deaf infirmarian called Placidus examined and then re-dressed the wound, clucking his tongue as he applied poultices and forced malodorous herbal concoctions through the knight's clenched teeth.

"You will bleed him?" Joseph cast a cautious glance at the instruments lying on the stand nearby.

"Ha!" the monk fairly shouted. "He has, I think, bled too much already! It is putrefaction I fear."

Friedrich suffered the monk's ministrations for the better part of an hour, his face the color of parchment, scarcely seeming to breathe. Then, slowly casting his good eye over the others in the room—Antony, Joseph, Robert, and Nicholas

Minor—he summoned the Scot closer with what strength he could muster.

"Leave me," he whispered. "But take Joseph and Robert. You must meet the ship."

A hurried exchange of glances between Antony and Joseph told Robert that Friedrich was right. But before either could speak, the room darkened. Yvette stood in the doorway, flanked by the older friars.

"Our sister would see Sir Friedrich," Nicholas Trevet announced quietly.

Friedrich's good eye turned to the door and widened in protest. Brother Placidus arched his bushy eyebrows almost to the fringe of his white tonsure.

"It is not . . . regular," Joseph said, glancing warily at Friedrich.

"I am charged to bear the treasure of the Temple," the beguine said in her low, resonant voice. "God wills it."

Again, glances quickly circled the room. At last Joseph spoke. "Admit her."

"I must be alone with him."

"That is not permitted," Friedrich objected weakly.

"God wills it," Joseph whispered to him, then bowed, turned, and left the room.

Brother Placidus gathered his bowls, knives, and dressings and, without a word, departed, scowling. Antony followed, and, in turn, Nicholas Minor and Robert, joining Mathilde and the two older friars. From the antechamber, Joseph pulled the door closed, then turned and stood before it, crossing his arms.

Silence fell among them. For the space of half an hour, Mathilde stood by the entrance, stolid as a baptismal font. Antony paced. The friars sat and, Robert surmised, told their beads. As perplexed as any of them, he leaned wearily against a wall, his eyes on the plank door behind the Turcopole.

Then, quietly, the latch clicked. Joseph turned and stepped aside as the door opened. Yvette stood in the opening, the flickering candlelight from behind outlining her cloak and wimple with a thin, golden aureole.

"He will be able to travel in the morning." She smiled for an instant, then left the room, passing through the astonished band of men like the Israelite host amidst the Red Sea.

Unable to remain still any longer, Robert rushed into the room, followed more cautiously by Joseph, Antony, and Nicholas Minor.

Friedrich was sitting up in the bed, looking like he had just awakened from a short, peaceful nap.

"God willed it," he said, and shrugged.

When the company left the monastery the following morning, Friedrich was once again mounted on Näscher, erect and alert as he had been the morning before. Standing by the gate, Brother Placidus watched them depart, puzzlement and suspicion warring in the folds of his face. Despite assurances given him and the abbot by the friars that all was well, Robert wondered if the old man was sniffing the air for brimstone. He, too, wondered about the night before, but by common, unspoken consent—or embarrassment—nothing more was said of it among the wayfarers that day or for a long time to come.

In two days' time, they passed through Châteaudun and Cloyes into the Loire Valley. Granted hospitality at the Abbey of the Trinity in Vendôme, they journeyed the following day to Château-Renault, and late in the afternoon approached the city of Tours.

Crossing the great bridge, they joined the procession of other pilgrims westward to the borough of Châteauneuf and the shrine of France's second patron. There they paid homage briefly at the tomb of Saint Martin, said the required prayers, and received their leaden badges.

Passing through the city, they found the narrow streets still filled with milk sellers, fruit peddlers, tinkers, and townspeople jostling one another, arguing, and shoving to get to the market stalls. Beggars crouched at street corners and in alleyways, their pleas mingling with the bolder cries of the apprentices and vendors playing their trade or seeking customers.

At the crossroads beyond the south gate of the city, Robert's eyes stung as he embraced each of the friars in turn, then watched them set out on the road to Châteauroux and Avignon, their black cloaks rippling in the light breeze. Nicholas Trevet turned once and waved a white napkin in benediction before the three Preachers rounded a bend in the road that removed them from sight.

Reduced by a third, the company passed on to Saint-Mauré, finding accommodation at the pilgrims' hospice. Another day's travel took them to Ozon, near Châtellerault. There they were received hospitably at the old commandery, still occupied through papal dispensation by elderly knights and sergeants who had accepted the offer of pension, provided they put off the habit and forswore the Rule, living out their days in prayer and penance.

The sad old men made their visitors as comfortable as they could, refreshed them from their own meager larder, and carefully stabled the horses out of sight of the road and the eyes of any curious passersby. Early the following morning, after a Mass celebrated by one of the aged chaplains and a rudimentary breakfast of dry bread and a little wine, Friedrich and Antony obtained directions to another former Templar enclave at Lavausseau.

Traveling southwest, they skirted Poitiers with its great churches and the tomb of Saint Hilary, avoiding the well-garrisoned palace of the Duke of Aquitaine, with its strong English ties. By pressing hard, they arrived before dusk at the small former commandery. The community of pensioners— here, clerks and farmers of the Order—gave the party a cautious welcome and were visibly relieved to see them off at first light. Robert wondered if they would ever live without the fear of arrest and summary condemnation lurking at the back of their minds after the events of that woeful October six years before.

Following the Route of Saint James, the travelers came the following evening to Saint-Maixent-l'École, where they found shelter at the hostel. Now within two days of La Rochelle, they still lagged a day behind. But the weather remained fair, and the next day's tide might do as well, if the sailing were delayed. At least so Antony hoped.

Crossing the Sèvre before Niort, they moved on without incident past Frontenay and halted at Mauzé. By mid-morning the following day, the wayfarers were now within seven leagues of La Rochelle, just beyond the village of La Laigne, where the road once again entered forestland. Cautious after the ambush near Bonneval, Antony sent Alisdair ahead to reconnoiter.

"A bailiff and a troop of sergeants lie just within the trees!" he reported on his return.

"Still searching for those of us who refused to confess to the blasphemies!" Friedrich muttered, his hand reaching for his ax.

"Peace," Antony said. "How many are there?"

"Perhaps ten or twelve."

"Heavily armed? Mounted?"

"From what I could see, three are mounted. The rest have halberds and arbalests."

"Do we fight?" Friedrich asked.

"We would need to kill them all to prevent their alerting the garrison at La Rochelle."

"And some of us will most likely be injured or killed," Robert suggested.

In the silence that followed, Yvette stepped forward.

"No one need die or suffer. But you must pass the sergeants in complete silence. I will guide you."

Niall's mouth fell open. "You mean, you want us to walk right up to them?"

"No, past them. Slowly. Lead the horses on foot and keep

them silent. On no account stop as you pass, and do not look at the soldiers. Have faith!"

"And so I do, by Jesu!" Antony said. "But this is surely madness."

Friedrich raised his hand before anyone else could speak.

"God and Eckhart have sent this sister to guide us. Do as she bids."

Without further comment, the big Saxon dismounted. "Muzzle the destriers," he warned Joseph and Alisdair. Then, quietly soothing his palfrey, he set off behind the beguine and her maid, who had already started down the road toward the forest.

Antony and the others gaped at one another in amazement. Robert shrugged and fell in behind Friedrich, leading Wahgemut. At worst he would be arrested and thrown into prison for the rest of his life. Unless they killed him, of course. There was always that.

Scenting horses ahead as they neared the edge of the wood, the stallion nickered impatiently through his muzzle.

"Softly, friend," Robert whispered. Wahgemut tossed his head in disgust but progressed quietly.

A short distance ahead, a squad of sergeants were deployed on both sides of the road. Several were on horseback. The lead figure, clad in mail and resting a spiked mace against his shoulder, urged his mount forward.

"Old woman!" he shouted, "have you seen anyone on the road today? A band of men with horses?"

The beguine paused and cupped one hand to her mouth. "I saw no one but these poor creatures," she called.

With rhythmic gestures, she waved her companions on. Silently, they ambled beside her, not daring to glance at the sergeants, who seemed interested only in the beguine.

When safely out of sight of the guards, Robert caught up with Yvette. "But how—"

"Men see what they expect to see," she said, and smiled.

"If they expect to see an old woman with cows, they see an old woman with cows."

Mathilde winked impishly at the astonished valet and followed her mistress down the road toward the city. Occasionally, Robert thought he heard her mooing softly and giggling.

The pilgrims arrived at the eastern gate of the city shortly after Sext. Their papers and licenses were given a cursory inspection, and they were allowed to pass unchallenged. Following the Rue des Merciers, they hurried through the busy market squares, past the Hôtel de Ville, and, coming to the Rue du Temple, filed under the shadow of the imposing commandery, on to the west gate and the port beyond. Antony again displayed their licenses, and the weary caravan was finally allowed to pass on to the quays.

The wharves were crowded with merchants, sailors, and dockworkers, all getting in one another's way and talking at once in a half-dozen tongues. A helpful if unsteady seaman pointed out the berth where the *Sainte-Vierge* was still moored.

Following behind Friedrich and Antony, Robert glanced up and whistled. "It's *huge*."

"A *carraca*," Joseph said. "What you Franks call a *huissier*. They are used in the Middle Sea to transport horses."

Stretching, it seemed, halfway along the docks, it was the only two-masted vessel in the harbor, the first Robert had ever seen. The carrack rode high in the water, its large lading port open. Ostlers were carefully leading horses and mules up the gangway. On the dock, teams of sweating workers were piling casks, chests, and bales of hay and straw near a treadmill crane, its arm poised over the waist of the ship. Crewmen with plaiting knives and tar-buckets in their hands prowled the decks and ratlines, tending to the rigging. Supervising all this activity was a solitary figure pacing the gallery of the aftercastle, shouting orders and gesticulating eloquently.

"Is it . . . *broken?*" Robert asked Joseph, eyeing the rakish-ly angled yard hanging from the shorter, aft mast.

"It is lateen-rigged, young sire," the Turcopole explained. "You northern Franks have not yet learned all the secrets of mastering the wind. Saracen galleys are always so rigged, and many Italian ships. This is a Genoese ship from the Middle Sea, fast and maneuverable for all its size."

"And also old, I fear," Friedrich said. "I *know* this ship. I have seen her before."

"She was at Acre, sire," Joseph said quietly. "Twenty years ago. She rescued many Franks and Arab Christians before the city fell to the Sultan."

"But it was not called the *Sainte-Vierge.*"

"Ships, like men, can change their names, sire."

"And age is not necessarily a sign of weakness," Antony added.

"I know little enough of ships," Friedrich confessed. "All I require is that it does not sink."

Bogo of Montferrand emerged from the welter of crew, passengers, workers, and animals thronging the quay, followed by a royal official carrying a white baton and seeming very con-scious of his authority.

"I feared you had been waylaid," he said abruptly as the official studied Antony's papers.

Friedrich laughed. "And so we were. But God saw us through."

He looked down at Yvette, who gave no sign, other than the flicker of a smile, that she understood anything beyond the plain meaning of his words.

"How many knights?" Antony asked.

"Thirty-one at present count," said de Montferrand. "Plus their retinues. Over ninety in all. There are also the crew, archers, twelve men-at-arms, and a few passengers."

"And the horses?"

"The captain has counted over one hundred. But there is

still stall space. It is a large ship. But we must be swift to catch the evening tide."

"Are these the stragglers, then?"

A burly figure was approaching with rapid strides. His gait had a peculiar roll to it, as if he had drunk too much wine and were trying to dance. Hatless, he had hair and a short beard, raven-hued and curly; his face was bronzed and weathered by wind and sea. Over high black boots, he wore a black leather doublet.

"Our captain," de Montferrand said with an uncharacteristic flourish. "Alain d'Arcachon. A Gascon."

"I know this man," Friedrich said, studying the captain's face. "He sailed with the fleet from Atlit and Cyprus."

"In truth, I did," d'Arcachon said, showing his teeth. "Though I was hardly more than a lad. Were you there?"

"I was there."

"*Eh bien,* my friend. On board with you now. We sail as soon as tide and wind allow."

With that, he turned heel and returned to the dock.

"Are you coming with us?" Friedrich asked.

De Montferrand shook his head. "Not I. There is work here yet unfinished. But I shall follow in time."

Friedrich searched the commander's face. "It is like Acre," he said.

"It is like Acre. Go with God."

When the last horses and mules were aboard, the lading port was closed and caulked. Heavier cargo and ballast were then cautiously lowered into the hold by the swinging crane. Gradually, the old ship sank deeper into the waters of the port.

When the last passengers were on deck, the gangways were pulled aboard, the mooring lines cast off, and a pilot boat began towing the *Sainte-Vierge* out of port. Two crewmen standing in the aftercastle heralded her departure with trumpets. Her planks creaked and groaned in reply. When she was at last released from the cable of the oared tow, a command from the captain caused her mainsail to be unfurled, then the lateen sail. Both cracked impatiently in the breeze as they filled.

Finally, accompanied by the cries of gulls gliding overhead, the ship headed for open water. Robert savored the tang of the sea, but felt no breath of the heaven-sent wind that propelled them.

Soon, the Pointe des Minimes appeared on their left. To the right d'Arcachon pointed out the Pointe de Chef de Baie. The *Sainte-Vierge* followed its curve, heading north into the Straits of Brittany under the leeward shore of the Île de Ré, which stretched like a finger toward the declining sun. A few fishing boats wandered lazily across the bay. Some, their sails furled, were already being rowed toward their berths.

But d'Arcachon posted sharp-eyed lookouts in the fore- and topcastles. Others scanned the shores of the Île de Ré from the main deck. Beyond the haven of La Rochelle, the danger of arrest was, if anything, more acute than ever.

The insouciant sun dipped lower over the island. Heartbeat by heartbeat, the *Sainte-Vierge* glided on under the steady breeze. Yvette, standing apart from the other passengers and even Mathilde, stared silently ahead, to all appearances alone unconcerned with their slack pace.

On the aftercastle deck with Antony, Friedrich, and Robert, d'Arcachon pointed to the blunt spires of the abbey church of the Châteliers silhouetted against the late afternoon sky. Beyond the moorlands of the Pointe des Barres, the limestone outcroppings of the Pointe de la Bergère came into view.

"The village of La Flotte lies within the cove," he said. "Were I in command of a galley, it is from there I would launch an ambush."

By heading north toward the coast of Brittany, d'Arcachon sought to put as much distance as possible between the carrack and the island while the light remained good, but soon a shrill cry from overhead sliced through the tension with cruel finality.

"Ship, ho!"

D'Arcachon swore eloquently, but it seemed to Robert that a great sigh, almost an expression of relief, emanated from the crew and passengers alike. The waiting was over.

"Galleys! Two of them! Off the larboard stern!"

In the distance, Robert made out two dark lines on the sea, moving out from the cover of a head of low cliffs.

"Are they French or English?" Antony shouted to the lookout.

"He cannot tell yet," d'Arcachon muttered. "What does it matter?"

Joseph climbed to the upper deck and came to stand by Robert's side.

"Can we outrun them?" Robert asked.

"The old carrack is swift," Joseph said, "but even with a good wind, it could not outpace large galleys."

"Will we fight?"

"We may have to. First, let us see how well our archers were trained."

Bowmen armed with arbalests took up positions behind the screens in the waist of the ship and along the stern rails of the aftercastle. Several climbed to the topcastle. Friedrich, Antony, the other knights, and their combatant squires began to arm themselves. Yvette ordered Mathilde to seek shelter with the other passengers, among them several women and children. The tough old peasant resisted until Antony fairly drove her into the hold, which already reeked from the stench of confined animals, wet straw, and fodder. But Yvette herself climbed to the forecastle.

Antony and d'Arcachon either took no notice or did not care to stop her as she crossed to the beam of the stempost. There, at the prow of the ship, she gazed toward the line of hills still two leagues away.

Although the carrack was moving at a rapid clip, the dark shapes in pursuit grew steadily larger. Soon, masts and oars were visible, and the shouts of the cockswains echoed faintly over the water. To Robert, the galleys looked like great scorpions striding over the waves, their many oars dipping and rising like long spindly legs.

Blood-red, the sun sank behind the pines and moorlands of the island. Still the galleys sped on, inexorably closing the vital distance between them and the *Sainte-Vierge*.

"Fog!" came a sudden shout from above. "Ahead! Ahead!"

Robert twisted to peer over the forward wales. Seeming to rise from the sea itself, twists of vapor were spreading over the waves in front of the ship, parting before her, then closing in her wake. As the deadly race drew on, the mist grew thicker, streaming up past the wales and lapping over onto the deck. It swirled into the shrouds and soon engulfed even the sails, although the wind did not abate.

"Captain!" the mate shouted. "We must reef the sails! Shall we prepare to drop anchor?"

But it was Yvette's voice that sounded through the eerie, muffled air.

"Sail on."

"We will run aground!" the mate cried. "There are sandbars and rocks— We cannot see ahead!"

"Sail on," Friedrich repeated, his good eye fixed intently on Antony.

After a moment's reflection, the Scottish knight turned to the captain.

"If God does not guide and protect us now, all is lost anyway. Sail on," he said.

D'Arcachon stared at him in disbelief, then crossed himself. "Sail on," he croaked to the mate. "But keep a sharp eye out!"

The carrack moved deeper into the fog, until Robert could no longer see the solitary figure of the beguine beside the stempost. The *Sainte-Vierge* seemed alone on a sea of billowing smoke. He wondered if the galleys, faced with that sudden wall of blankness, had turned back. Not so much as a single arrow had emerged from the dense wall of cloud behind them. Or would their pursuers, too, defy reason and dare Providence in order to overtake and attack their slower prey?

At his post in front of the aftercastle, the steersman gripped the tiller tightly, unsure which way to turn the ship. Feeling her change tack periodically, as if moved by the wind alone, he loudly invoked the Virgin Mary, Saint Nicholas, and Saint Elmo, the Patron of Seamen.

"It lifts!"

All eyes followed the shout to the topcastle, still half-hidden in the haze. But farther overhead, past the eye-strained lookout and archers, hints of azure flickered behind the roiling tatters of mist. Moments later, the carrack passed out of the fog bank into a clear, summer evening. Behind her, however, the mist still stood like a dark wall of cloud separating the *Sainte-Vierge* from her pursuers.

In the silence that followed, pierced only by the cries of the gulls soaring overhead, all eyes slowly turned to the figure standing on the forecastle, still facing the bright sea ahead. One by one, the passengers and crew crossed themselves. Some also kissed their thumbs to ward off the evil eye.

"Keep a sharp eye abaft," d'Arcachon called. "We are not out of danger yet!"

Even so, favored by southeasterly breezes, the *Sainte-Vierge* sailed untroubled up the coast of the Bay of Biscay, around the jutting points of Finistere, and into the great and fearsome expanse of the endless ocean itself, on a heading toward the southern coast of Ireland. Each day, carrying her casket, Yvette mounted the companion ladder to the forecastle and stood until nightfall at the forward rail, her free hand resting on the stempost as she silently studied the sea and sky ahead. Most days, Mathilde squatted at the bottom of the companion ladder sewing or, more likely, fretting. And on most days, Robert found his gaze wandering frequently to the forecastle.

"Methinks young Robert has developed a new sense of devotion since the beguine came into our midst," Niall gibed lightly one midday, as the companions dined off their tin plates.

"It is hardly a surprise," Joseph said. "Saving the children, he and the Lady Yvette are the youngest of our company. It is only natural."

"But not permitted among the Poor Knights of Christ," Friedrich said with a warning glance.

Blushing, Robert filled a cannikin with water and carried it to the forecastle. As always, Mathilde squatted beside the companion ladder, frowning in her baffled efforts to sew a patch on her skirt against both the wind and the rolling of the ship. Above, Yvette stood by the stempost. As Robert approached, followed, as always, by the watchful chaperon, a sudden gust, fraught with salt spray, tore at Yvette's wimple, lifting it from her coif and sending it flying.

Robert lunged and tried to snatch it from the air. He missed it by inches, splashing himself with the water, to the unexpected merriment of both women.

Still laughing, Yvette unlaced her coif and pulled it off. She shook out her auburn hair, luxuriating in the momentary freedom. Then she handed Mathilde the casket, captured the flowing tresses with both hands, and gathered them behind her head.

"Quickly," she said, "a ribbon!"

Somewhere out of her ample skirts, Mathilde produced a riband of blue silk. Snatching it with one hand, Yvette corralled her errant locks with the other, binding them tightly.

"God will not mind," she said to the wide-eyed youth. "I think God likes to see hair. Why else would he have given us so much?"

Retrieving the casket, she took the half-empty cup of water and thanked Robert with her eyes.

After a day out of sight of land, the lookout spied the Isles of Scilly on the horizon. Two days later, the craggy fingers of Cork could be seen off the steerboard bow. Two more days of fair sailing round Munster and northward brought the carrack to the port of Galway, where they put in to take on water and fresh provisions. Even then, Yvette remained fixed at her station on the forecastle, wrapped against the night in her woolen pilgrim's cloak. A few dockworkers stopped to stare at the strange unmoving figure, but the sight of Friedrich or Joseph standing guard nearby, armed and fierce-looking, prompted them to move on quietly.

On the twenty-fourth of July, the carrack set sail again, rounding the sheer cliffs and thickly wooded promontories of Connaught, skirting the desolate forelands and green coast of Donegal, then heading into the cold North Sea toward the Sea of the Hebrides.

"Fàilte ort a dh'Albainn," Antony said with a sweep of his arm when the line of Islay appeared between the cobalt waves and the clear azure sky. "Welcome to Scotland."

The exhilaration of entering the final leg of the long voyage spread among passengers and crew. But on the afternoon of the following day, as the ship approached the Firth of Lorn, just under the Isle of Mull, the chill cry of the lookout sounded again.

"Two galleys athwart the steerboard stern!"

"Edward's, or I am a Saracen slave!" Antony stormed, peering at the pennants streaming behind the long, narrow ships. "Can we run or shall we engage?"

"Both, I suspect," d'Arcachon said, grimacing. "But we have the advantage of height and a full complement of archers. We can make them pay for harrying us."

They were not huge like Philip's galleys, but fast and, from what Robert could see at three hundred yards' distance, well armed. Diverging, they approached the *Sainte-Vierge* from both sides, planning, d'Arcachon warned, to catch the carrack in the cross fire of their arbalests.

Soldiers rather than slaves, the rowing crews of the galleys greatly outnumbered the fighting men aboard the *Sainte-Vierge*. But to take her by combat, they would first have to grapple and board. Archery would first try to reduce her ability to resist—for thirty knights, a dozen men-at-arms, and a squadron of archers could still offer a formidable defense, especially in view of the carrack's towering height.

Arrows and bolts began raining down on the *Sainte-Vierge* as soon as the galleys drew within range. Most whistled harmlessly overhead, falling into the sea, but several tore through the sails and a number thudded into the hull and decks. One or two glanced off the masts or spars, careening down onto the crew and officers and those passengers who had not had the fortune to find shelter. Shouts and cries told Robert that some found their mark.

D'Arcachon and Antony herded the remaining passengers and as many knights and squires as possible under the castle decks and even down into the reeking hold. The archers returned fire relentlessly into the galleys. Helmeted crewmen hoisted stones, gads, and javelins aloft to the top castle in preparation for closer engagement. But like hounds coursing a stag, the smaller, faster vessels maintained enough distance to render these weapons useless.

In the waist of the ship when the attack began, Robert sighted Joseph behind the steerboard archery screen with his arbalest. Pushing to his side, he shouted over the noise surrounding them. "Yvette! Where is she?"

"Still on the forecastle deck," Joseph shouted back, retracting his bowstring with the hooks and pulleys suspended from his belt. "Do not try to reach her, young sire. God will protect her."

Turning, Robert saw Mathilde scrambling frantically up the companion ladder, shouting for Yvette.

"God may be busy elsewhere," he muttered and dashed after her, praying for more mist or some other miracle.

He had just gained the forecastle deck when, with a piercing cry, Mathilde stumbled and pitched forward, the shaft of an arrow protruding from her neck. Spinning around, Yvette looked first to Mathilde; then her eyes locked with those of Robert, still frozen at the threshold of the deck.

As the beguine stepped forward toward her companion, clutching the casket to her breast, Robert heard the rising whistle of another rain of arrows. He leaped over the dying woman toward Yvette. As quarrels hissed overhead and slammed into the deck around them, Yvette raised her head and looked up at Robert, tears streaming down her cheeks. Then she gasped and fell backward.

"Mistress!"

At first, Robert thought she had only lost her balance. Then, in horror, he saw the fletching of the bolt jutting up from her chest, near the left shoulder. Her eyes were closed tightly against the pain.

Robert shielded her with his body through the following hours, aware only of their hearts beating together—his throbbing loudly in his ears; hers, he feared, growing weaker. He had no idea how much time had passed when strong hands at last pulled him away. Yvette lay huddled against the stempost, her casket gripped tightly at her side.

"Young sire, allow me to attend her," Joseph said.

Rising to his knees, Robert first realized it was now dark. Mathilde's body was gone, and the deck freshly scrubbed.

"Do not attempt to move me," Yvette warned them, "or I shall surely die."

"But you cannot stay here, mistress," Joseph said. "You are sorely wounded and will perish from the cold and wind."

Antony and Friedrich had climbed to the forecastle, followed by Niall and Alisdair. Robert warded them off with a gesture, and they stood, watching with mounting concern.

"Bring me my cloak," Yvette said softly.

The knights watched, baffled, as with Robert's help, the beguine wrapped herself in the gray woolen garment.

"Now," she said, "bear me to the rail."

Fearfully they supported her as she made her way, one slow step at a time, to her former station. She placed one hand on the rail and clutched the casket with the other, but said nothing further.

At last, the others returned to the main deck. A line of pale fire simmered on the western horizon. The *Sainte-Vierge* moved alone now over the restless waves.

"What became of the galleys?" Robert asked.

"They harried us sharply for hours," Antony said. "Then, of a sudden, the lead ship veered sharply into the path of the other. The captains tried to avoid a collision, but their oars became entangled, and the second ship finally rammed the first."

"One of our archers may have killed the steersman," Joseph suggested. "Or, as it seemed, they changed course to avoid the rocks."

"There were no rocks," Antony said. "We were sailing close to shore, but there were no rocks."

The Turcopole smiled wistfully. "Not that *we* could see."

Later, Robert brought Yvette a steaming plate of matelote from the ship's kitchen. She drank a little water mixed with wine but would not eat. "It is not possible now," she said. "Nor is it necessary. Soon I will be home."

"May God grant, mistress."

By midday, gray clouds were racing overhead, low enough, Robert thought, that he might almost touch them. Whistling in the shrouds, the wind stung his cheeks with rain and salt spray as he stood vigil at the rail next to Yvette.

"I was given three graces," she whispered hoarsely. "One for Friedrich, one for Antony, and one for myself. This is the third grace."

"How can you call it grace?" he said. "It is a curse!"

"In life, nothing of value is achieved without cost. With God, it is not so."

"You were to bear the treasure of the Temple," Robert protested. "Was that to be without cost?"

"Men added the cost, Robert. The graces were bestowed to offset it."

Favored by fair weather, the *Sainte-Vierge* continued north past the crags of Skye, the towering peaks of Assynt, the golden beaches of Sutherland. Skirting the cliffs of the Cape of Wrath, she sailed calmly along the gentler shores of northern Caithness. Even the crashing waves of the Firth of Pentland failed to daunt the old carrack as she rounded Dunnet Head before the last, long run toward Ross.

"Mark me, I still mislike much of this," d'Arcachon confided to Antony and Friedrich as the evening shadows crept over the waves from the hills beyond Helmsdale. "We have lost only three more horses in as many days, and the weather—! The wind has hardly shifted since we rounded the Cape of Wrath. There has been no storm since we left La Rochelle. The crew is uneasy, and I am none too comfortable. There is talk of witchcraft."

"Not witchcraft, sir captain," the Saxon said. "Grace. Let there be no further chatter about magic."

"Look—above!" someone shouted.

Bright blue wisps of light were dancing on the masthead and topcastle railing. The shimmering glow leaped to the yards and rigging, then ran bristling along the rails of the forecastle and the stern gallery. Many of the knights and their retainers fell to their knees, praying fervently.

Robert felt his pulse begin to race. The hairs on his scalp and neck tingled, and gooseflesh rose on his arms and legs. Even Antony seemed about to panic. Joseph remained impassive, a smile hovering on his lips. The crew, however, murmured approval.

"It is the benison of the Holy Preacher, Saint Elmo," an old seaman explained, lifting his knife high overhead to catch the cold fire on its tip. "The favor of heaven is with us."

"So may it be," d'Arcachon muttered. "But I fear there may also be a storm coming."

"You wonder about the treasure, do you not?" Joseph asked that night. He had found Robert gazing across the waist of the ship to the forecastle, where the solitary figure of the beguine was now and again silvered by the moon as it passed through the gathering clouds.

"I wonder about Yvette. Might she herself be the treasure?"

"And the casket? The Jews, it is said, convert their wealth into gems, so they can carry it with them when expelled from their homes. Perhaps the Templars did so as well."

"But why entrust such wealth to a mere maiden? Better a knight, like Friedrich or Antony."

Joseph nodded. "Some think it might hold earth from the Holy Sepulcher. Or perhaps the heart of Hugues de Payens, as Friedrich believes."

"The casket does not hold the treasure."

"Perhaps you are right, young sire," the Turcopole said thoughtfully. "But," he added very quietly, "perhaps not."

They stood in silence for a while. Then Robert asked, "Will she live, Joseph?"

"Her life is now in the hands of God alone."

August began on a gray morning overshot with brooding clouds. Sailing close against the wind, the carrack moved briskly down the ragged coast of Caithness. Fragrant smoke from hillside fires mingled with the tang of the North Sea.

"The celebration of the old god of light," Antony explained. "In the hills, they will leap over the fires tonight."

"If they can light them," Friedrich said, as a squall danced madly over the sea behind them.

Sped by the wind, the ship cut across the Firth of Dornoch and around the narrow head of Tarbet Ness as they moved on a southerly tack toward the Black Isle.

"We will dock at Cromarty harbor this evening," Antony said. "There is little to be gained by sailing into the Firth to reach Dingwall. And much to be lost if the ship is trapped within the headlands."

The sky was clearing by the time the *Sainte-Vierge* docked at the small port, occupying the entire length of the pier. The passengers and cargo were first taken off. Then, when the ballast had been jettisoned, the lading port was opened and the horses and mules were carefully led out, staggering and gaunt from their weeks in the dark, fetid hold. Robert returned often in those hours to the forecastle. Each time, Yvette was as he had left her, one hand on the rail, the other clasping the casket. In the end, he, too, remained on the deck.

"I do not understand any of this," he said. "Why must it end so?"

"You speak thus because you do not see with the eyes of God."

"And what does God see?" His voice was bitter, he knew. But masking his despair was now beyond his power.

"Master Eckhart says God sees everything. But our eyes are too weak. Look!"

Turning, Yvette opened the casket, and, for a moment, he did see—or, rather, as he looked into the darkness, he *knew*—something nameless, yet so vast, so ancient, so complex, and yet so elegantly simple that it was both dizzying and exhilarating.

When she closed the lid, the vision departed.

"No—wait!" Robert protested. "Just a moment longer . . ."

Wearily, Yvette smiled. "You would never have enough time to see it all."

"The ship is now almost wholly empty," said Joseph, who had approached unnoticed.

D'Arcachon and his officers were the last of the crew to debark. Antony and Friedrich then mounted the forecastle. Behind them, Niall and Alisdair watched from the top of the companion ladder.

"I may not depart until all have gone ashore," Yvette said.

"Fetch a priest from the nearest church," Friedrich said through clenched teeth. "Drag him here if you must."

Antony signaled with his hand. Alisdair trotted to the gangway and down to the pier, disappearing in the direction of the town. One by one, the others followed off the ship, glancing back furtively.

Together, Robert and Yvette watched as, on the darkening shore, ostlers and grooms led the enervated horses toward pasture and fresh water. Robert tried without success to make out Wahgemut and Näscher among the dozens of destriers, palfreys, rouncies, and pack animals. Knights and squires wandered among them, seeking their mounts, soothing them with gentle praise, offering apples and handfuls of fresh grass gleaned from neighboring farms. Others, bereft of their mounts by the rigors of the long voyage, gathered in small groups, silently watching.

"I have carried the treasure to Scotland as I was bidden," Yvette said weakly, hugging the casket to her breast. "Now, you, too, must go, Robert."

"No, mistress. I will not leave you!"

"Where I travel now, I can only go alone."

He had begun to understand. But as the sun descended into the haze rising over the distant Highlands, Robert stood alone on the pier and watched uneasily. With increasing insistence, the carrack tugged at the cables tethering it to the familiar, solid world.

Suddenly the mooring lines drew taut as bowstrings. With a crack, the first stout rope snapped in two. Robert had time only to duck as the landward portion scythed overhead, hissing like an arrow in flight.

With a splintering wail, the iron ring holding the second cable tore loose from the planks. Crazily, the carrack lurched free, rocking in the breeze. The gangway, pulled from its seat, splashed into the sea.

Then, as if the reef knots had been loosed by unseen hands, the mainsail dropped with a retort, billowing as it caught the wind. Behind him, Robert heard the shouts of the captain and crew as they ran toward the pier. Turning briefly, he saw Alisdair loping toward the beachfront, followed at a distance by a corpulent, dark-robed friar.

Despite the rising wind, wisps of fog took shape, ascending, it seemed again, out of the sea itself. Stained lavender and rose by the dying sun, the swirling billows parted playfully before the prow of the old carrack.

For only a moment longer, he saw Yvette, still on the forecastle, still as immovable as a carving on the façade of Nôtre Dame. Nor did she look back when the rising vapors gently enfolded the *Sainte-Vierge* as it began moving out to sea.

In years to come, despite rumors that Robert heard from time to time of a derelict vessel floating somewhere in the North Sea, neither ship nor maid were ever seen again.

INTERLUDE FOUR

The ultimate fate of the Templar fleet is unknown, but we can assume that at least a portion of the Templars' wealth was aboard when the fleet sailed from La Rochelle in the predawn hours of October 13, 1307. We know that the Preceptor of France, though later captured, spirited away fifty horses from the Paris preceptory—presumably laden with treasure, since that treasury was empty when Nogaret swooped—and put them to sea with eighteen galleys, none of which were ever seen again. More consignments may well have been hidden in other places throughout France until they could be smuggled out.

Given the near certainty that many Templars found refuge in Scotland after the suppression of the Order, and that they fought for the newly crowned Robert the Bruce in the years to come, it is entirely reasonable to assume that men, equipment, horses—and other treasures—may have been part of the cargo carried away in various stages, to avoid confiscation by the French authorities. Since Scotland was under papal interdict at the time, the Bruce refused to let legates serve the formal writs; indeed, though Scotland's bishops later went through the motions of a formal inquiry, all the charges were found to be "not proven," in the classic Scottish verdict, and all those questioned were released unharmed. Tradition has it that a significant Templar force fought alongside Robert the Bruce at the Battle of Bannochburn, very shortly after Jacques de Molay was burned at the stake, and helped him win the day. In what may be a link between the Knights Templar and Freemasonry, the Bruce is then said to have established the Royal Order of Scotland at Kilwinning to honor these knights—and "Mother Kilwinning" is generally regarded as the very oldest lodge of Freemasonry in Scotland.

Meanwhile, former members of the Order who did not go underground in various ways either joined other Orders (some of which were essentially Templars under another name, such as the Royal Order of Christ in Portugal—whose red Maltese cross emblem graced the sails of Christopher Columbus when he sailed in search of the New World) or were pensioned off. Many joined the Teutonic Knights, fighting pagans in the North, or were transferred to the Order of St. John, which received many former Templar properties.

But questions remained regarding both the Order itself and the fate of certain individuals involved in bringing the Order down. Jacques de Molay's dying curse, just before he succumbed to the flames on March 14, 1314, had called both the pope and Philip of France to join him before the tribunal of heaven within the year—and they did so: Pope Clement V on April 20 and King Philip IV on November 29.

Rumors regarding the deaths began immediately. Speculation varied between mere coincidence, supernatural intervention, and simple vengeance by outlawed, very human Templars. Ten years later, Pope Clement's successor, the eighty-year-old Pope John XXII, summoned to Avignon the Franciscan theologian William of Ockham, O.F.M., ostensibly to have him questioned by a papal tribunal over the possible heretical nature of certain of his philosophical writings. This is historical fact, but given Brother William's reputation for incisive thinking and the ongoing whispers about the curse of Jacques de Molay, it is entirely possible that Pope John had an additional agenda.

Occam's Razor

Robert Reginald

"Find us the Templar treasure," said Pope John, tapping his cane on the floor to punctuate his speech, "or you will experience firsthand the flames that consumed that devil-worshipper Jacques de Molay!"

Our adventure had begun six months earlier in England. I have previously recorded several of the investigations of my illustrious master, the Doctor Invincibilis William of Occam, O.F.M., into matters insidious and criminous; but I could not relate until now his greatest feat of cogitation, for he charged me with the holiest of oaths never to speak of this affair again while he yet drew breath. The Black Death having claimed his dear life this past year, I am finally free to set down the story of the remarkable events that threatened our very lives and souls.

In November of the year 1323 my master received a summons from the Holy Father, instructing him to appear before a Tribunal at Avignon no later than the first day of May following. This was in response to a circular letter issued by Master William supporting the Declaration at Perugia of his friend Michael de Cesena, Father General of the Franciscan Order, that Jesus Christ and his apostles had owned nothing but the clothes on their backs, a position subsequently condemned by the Pope, who now threatened both Cesena and his followers with excommunication. Accordingly, my master took formal leave from his teaching position at the University of Oxford, with every intention of returning there as soon as he had been cleansed of any theological taint.

We made a March crossing to Calais during a break in the weather, and for the first time I understood full well the torments awaiting evildoers in Hell. The town of Avignon is located in the southeastern corner of France, and given the foul condition of that country's roads, it took us almost six weeks to find our way south, making several stops along the way.

We entered Avignon near the end of April, and took lodging at Saint Anaclète, an establishment of our Order of Friars Minor in the southeast section of the town, just outside the walls. The town had been leased by Pope Clement V in 1309 as a fief from the King of Sicilia, but it always seemed to me a small and very crowded place, eminently suited to the poverty of mind exhibited by its rulers.

Tucked into a bend of the Rhône River, the city had developed from an ancient settlement on the Rocher des Doms, an oblong hill protected by a decaying Roman wall. On it four great structures fought for space: the Citadel itself, overhanging the river; the official residence of the Bishops of Avignon, west of the Citadel; the Cathedral of Nôtre Dame des Doms, south of the Citadel and north of the Papal Apartments; and the Palais des Papes, a large complex of buildings covering the south end of the crag. As the town had expanded, a second wall had been erected to protect the settlements south of the Rocher, but it too was soon eclipsed by new developments pushing beyond the limit of the battlements.

On our arrival, Master William dispatched a note to His Holiness, informing him of our presence. For two weeks we received no response. Then—I remember the occasion well—a messenger dressed all in black banged on our door just after sunrise and handed my master an official letter:

Feast of Saint Matthias the Apostle
Ad Gulielmum Ocami, O.F.M.
Brother: Thou shalt submit thyself to the authority of the
Holy Father at the IIIrd hour of the morning II days hence.
+*Joannes XXII PM*

At the stated time we appeared before the Papal Palace, and were escorted to a private meeting room, not without some controversy, for I would have been excluded had not Master William insisted on my presence as a witness. An hour later the Holy Father shuffled into the room with the help of a cane. I had never seen his portrait and was surprised to discover how frail he had become. At this time he had already reached his eightieth year and was bent over with affliction. His white bushy eyebrows and cherubic face minded me of the elves my grandfather had described to me as a boy in the West Country. The Pope took his seat on a dais to the right, and then stared at us for several minutes.

"So, even in this small matter you disobey us, Brother William," he finally said, in a barely audible whisper.

"Forgive me, Holy Father," replied my master, "but I have come to rely so heavily on Brother Thaddæus that I could not conceive the idea that he might be excluded."

"Then he may remain," the Pope said. "Tell me, Brother William, did you ever meet the heretic Jacques de Molay, last Master of the Order of the Knights of the Temple of Solomon?"

My master started. "No, Your Grace. I was a young man when he was arrested, and still a student when he was executed in 1314."

"Yes," the Pope replied, "but your Master at Oxford knew Molay, and through him you have been tainted."

Master William hesitated a moment before answering. "What you say is true in the first part, Holy Father, but I never met the man, and I know very little about him except what idle gossip has reported."

"The Templars are everywhere!" the Pope said with a scowl. "Their evil has never been extirpated because the wicked idol they worshipped was never found by King Philip. Now they are circulating rumors that *we* were somehow involved in the death of their Grand Master a decade ago—and even of our predecessor and the King himself later that year. These are lies. Yet even lies can harm the innocent, and should these tales continue unabated, our Papacy itself could be at risk.

"We have heard of your investigation into the poisonings of the Oxford dons, and how you uncovered the foul murderer of young Vincent Garnier two years since, and we have equal need of your services. We therefore charge you to examine the deaths of Clement V and Philip IV of beloved memory, to determine whether their passings were unnatural; and if so, who killed them and why. We should not be displeased to hear that the Templars were involved.

"You are further ordered to recover the Templar treasure and to bring it to us privily." He drew a parchment sheet from his robe. "This warrant gives you the authority to question anyone in the realm, even King Charles, regarding these matters." He handed it to Master William, who considered his reply carefully.

"Holy Father, these matters are perhaps best left to God's discretion," he said. "It has been a ten-year since the last Preceptors were executed or imprisoned, and longer than that since the Templars were suppressed. Scarce anyone who held a position of authority in the Order still lives. I have found through experience that the quicker such inquiries are made, the greater the probability of success. I do not believe that success is likely in this case."

Pope John sniffed. "We are not concerned with your reservations," he said. "If we are dissatisfied with the speed of your inquiries, we may undertake the suppression of a second order, the Friars Minor. Your Master Cesena has already defied our writ, and we have summoned him here to account for his actions. His fate, your fate, even your young companion's fate, are entirely in your hands. Do not disappoint us, Brother William. The pyres can easily be relit. Now kiss our ring and be gone."

And we were thus dismissed.

Later that evening we sat in our quarters, somberly sipping herbal tea and dining on hard bread and harder cheese. Master William had been uncommonly quiet much of the afternoon, and I had learned never to disturb his contemplations.

"Well, young Thaddæus," he finally said, "what do you make of this day's events?"

"His Holiness is a hard taskmaster," I replied.

"Indeed. But the challenge is still the most daunting we've faced since the Ebanus Equerry. Yes, we need a plan." He began pacing up and down the small room, his hands interlaced behind his back, his brows drawn tightly down over his eyes in concentration.

"The lapse of time means we can gain no firsthand impressions from anyone," he said. "Even those who may have actually witnessed the events will have selectively edited them in their own minds during the ensuing years. Some may have even been ordered to do so.

"As always, we must ask ourselves these questions: If a crime took place, who had the opportunity to commit it? Who, having the opportunity, also had the will to effect it? Who, having the opportunity and will, had the means to carry it out? Who, having opportunity, will, and means, would have benefitted from its possible commission?

"The answer to the latter question may be the only one we can truly satisfy at this late date. However, we must first determine the circumstances of each death, and who of those in attendance at each passing might still be living." He turned to me.

"As usual, Thaddæus, I will require you to record in detail everything you see. Now, my boy, let us consider the final mystery placed before us. Please fetch me the speculum."

I carefully removed the instrument from the backpack where it had been specially cradled. It was a curved piece of metal, almost round in shape and highly polished to a supernally bright sheen. The alloy was quite unlike anything I have seen before or since, having a slight greenish tint that seemed to glow from within. On its back were inscribed a curious set of characters, like Roman letters in reverse, in a language I could not translate; my master never told me where he had acquired the piece, although he did claim familiarity with the words.

Master William placed the mirror on his knees. As he made his preparations, he asked me: "What do you know about the Templars, Thaddæus?"

"Oh, sir, there are many stories about, most of them bad. I do know the Order was suppressed by Pope Clement the year I was born. They are said to have practiced unholy rituals upon each other, and the foulest kind of black magic, and to have worshipped an idol of Satan in the form of an obscene head."

"Don't believe everything you hear," Master William replied. "Every Order has its stray sheep, certainly. But I am utterly convinced that the Knights Templar were mostly righteous men who were unjustly accused of crimes they never committed, and that their chief accuser, King Philip le Bel, profited greatly by their suppression. Now, let's see, where are we?"

He fiddled with the device on his lap, and suddenly it began to turn, slowly at first, then picking up speed. I could not see how it was being impelled, but Master William held his hands equidistant from the speculum as it rose slowly up from his legs. It began to whine as it glowed brighter and brighter, then turned on end so its top was facing outward toward me.

"Don't be afraid, lad," my master said. "Come closer and gaze into the mirror."

I crept nearer and looked in wonder upon the bright image of the thing. It seemed to me that a picture was forming on its upper surface, a vision of men dressed all in armor, wearing snow-white robes ensigned with a bloodred cross, crowded around a curious reliquary containing the faint outline of a face drawn on a white backdrop. There was no doubt in my mind that the picture was that of a bearded man, although the shading somehow seemed all wrong.

The men appeared to be praying to the relic. Their expressions reflected joy and sanctity, not depraved debauchery, and they treated the object with great reverence. I could not tell where they were, except that the room was small and fully enclosed, lit only by flickering candlelight. I wanted to reach out and touch the image, but when I tried to do so, one of the knights turned and looked me straight in the eyes, as if he could actually see me. I woke with a start from my trance.

"What did you experience, Thaddæus?" my master asked.

After I had related my vision, Master William pondered these wonders for a few moments before saying: "What you saw was the present, not the past. Those were Templars praying within their Temple, reduced though it might be in pomp and circumstance. If we can find that place, we will also discover their treasure, although I do not think the Holy Father will thank us for our efforts." He sighed. "Sufficient unto the day is the evil thereof. Off to bed with you, son. We have much to do on the morrow."

The next morning, I awoke at sunrise to the droning of my master's prayers, rousing myself reluctantly from my warm bed. After a brief repast, we hied ourselves to the Papal Apartments, where we began questioning the papal servants, quickly determining those few who had served under the previous administration. Chief among these was Frère Ambrosin, a man of some fifty years who now had achieved the position of majordomo to the papal household. A fringe of gray hair surrounded his pointed bald pate, making it look like nothing so much as a large, naked boulder poking up through dried, faded grass, the rock cracked and weather-stained by the elements.

"I'm a busy man," he said. "Whatever do you want?"

"Just a little of your time, Brother," my master replied. "And some of your memories. His Holiness has given me leave to question you on these matters. During the time of Papa Clemens, God rest his memory, you were serving in the household here, were you not?"

"In truth, sir, I entered the Pope's service in the year 1303, when he was still Archbishop of Bordeaux: Bertrand de Got, as he was known then. He was a kind master to me, and I stayed with him when he was elevated to the papacy two years later." He scratched his bare head. "What's this about, sir? Have I done something wrong?"

Master William smiled. "No, nothing, Brother Ambrosin, please reassure yourself on that account. I just want to know something about the late Pope's health."

"His health, sir?" The majordomo looked puzzled. "Well, it was never very good, even from the beginning of his reign. He had the first of his 'spells,' as he used to call them, about a year after his election, following an argument with King Philip over those devil-worshippers the Templars. He lay abed for a month and was ill for more than four. Thereafter, the 'spells' came upon him at irregular times, often after some unpleasantness or other. Men in high stations seem to have an unending stream of such difficulties. Over the years these attacks steadily got worse, and finally he died of the last of them."

"Tell me more about these 'spells,' " my master said.

"Oh, they were terrible, sir," the monk replied. "He'd have these pains in the belly something fierce, and he'd be doubled up and tossing about all night, often getting no rest at all, and he couldn't keep anything down, sometimes for days on end. Oh, we often prayed to God Almighty for his relief. I thought the first 'spell' would kill him for sure, it went on so long, but he finally recovered some of his health early in 1307, though never like before.

"The attacks began again two years later, and with each one

he gradually weakened, until the final episodes caused him to shit blood and spit black bile sometimes. He suffered as much as any holy martyr, sir, I can tell you." He crossed himself.

"Who treated him when he had these attacks?" asked Master William.

"Well," said Ambrosin, "the Holy Father put great store in the physicians. One of them who provided him with some relief was eventually made an archbishop, I think—somewhere in the Germanies. So there was always a well-trained doctor present, and I can tell you he received the best of care. In the end, even the King took an interest."

"Indeed?" my master replied.

"Oh yes. You see, the Holy Father left Avignon early in 1313 to visit his nephew at Carpentras, staying at Castle Monteux for over a year. But his health continued to decline, until finally King Philip became concerned and sent his own physician from Paris. The King himself visited the Pope before Christmas, making a hard winter's journey to comfort a sick friend." He looked around the room, and lowered his voice: "They had a terrible row, you know."

"Really?"

Ambrosin nodded his head. "The King wanted Papa Clemens to sign some document or other regarding those Templar people, which he finally did, because I had to witness it, and King Philip thought I couldn't read." He chuckled to himself. "Those great men never thought very much of me, just because I was born a peasant. They would talk around me like I wasn't even in the room. All except the Holy Father.

"But the Pope continued to worsen, and the following spring he decided to go home to his family in Gascony. Just after starting out from Carpentras, he received a letter that upset him greatly, and he took to his bed that evening, never to rise again. They were able to carry him to Roquemaure-on-the-Rhône before he expired. Oh, sir, I tell you he died in God's good grace."

My master was appropriately somber: "Brother Ambrosin, was there anything about his final illness that seemed at all unusual?"

The majordomo considered before responding. "Now that you mention it, sir, I tended the Holy Father during his last days, and I did notice his fingertips becoming somewhat discolored. I didn't think much of it at the time, because he was so clearly failing. Also, I combed his hair daily, and it began to come out in clumps during that final week. But he had a fever, and sometimes sick people do lose all their hair. So I don't know any more."

"You mentioned a letter that Papa Clemens received near the end."

"Yes, sir," replied the monk, "but it was never found after he died, and I have no knowledge of who sent it or what it contained."

"Thank you, Brother Ambrosin," Master William said. "You have been most kind."

We next interviewed the Chief Cook, one Master Manosque, a rather thin fellow who looked as if he'd never eaten a good meal in his life. His whole face was a frown. Again Master William introduced himself and asked Manosque about his service.

"I cook for Clemen-Pope six years," he replied. "I cook good."

"I am quite certain that no one would criticize your cuisine," replied my master, "but I would like to know about the Holy Father's stomach problems."

"Bad, very bad," Manosque said. "Tummy make noise all time. Pains, gas, loose turds. All bad. Sometime no can eat. Not my food. My food good. My food fresh." He waved his arms around like a windmill, obviously much agitated.

Master William stifled a smile. "I have heard nothing but praise about your fine dinners. Now tell me, who prepared the Pope's meals when he left Avignon?"

"Pope leave 'Vignon?" asked the cook.

"Yes, you remember, the year before he died, Papa Clemens went to his nephew's castle."

"Ah. I fix. I fix all Clemen-Pope's food. No one else fix," Manosque responded.

"And was he well there?" asked Master William.

"No, no, very bad at Montus. Eat little, burp much. I fix good food, but . . ." The chef's shoulders lifted in resignation.

"What about when the Holy Father left Carpentras to go to Gascony?" my master inquired.

"I follow. Pope eat bad. I bring good food, but he all white. He have paper in hand. Hand shake. He fall on floor. He cry for God. God come." He crossed himself, and we followed suit. "Very sad. He good master. New master mean. Very sad."

And that was all we were able to get out of the eloquent Master Manosque. We talked with several other members of the Pope's staff, but they could add little, until we reached Brother Daniel Jacquelot, a man in his forties shaped like a pear, with bulging stomach and normal-sized chest and arms.

"Brother Daniel," my master began, "can you tell us anything about Papa Clemens's passing?"

Jacquelot had a way of answering every query with another question. "Well, he'd been ill for some time, hadn't he? I didn't have daily contact with him, no one did, despite what they might say. When he was sick, which was often, he eschewed the company of everyone except a few relatives and confidants—and he had promoted so many of the former into the latter that there were always a few cousins and nephews about.

"I think what brought on the crisis was the business over the Templars. The Pope was a good man, don't misunderstand me, but he wanted to be loved, and King Philip le Bel utterly dominated him. In the last year of his life, he became increasingly unhappy about what he had been forced to do to these knights. He never believed the stories about their supposed misdeeds. On several occasions he told me that he just hoped

Molay and his cronies would die peacefully in prison and solve his problem. After all, they were all old men, as old as the Pontiff.

"But they didn't die, and finally the King came to him at Carpentras and demanded that Molay and Charney be publicly tried. You see, under the law, Philip had to have the Order suppressed and its leaders condemned by the Pope, in order for the Templar property that the King had already confiscated to remain legally in his hands—supposedly for a new crusade, a crusade which never materialized.

"Then the King's man, that snake Nogaret, came to him after we had left Carpentras for Gascony, and gave him a message, perhaps from his master. The Pope yelled something at him, then collapsed and never recovered."

Master William paused for a moment before asking, "Did the Holy Father experience any unusual symptoms during his final days?"

"Who could say for sure?" Brother Daniel replied. "I saw him only once or twice that week, and he looked pale and very ill. I do remember that when we prepared his body for transport a few days later, it seemed to me somewhat discolored, at least compared to others I had seen, and this quite shortly after death; but each corpse tells its own story, doesn't it?"

Brother Daniel had nothing further to add, and we could find no other servants or staff to provide us with new details about the long-ago passing of Clement V. Later that evening, my master asked my opinion about the day's proceedings.

"Well, sir," I said, "it's obvious to me that the Pope had been sick for many years, and that he probably died of his ailment, whatever other factors may have contributed to his death."

"Perhaps" was all Master William would say. "But still I find it curious that his persistent illness seemed to produce such contrary symptoms near the end."

* * *

We spent a day settling our accounts in Avignon, then journeyed north to Paris to interview the King and his ministers concerning the death of King Philip IV and the Templar treasure. When we arrived, we took quarters at the Franciscan Monastery of Saint Tiron, and sent a note to the Palace requesting an audience, which we received three days later. Charles IV, called le Bel after his father, was then about thirty years of age and, like all of his family, strikingly well formed. He had succeeded his brother, King Philip le Long, in 1322—who previously had succeeded another brother—and was now calling himself Holy Roman Emperor, following the deposition of Emperor Ludwig by Pope John just two months earlier. Common gossip held that great sums had changed hands for this little favor.

We were led to a private antechamber, where we made our obeisances, and my master gave our warrant to His Majesty, who passed it to his minister for consideration. They conferred for several minutes before returning the document.

"What do you seek, Brother William?" the King inquired.

"Only the truth, sire," my master replied. "His Holiness wishes to know the circumstances of your father's passing ten years ago."

"Does he indeed? There are many truths, Frère Guillaume, some of them truer than others. Our late father died cursed by that devil-worshipper Molay, and he suffered greatly for his sins. But did you know that he also died cursed by his three sons? Ah, now *that* surprises you."

The King's expression hardened.

"Early in the year 1314, Philip the un-Fair arrested our wife and the wives of our two royal brothers, accused them of adultery on the false witness of our sister, Isabella of England, and then had them imprisoned. Our lovely Blanche was scarcely eighteen years of age. She was pure and innocent and guileless, and there was nothing we could do to save her. She was taken away to a nunnery at Maubuisson, and we had to divorce her. So do not ask us of our father. He died unlamented by his family."

Master William considered his next words carefully. "But what were the specific circumstances of King Philip's passing?"

"You vex us, Frère Guillaume, you do not listen to what we say," the King replied. "Yet, out of respect for the Holy Father who has given us so much, we will answer. *Nota bene:* The King our father had gone to hunt at Pont Saint Maxence in early November, and he took ill in the woods there on the fourth day of that month. We saw him stop suddenly beneath a tree, turn white, stiffen, clutch his head, and slump over his saddle. There was no doctor present, but his aide, Master Rodolphe, went to him immediately and said he had no pulse. However, he soon recovered his wits and was taken by boat to Poissy, thence by horse to Essonnes, and then by litter to Fontainebleau. By this time he had suffered a second attack, worse than the first, and he finally succumbed there on the twenty-ninth."

"Who visited him *in extremis*?" my master inquired.

"Those of the lords temporal and lords spiritual who arrived in time came to his bed to receive his blessing," the King replied. "They included the Archbishop of Bourges, the Cardinal Bishop of Avignon and Porto, the Abbot of Cluny, the Count of Poitiers, the Archbishop of Embrun, the Viscount of Lomagne, the Cardinal de Got, and a few others of lesser rank. He then called our brother, Louis X of blessed memory, to his side, and said to him: 'Ponder these words, young Louis: "What is it to be King of France?"'

"Much of what he said during that last week made no sense. A few days later he perished, and his body was returned to Paris."

"Your Majesty mentioned Lomagne and Got. Were they not related to the late Papa Clemens?" asked Master William.

"They were. Lomagne was his nephew, we believe. As you may have already heard, the Pope had a certain affinity for his own family," the King noted with the flash of a smile that quickly vanished. "Now, we have other duties to which we must attend. There is nothing further we can tell you about this matter. We wish you *bon voyage,* Frère Guillaume." And he waved us away.

Later that afternoon we questioned the Court Physician, Odonar d'Artevelde, who had served the Kings of France for a quarter century. The doctor was a pompous little toad of about sixty years, with a long gray beard, balding pate, and flamboyant robes. I would have thought him a magician or wandering actor had I not known otherwise.

"You were not present when the King suffered his first attack?" my master asked.

"Indeed, I was not," Odonar replied. "The King was on holiday, and I was in Paris. Of course, when I heard that His Majesty had fallen ill, I left immediately and reached Fontainebleau on the same day that the King's litter arrived."

"And what was the King's condition when you first examined him?" Master William inquired.

"His humors were clearly out of balance, particularly the choler, giving his skin a yellowish cast. As a result, he had suffered a slight paralysis in his left side, making it difficult for him to sit long in the saddle, although he could speak and reason without impairment. I was told that the first attack had affected his heart, and this I could confirm with my trained eye— that there was still a weakness of limb and shortness of breath common to those afflicted by such ailments.

"Yet, even with all of these difficulties, he seemed in very good spirits and on his way to a good recovery. Overall, his body was still strong and virile, and I felt that he had an excellent chance of living at least another five or ten years, if he could avoid excessive strain and excitement; and I did not hesitate to tell him so. However, being the prudent man that he was, he updated his will and made his confession to the Cardinal."

"The Cardinal?" Master William replied. "Oh, do you mean Got?"

"No, no, the other one, you know, Duèse. He and the King were old friends, and he had hurried up from Avignon when he heard about le Bel's misfortune. Ha, he must have ridden a few horses to death to get there as quickly as he did, and he a man of seventy." He chortled to himself, then sobered.

"It was a funny thing, though. After that, the King just seemed to lose heart. Within two days, it was obvious he was dying, and he called his children around him to give them his final blessing. I did everything I could. But he broke into a rash and the phlegmatic humor overwhelmed the others, filling his lungs with fluid. I've never seen anything quite like it. He should have lived." The physician's shoulders slumped.

"And then his sons followed him to the grave one by one, all young men, too—first bold Louis and then Philip the Tall, with little Jean squeezed in between, just five days old at his death. The family is cursed, no doubt about it.

"It was those thrice-damned Templars. Molay jinxed the King and his sons as the flames claimed him. I was there, and I still have nightmares about it. I remember Molay politely inviting the Pope and the King to join him before God's throne by year's end, and then the Preceptor Geoffroi de Charney shouting out: 'The shroud shall claim you, my Lords, you cannot escape the shroud.' It was chilling, I tell you." He shuddered.

Master William thanked him graciously for his time, and we retired to our cells at the abbey for the evening.

"Master," I said, after we had eaten our simple meal, "I don't understand. Both of these men seem to have died natural deaths, and yet the Holy Father seems much concerned about the circumstances." This, one must remember, was decades before the terrible scourge of the plague had made death a commonplace visitor to our households. "I also don't see how we will ever find these Templars, if indeed there are any members of that Order still living."

My kind and wise teacher just smiled, startled from his musings, and replied: "As the Lord said to Job: 'Who is this that darkeneth counsel by words without knowledge?' Never fear, dear Thaddæus. All things come to those who wait."

Sometime in the middle of the night I came suddenly awake, shivering for lack of a cover, and abruptly realized that I was lying on a rough animal skin spread carelessly on the cold stone floor of a strange room, a place that I had no recollection of reaching. My master lay supine beside me, snoring gently. The last thing I remembered from the previous evening was drinking a cup of wine freshly spilled out from a newly tapped skin, and then toddling off to bed. Now my head ached abominably, as if Satan himself were stabbing it with a large pin, and I found it hard to gain my bearings. Nearby a solitary candle barely illumined the area where we had been placed.

"Master," I said, "Master, wake up."

Master William groaned and tried to sit up. "Where are we?" he asked. "What is this place?"

A voice behind us replied, "Welcome to the Paris Commanderie of the Military Order of the Knights of the Temple of Solomon. I regret that our accommodations are not what they were, but we were never slaves to comfort. I regret also the deception used in bringing you here, but no one must ever know of this place. However, we did obtain a set of your robes for your comfort."

While we quietly dressed, several of the brethren beyond the sphere of light began lighting the torches placed around the walls of the room, and I gasped when I realized that it was the same place I had seen several weeks earlier in my vision. Gradually the figures became distinguishable, and I realized that they wore the same white robes as before. Their faces were covered with plain black masks.

"Master William, I believe you have some questions to ask us," said their leader.

"Who are you?" my master asked.

"You will pardon me, sir, if I limit myself to saying that I am the Grand Master of the reconstituted Order, duly elected by its surviving membership."

"The Templars were officially suppressed by Pope Clement twelve years ago," my master said. "By what right do you claim that usage?"

"By the rule established by the Council of Troyes, and by the traditions established by Hugues de Payens and the Nine Founders. Although we respect the Holy Fathers, past and present, they are only men, subject to the fallibility of the flesh or even, on occasion, to the wiles of the Devil. The evil that was done to us seventeen years ago was not the work of God, but the actions of two such men, one a King eager to fill his coffers, the other a Pope eager to curry favor with the King. God could not have sanctioned actions so abhorrent to everything taught us by our Lord Jesus Christ.

"This being the case, the Holy Father was in error, and his suppression of our Order, while legal under the canons of the Church, was contrary to God's will. Therefore, those of us who survived the King's depredations have continued the traditions of our brethren, and have reestablished the Order as a secret society devoted to maintaining our special knowledge for the benefit of mankind. In this we have the blessing of Almighty God and his son Jesus Christ. We shall not again be destroyed."

Master William rubbed his eyes in weariness. "What of the charges levied against you?" he inquired.

"Lies and fabrications," replied the knight. "Oh, we do not claim perfection, sir. We are sinners all, imperfect vessels at best, to be filled with God's grace. But we are innocent of the accusations made against us, as proven by the actions of our Grand Master, Jacques de Molay, who died the martyr's death with Geoffroi de Charney. God has punished the instigators of these crimes, and He will continue to punish them unto the thirteenth generation. Yea, I tell you that this Kingdom shall soon pay a fearful price for the iniquities of its Kings, and like the ancient land of Egypt under the Pharaohs, it shall suffer a hundred years of plagues and wars and famines.

"As for the so-called Supreme Pontiffs, your young companion shall live to see two men calling themselves Pope, each supported by half the civilized world, one residing in Avignon, one in Rome. That schism shall forever destroy the power of the Popes."

"And what of the idol, the head men claim you worship?" my master asked.

"Now that is the greatest lie of all," replied the Grand Master. "And yet there is a certain basis to the tale, for the Devil often mixes truth with falsehood to seduce the unwary. In the time of Christ, the King of Edessa was a leper and sent a letter to Jesus pleading for relief from his illness. But the Son of God had already been crucified by the Jews and Romans, and so one of the lesser disciples, Addai, was sent to Syria to convert that land. He brought with him a cloth that had covered the blessed body of Jesus in His tomb, and with it he cured King Abgar of his affliction. The monarch and his land embraced Christianity.

"The shroud remained in Syria for nine hundred years, until Samosata was occupied by the Saracens. They reluctantly traded the cloth to the Byzantine Emperor for several hundred Muslim prisoners, and the artifact was brought to Constantinople in 944, where it was most joyously displayed in Santa Sophia. The Mandylion, for such was its name, remained there until the city was sacked by the crusaders in the year 1204, at which time it was acquired by the Order of the Temple. When Acre fell in 1291, our treasures were moved to Cyprus, and thence to France.

"Everything that I have told you here is true. Yet these are just words. I could be lying, I could be deceived, I could be wrong. So let me show you the proof of what I say."

I saw him signal slightly with his left hand, and the ranks of the brethren abruptly parted. There I saw the face of my vision—the haunted visage of a thin, bearded man, his fore-head crowned with thorns. The shroud was housed in a box that displayed the head only, the rest being folded underneath. I was overwhelmed with emotion, for there was no doubt in my mind that this cloth had once covered the blessed face of our Savior. I fell to my knees in reverence, my master and the knights around us following suit.

"We have been told that the cloth must now leave us for a brief time," the Templar continued, "and that young Thaddæus here shall serve as the instrument of God's will, since he is innocent in both body and soul. Therefore, see now the mira-cle of the shroud!"

He reached into the box, unfastened the cloth, and slowly, very gently drew forth the entire length of the burial covering, and I gasped again, for the image of Christ's body and the pun-ishments it had suffered at the hands of the ignorant heathen were plainly evident for all to see, albeit shaded and delineat-ed as if reversed in image. Here and there the fabric was spot-ted with Jesus' holy blood.

My master crossed himself and exclaimed, "Glory be to God that I have lived long enough to see such a wonder first-hand! But you say we are to take this great gift away with us. Why? The Pope will only confiscate it if we bring it to him."

The Grand Master of the Templars replied: "All I can tell you is that you will have need of it soon enough. As for the cloth—well, God protects his own, as he has protected this free Temple from discovery by the King. The shroud will even-tually be returned to us unharmed. We have seen this in the visions God has been gracious enough to grant to us, and we also know that you, Gulielmus Magus, are his agent for good in the world, now and in the years to come. Let Brother Thaddæus be the carrier, and mark well my words: Do not touch the shroud yourself, do not let any other person handle it except your young ward. *He* is the chosen."

Then he stretched out his arms and embraced Master

William, kissing him on each cheek: "Peace be unto thee, Brother, and good journey to you both."

The next morning we left Paris for Avignon, reaching the town in early June. The days were warm and fair on our journey, and I felt as happy then as I ever have, content with my life and what it had to offer. Every step of the way south I could feel the shroud burning on my back, folded there into its leather carrying case, but it was a pleasant warmth, reinforced by the sun's rays, and making me feel for the first time that I had much to contribute to the world. All roads were open to me.

As we drew ever nearer to that old man tap-tapping his way around and round his gilded prison, I realized for the first time how sad a little life he must live, how constrained he must feel, and how joyless was his existence. I determined then and there to do something worthwhile with my life, and vowed to God that I would become a Templar if that were possible.

Pope John must have had spies watching for us, for no sooner had we returned to our cells at Saint Anaclète's when we received a message summoning us to audience first thing the next morning. This time we were led to the ornate reception room of the Palais des Papes, where the Supreme Pontiff perched high on his great throne, surrounded by his cardinals and councilors. We entered and paid due homage to the leader of Western Christianity.

"Have you fulfilled your quest?" asked the Pope.

"We have, Your Holiness," my master replied.

The Pope waved his hands at the others in the room: "You may leave us." When they were gone, he said: "Make your report, then."

Master William formally bowed, clasped his two hands together as if praying, and began:

"You set us three tasks. As to the first, we have investigated the death of your predecessor, Clement V of blessed memory, and have made certain determinations." He then explained whom we had questioned and why, giving detailed summaries of their answers.

"Was he murdered?" the Pontiff inquired.

"Possibly. His illness did change somewhat in his last days, following his meeting with Nogaret." Master William paused, as if considering his words more profoundly, and then I heard him expound for the first time that statement for which he later became most famous.

"Yet I think not, for what can be done with fewer assumptions is done in vain with more. My own judgment is that Papa Clemens died a natural death, albeit one made severe with anxiety. For the King had no need to dispose of him, since he already was the most pliant creature in all of France."

"Be careful what you say, Brother William," replied the Pope. "Be very careful. And what of the King's death?"

"Ah, yes, Philip le Bel. Now *that* is a problem of an entirely different order. The King suffered an attack of paralysis early in November and, despite a slight recurrence a week later, appeared to be recovering his health, with perhaps some slight weakness remaining in his side. Then his symptoms changed completely, following the visit of one of his friends, and he died very quickly thereafter. The simplest explanation for this is that the King was poisoned."

"And who killed him?" the Pope inquired.

"Why, *you* did, Cardinal Duèse," my master retorted.

The Holy Father started, and I expected him immediately to call in the guards and have us both arrested and executed on the spot. But he did no such thing, much to my surprise. Instead, after a moment's silence, he asked:

"Why would I do such a thing?" He used the personal pronoun for the first time.

"Because you wished to be Pope, and you knew that the King had withdrawn his support of your candidacy, since he could not control you. The College of Cardinals was deadlocked, and the King was about to insist that his own man be elected. Without Philip, you could keep the balloting going indefinitely, until a compromise could be reached. It took you two years, but you finally achieved your goal."

"You have no proof of these . . . speculations?" the Pope said.

"No, none."

"Then you will keep them to yourself on pain of death, and we shall make certain that you have no chance to recite them in a court of law. Now, what of the Templar treasure?"

My master smiled a strange smile, turned up at one corner of his mouth. "Oh, we found it, Your Grace."

"What?" Clearly the Holy Father was not expecting this answer. "Where is it? I see nothing."

"You must open your eyes to see, Pontifex." He turned to me: "Thaddæus!" he commanded.

Then I retrieved the pouch from my back and carefully pulled the cloth forth where the Pope could not see. As I turned around, I allowed the entire length of the shroud to unfold, holding it up as high as I could reach. And it seemed to me that the figure etched on the linen writhed and moved, and a deep voice spoke forth quite clearly, filling the room with Its presence: "John, John, why persecutest thou me?"

The Pope screamed then, quite loudly for one so old, as if he had looked into the depths of Hell itself and seen his own place well prepared, and he yelled again, almost incoherently, "Take it away, take it away," spittle dribbling down his chin, his right hand waving futilely in the air.

At a nod from my master, I carefully folded the shroud and reverently put it away into its leather case. Guards and officials had already begun to respond to his shouts, and they seized us immediately.

After he had regained his composure, the Pope ordered us released and again cleared the room, save for a secretary. He looked down upon us sternly before pronouncing judgment.

"Brother William, you will forget everything that has happened here, and you will swear never to reveal what you have learned to another soul, on pain of instant excommunication and death by fire for you and your assistant."

My master had no choice but to give his oath to that effect.

"You may go for now," said the Pope, "but you will both remain within the boundaries of Avignon until I release you."

And once again we were dismissed.

Later that day we were walking in the garden of the abbey, and I asked Master William, "Sir, I don't understand. Why did the Pope let us go?"

He replied with a quote from Scripture: "'Many prophets and kings have desired to see those things which you see, and have not seen them; and to hear those things which you hear, and have not heard them.' The Holy Father knew that he could not cross a certain boundary, that the shroud would protect its own. That does not remove the danger entirely, my son, for popes and potentates have very short memories, and while we are within John's easy reach, we shall have to walk the walk of righteous men. Now it is time for prayers, and I suggest to you that both we and he have urgent need of them."

He smiled broadly at my consternation and tossed my hair. "Never fear, young Thaddæus, the truth shall not easily be suppressed, and there shall come a day when the Templars and their shroud can once again be seen openly in the world."

Now these events took place a quarter century ago, in the Year of Our Lord 1324, when my wise and good master, William of Occam, was just beginning to formulate his philosophies, and when we had many great adventures yet to come. I look back upon those days with wonder and with gratitude, and thank God Almighty that I had the chance to walk with giants upon the earth.

And when I gaze into the speculum that Master William left me, I can see the cross on my surcoat reflected back at me, and remember his dear face which I miss so much. Amen.

INTERLUDE FIVE

Whatever the nature of the pope's meeting with William of Ockham, it is historical fact that the two became implacable enemies thereafter—though heresy charges against Brother William were eventually dropped. The pope continued to disagree with certain radical elements within the Franciscan Order, but the Franciscans continued to grow in strength, occupying a position of influence comparable to that of the Dominicans. A group of Franciscans accompanied Columbus on his voyage to the New World, but fugitive Templars may well have been there before them. It is even possible that at least one ship of the vanished Templar fleet eventually reached landfall in the New World, as this American legend suggests, carrying a particular Templar treasure.

Stonish Men

Andre Norton

I buried Osbert this morning. It was a long, hard task, my age-aching bones complaining bitterly. But as a true Templar he deserved as good a resting place as I could contrive. I am the last now, and there have been signs that the natives are growing bolder. It will be soon that they will come to this, the first and last Templar stronghold in this strange and unknown world. I only trust that I shall be able to meet them armed, and with sword in my hand as a true Knight of the Lord. Our treasure is hidden well, and I do not think it shall ever be found.

It all began with a grim hunting, leading to torture and death. I was but a senior novice of the Temple then, Owen de Clare, professed and vowed in my native England to the finest barrier Christendom could raise against the infidels—the Poor Knights of the Temple. We grew too great, too mighty, for that thrice-damned Philip of France. He wanted to dabble his hands in our treasure chests, and the fact that we owed him no allegiance—being answerable only to that Voice of the Almighty, the Pope himself—irked his arrogant pride and outreach for power.

They came upon us without warning. It had been subtly and secretly planned, and the Pope himself helped in the beastly death hunt that was turned against us. Many of us died by fire and torture.

But our Temple, a hardly known one, was on the seacoast and we had ships to hand. Yes, we had hunted the Infidel by sea as well as land. I was with the Knight Commander when he saw there was nothing ahead but our taking. And it was to me, yet a boy scarce out of training, that he entrusted our treasure. Not the gold and gems the king's butchers wanted, but the Casket. Sealed shut it was securely and always was, save at certain Great Days when it was revealed only to those who were full sworn.

"Go," he ordered me. "Take the way over the rooftops. You are still agile and sturdy enough to dare those. Get to the harbor and the *True Spirit* and give the order to make sail at once, lest the last of our brothers be caught in this trap."

Go I did, and that climb over the rooftops was sometimes as perilous as a seldom-dared mountain path. But it was made, and I carried the Casket to the *True Spirit.* As with all others of our fleet (we swept the Infidels from the inner seas even as we had overwhelmed them on land), we set sail.

Hope held for us refuge among the Scots, some of which wore our device. Thus we set a course out of the inner sea and to the north.

But it would seem that the wrath of the Dark and the Evil still stalked us, for we were caught in the greatest of storms, our small fleet scattered.

The winds drove us hard. Three men were carried overboard by the waves. But the power of that which lay within the Casket brought us through, though our course the sailing master could not guess. In the end, when we were lacking in water and food and might die aboard our craft, land was sighted to the west. To that we headed, coming at last into a narrow inlet between shores that sloped sharply upward and were crowned by the greatest trees I had ever seen.

We came to anchor there—forever. Our ship had been so battered that we dared not turn again to the sea. This was the edge of the world itself, and perhaps we were the first of our kind to set foot on it.

There was a sharp, steep climb using a narrow ledge to the cliff top, and we stood wonderingly among the trees. Not far away a deer raised its head to look at us inquiringly, as if our kind were unknown to it. Osbert, my sword brother, was quick of eye and ready with bow, bringing it down.

So we filled our bellies, and drank from a stream seeking the sea. Thus we became wanderers, ever seeking a place we could hold.

For there were men after all in that forest: strange, half-naked of body. They would have brought us down. However, their stone-tipped arrows, the flint-pointed spears, made no dents in our armor, which we had worked hard to keep at its best.

Thus using the stream as a guide, always aware of the need for careful watch, we traveled westward, seeking a resting place. For each of us in his heart knew that there would be no returning.

With us went the Casket of the treasure, each man being honored to carry it in turn. It gave a core of strength that banished our despair, for we believed that it was indeed our leader in some way.

Ever we sought a place that might be easy to defend. Two of our company we had lost along the way. One was brought down by a huge bear that only the ax of Wulf could end. And Piers ate some berries that were the seeds of a demon that racked him into the quiet of death.

Then we found what was our goal—an isle in a wide river. There were rocks on that river island; and we labored, knight, novice, and seaman, to build our crude fort. The heart of it was the place of that treasure that had been given us to guard.

Years passed; the commander died of a coughing rheum, two who went hunting in the woodlands never returned. We were a handful, still faithful to our trust. By the Blood shed by our Precious Lord, we so held to our faith and honor.

So we dwindled, and today I have buried my sword brother, who was as dear to me as blood kin; and I stand alone—to wait for the coming of the savages who have showed more and more boldness. There will be none to bury me, yet I hold my honor to the end, for that which we guarded is safe and in a place where no naked savage can find it. Perhaps in time—all things are ordered by our Lord—there will come one fit and needful to take up the task again.

They were a small party to dare the river, though recent reports had not suggested that hostiles had made forays in this direction. Somewhere ahead of their clumsy craft, which rode the current erratically, was the outpost of Deerfield. Three of them were aboard: Galvin Rodder, rafter, trapper, guide, or whatever he chose to turn hand to, had been wary all morning, sniffing the air like a hound on trace. He spoke to his companions, Matthew Hawkins, man of God, and his son Owen:

"Preacher, we-uns may be in for trouble. An' I'd like firm ground under me when it comes. Maybe that there isle up ahead. That there they say is a ghost place. The Injuns swear it was held by the Stonish Men."

Matthew Hawkins was alert at that moment more to Rodder's hint of legend than to what might be behind them. Though he was pledged to bring the Word to heathen souls, he could not always restrain his own private hobby of gathering all the queer stories and legends that seemed to abound in this land of trees hardy enough to resist only the most determined of invaders.

"Stonish Men?" he now queried.

Already the raft was heading toward the island where ledges of rock broke through the general green.

"They was supposed to be hereabouts. The Injuns swear as how they had stone bodies—no arrow nor spear could bring them down. I tell you, Preacher, we-uns were not the first white skins to travel west—there's a capful of tales like to this."

Behind him Owen Hawkins was listening, but he was more intent on watching the shores on either side. His hand tightened on his rifle. Maybe it wasn't proper for a man of God to go armed, but nothing said his son, who had taken no such vows, could not make himself well acquainted with the best weapons he could afford.

He had little interest in the old stories his father liked and sought. Most of it must be rubbish. This land hid far more forceful dangers, and that odd feeling he always had as a warning was stirring.

From the cloaking of forest behind them came the boom of a shot. Galvin grunted as a red splotch appeared high on his shoulder.

"So they's nosed out our passin', an' now they is ready to make their move," he gasped. "This here raft ain't no place to make a stand—it's gotta be th' island. We got no chance in Hell (pardon, Preacher) of outrunnin' them. An' in the open, they can pick us off just as they please."

"The island will prove a shelter, then?"

"I ain't sayin' yes and I ain't sayin' no—it's a maybe thing. But I sure don't want to lose what hair I've got me left!"

He poled their unwieldy craft at a faster swing, the red spot on his shoulder glistening in the sun.

"Head to the right, behind that point there." Owen found himself saying those words as if repeating some suggestion from another.

Galvin's bushy eyebrows lifted as he demanded: "How come you knew there was this here place waiting?" They had slid behind an outstretched hook of rock stretched like a beckoning finger and were certainly, for the moment, no longer clear targets.

Owen flushed. "I didn't know," he protested.

But Galvin had no more time to ask questions as he swung the unwieldy craft into what did seem almost like a pocket-sized harbor. They united to pull the raft halfway up the bank. Then his father insisted that Galvin have his wound, not a deep one, tended. As much as preaching, Matthew Hawkins knew something of the healing art.

However, once the task of transferring their stores ashore was accomplished, Owen had to yield to that which had pulled at him stronger and stronger from the moment he set foot on this isle. He headed inland with the skill of one who knew exactly where he was.

Rough stone walls confronted him. No redskin he had ever heard of did that kind of building. Most of it had tumbled this way and that through the years, but enough remained to mark out a square. He jumped one of the fallen walls and stood in that square. For a moment he was giddy, as if something had struck him on the head, and then he turned—someone might have caught him by the shoulder to urge him so—to the one portion of the wall that sturdily resisted the attacks of time.

When Galvin and his father caught up with him, Owen was down on his knees, running his hands back and forth to brush away moss and reveal the lines deep graven there.

It was a cross slightly different from any he had seen before. A grave? It might well be. Then his father's shadow covered the patch he had cleared.

"What have we here?" Matthew Hawkins went on his knees beside his son. "Spanish? Never heard they came this far north—"

But that same force that had brought Owen here set him now to digging swiftly—and with all the strength he could summon—at the edges of that crossed stone.

Galvin had loaded all three rifles and had them well to hand.

"Good-enough place," he observed.

There came the call of a jay, and he stiffened. "Seems like that there old story isn't goin' to help us, Reverend. You and the boy better get to the guns. We've got the best cover in this part anyhow."

The stone moved at Owen's tugging and then fell to the ground, barely missing his knees. The space within was small, but he could see the box inside, and eagerly he pulled at it.

"Well, I'll be!" Galvin gave the find a long glance, and then his head snapped around as a birdcall came from some rocks.

The trailing party was slow to show, or perhaps some last remnants of superstition kept them from charging. Owen hefted the heavy rifle. The box was between his feet, and now in the full light it gleamed and sparks of light made patterns at the corners of the lid.

There followed no time for treasure hunting. Their trackers suddenly took heart and came leaping into view. There was one among them who wore a tattered hunting shirt, and whose greased-back hair was a dirty red. A renegade.

Perhaps they never had a chance from the very start, but they took out two of the attackers before they were pulled down in turn and looked up into wolfish faces dabbed with paint. Better dead than captive, Owen knew, and shivered.

"Wall, now." It was the renegade who stopped and caught up the box. "Got yourself a pretty, boy. You won't git no chance at it now. I, Hawk Haverage, gits this."

They were already pulling that about. Galvin's eyes were closed, and there was a thick smear of blood down the side of his face. Owen could see only his father's feet being bound with rawhide thongs.

"Let's see what's in this pretty of yourn." Haverage swung it back and forth by his ear, listening. Perhaps for a rattle of contents. Then he applied the point of his knife to the edge of the box, prying it up on all four sides.

The Indians had stopped their own looting to draw closer. Finally the lid rose, and Haverage looked confounded.

"Old sandal. Look, it's old enough to be just dust." He turned the box upside down and shook it. Dust did come out, but it did not fall. Rather, it spread and thickened—thickened enough to form bodies. Bodies bursting from that fog. There was a shrill screeching as the Indians took off, scrambling wildly over the broken walls.

Haverage was of stronger stuff. He flung the knife he still

held at the nearest figure. It struck true enough, and Owen was sure that he heard the ring of metal against metal before it fell.

They were no longer things of shadows, those who gathered here, but rather like some of the pictures he had seen in those books his father sometimes found to borrow. Knights!

Knights from a different world and time. The leader had reached Haverage. A sword as solid as any normal steel swung up and came down. Though his body showed no visible wound, the renegade collapsed and lay still.

Then that silent company out of time gathered around the box. They knelt, holding their swords by the blade before them. Owen could see their lips move, though he caught no sound, and he believed they were praying.

Slowly they arose and then they marched into the fog that had been hanging like a curtain. There was a feeling of withdrawal, as if something utterly precious had come to an end.

The fog was gone, and with it the knights. Haverage's body lay unmoving by the wall, but his father said sharply:

"Owen, that knife, can you get it and cut yourself free?"

It was an effort, but he achieved that at last and, making a wide circle about the box, went to free his father. Galvin groaned and struggled up on one elbow with his bound hands, which Owen quickly freed, to reach his head.

Once more Matthew tended a wound that, as the blood was washed away, proved to be less serious than they had feared. But instead of watching his father's labors, Owen kept his eyes upon the box that lay by Haverage's inert body.

Finally he made himself move to pick it up. Its interior was clear of dust, but there was writing engraved on the lid. He knew a little Latin, all his father could drive into his head on occasion when there was time for schooling.

His father came up behind him. "Now that has the look of a Popish thing—"

Galvin was sitting up, and now he said weakly: "What's it for, Reverend? Looks like gold, don't it?"

"They were used to hold holy things—bones of saints and the like."

Owen pushed it into his father's hands. "There's writing on it—Latin, maybe."

His father studied the engraving, carefully brushing away a film of dust from the lines.

"Where His Holy Feet pressed let all remember the courage of Our Lord." Then Matthew pointed to a last symbol. "A Knights Templar seal. They were always thought to have found great treasures of the spirit in the Holy Land, and guarded such to the end. . . ."

"But Haverage said there was only an old sandal inside. . . ." Owen said slowly. That odd sense of being one with someone else grew stronger and then was gone.

"'Where His Holy Feet pressed.' Remember your scripture, boy. When Our Lord was sent to the cross, did not the soldiers on guard throw dice for His robe—and perhaps His sandals? Only our Holy Father knows the secrets of this world. Templars came here fearing the wrath of those roused against them.

"They were the Stonish Men in truth, keeping guard until death. But today we saw them return, that their treasure not fall into evil hands."

His father knelt, and Owen followed quickly. With the ease of long practice his father spoke those lines intended to ease the passing of those who died in the Light—far from home—deep in time.

Owen did not even realize that he was moving until his hands closed about the Casket and he was kneeling, to set it in its old hiding place. He fumbled with the heavy stone and urged it back into position. It was empty, but it had once held very much. It, too, must not be any longer troubled by the greed of men.

INTERLUDE SIX

As one's oeuvre as an author grows, over the years, it is always a source of wonder and delight to see what happens when another author picks up on an aspect of one's previous work, melds it with the concept for another project, and comes up with an idea that is both compatible with the original conception *and* fresh and exciting. Back in 1982, when researching my World War II thriller *Lammas Night,* my interest in the Knights Templar arose from a perspective still largely historical. The protagonist of that novel, John Graham, must have known about the Templars' contemporary incarnation as an esoteric body similar to the one in which he worked—but he hadn't yet told me. As his own Templar connections emerged in *The Templar Treasure,* which I coauthored with Deborah Turner Harris in 1993, it became apparent that modern esoteric Templars also must have been working their own magic to stop Hitler during World War II; Graham just hadn't seen fit to mention it at the time.

But Brad Sinor figured out at least part of what they were doing. And his Templars seem to have an ability similar to John Graham's, to travel on the Second Road—and for a very important reason.

Dreams and Nightmares

Bradley H. Sinor

Preceptor! Preceptor!"

That it hardly seemed more than a minute or two since he had closed his eyes, trying to snatch a few hours' sleep, before he was shaken awake was no surprise to Geoffroi de Charney.

Indeed, it was a rare thing for him, as the Preceptor of Normandy for the Knights Templar, and the second-ranking member of the Order, to get an uninterrupted night's sleep. And in this troubled summer of 1307, those moments had grown rarer and rarer.

"This had better be something at least as important as the Second Coming," he muttered into his pillow.

"Preceptor! Preceptor!"

Reluctantly de Charney pried his eyes open. The voice calling him belonged to a young man dressed in the robes of a novice brother. The small candle in his hand seemed to cast as many shadows as it dispelled.

"Preceptor de Charney. Are you awake?"

"Yes, yes, I'm awake. Stop your yammering and tell me why you are disturbing me."

In the past month, de Charney had been awakened more than once by demands from one or another of the local villagers for him to help find stolen livestock or capture the looters of several barns. It was something he would have done willingly—and had, many times in the past—but with the current problems faced by the Order, such demands seemed more an annoyance than anything else.

"Preceptor, you must get up."

"Who told you to get me out of bed?"

"Sergeant Brother Zael. He also instructed me to keep after you until you were actually on your feet. Otherwise you might go back to sleep. He said I was to do that even if you were to order me not to."

That the young man was terrified of his superior's reaction was evident. That he was even more terrified of Sergeant Brother Demetrious Zael was equally obvious. De Charney couldn't help but smile. Zael had been terrifying young recruits to the Order for more than three decades. In the process, he had also made them some of the best soldiers ever to have worn the white tabard of the Templars.

Reluctantly the Preceptor of Normandy pushed the blanket back and stood up. He twisted first one way and then another to work the kinks out of his muscles.

"There, I'm up. We wouldn't want to get you in trouble with Sergeant Brother Zael."

"Thank you, Preceptor," the novice said meekly.

"So what's the problem?"

"A messenger has arrived with dispatches from the Grand Master. Less than an hour ago."

"From de Molay?" Geoffroi did not like the sudden feeling he had in the pit of his stomach. "Where are these dispatches?"

"The messenger still has them. He refuses to hand them over to anyone but you, Preceptor."

De Charney sighed. That sounded like the sort of instructions that the Grand Master would give—and given the political atmosphere in France, it was only prudent.

"Very well. I will see him. What time is it?"

"It was just after one when I was sent to fetch you."

"All right. I will need a few moments to prepare myself. Have the messenger brought to the library. I will be there momentarily."

"Yes, Preceptor."

Drake Constantine had allowed the world to fade around him until there was only the tabletop with its single flickering candle remaining. For three hours he had been preparing himself for this moment. Though he had utter confidence in his own ability to do what was needed tonight, he was still a bit afraid.

It must be done, he reminded himself, wrapping himself in the flickering shadows cast by his candle.

Continuing to gaze into the candle's flame, he drew slow, measured breaths as he centered himself, letting his mind and heart reach out. From off to his right came the sound of a door opening.

"I thank you for delivering these," de Charney said to the messenger waiting in the library. "Brother Rameriez will see that you are fed and given a place to rest. It will take me several hours to prepare a reply for the Grand Master."

"Thank you, Preceptor." The young man turned and followed the older Templar who had escorted him to the library.

De Charney listened as the sound of their footsteps receded down the hallway. Moving closer to a lantern hanging above the table behind him, he looked down at the three letters that had come from de Molay.

The political situation was growing even worse than de Charney had thought. For a moment he caught himself longing for the hot, dry deserts of the Holy Land. In Outremer, things had seemed much simpler.

"Or perhaps I was simpler then," he muttered.

He looked around the library, its shelves bare and lonely now. Once it had overflowed with riches. There had been more than three dozen books. But, as the summer had worn on, the Grand Master had ordered that all the books and records of the Order be removed and taken to a more secure place, lest they be used against the Temple. De Charney suspected that they had been not hidden, but burned.

Sighing, de Charney dropped the letters on the table and bent to pull a stool closer, but a sudden chill ran through him before he could sit. His hand dropped to the hilt of the dagger at his waist as the same instincts that had saved his life time and again in battle blazed to life.

The light that filled the room seemed suddenly more than should be coming from the lantern above him, and sitting across the table from him was a man dressed in black shirt, silver vest, and boots. Unlike de Charney, he was clean-shaven, and his hair was touched with gray.

"Geoffroi de Charney. I have been waiting a very long time to meet you. We have much to discuss," the man said.

De Charney found himself easing the dagger from its sheath.

"Who are you, sir?"

"I am a friend."

"How did you come to this place that only members of this Order have the right to enter?"

"I come in peace, and when I depart, I swear before all that the Temple holds true, that none shall have been harmed."

"The devil can speak with a smooth tongue, sir, and make promises that please him." It came to de Charney that the stranger had spoken not in Norman French but in English—a language that de Charney knew but little. Yet he understood every word that was said.

"Do you think I am the devil?" the stranger asked. "I believe that King Philip has claimed that the entire Temple may well be devils."

"I am all too well aware of what Philip has said." De Charney's voice carried the venom and fear that he felt. He reminded himself that a Christian man should be more forgiving.

The stranger inclined his head. "My name, Geoffroi de Charney, Preceptor for Normandy of the Poor Fellow-Soldiers of Christ and the Temple of Solomon, is Drake Constantine. As for my right to be here, I have every right."

Reaching into his vest pocket, the man brought out a small medallion that he laid on the table near the candle. It showed two knights sitting on a single horse. The Latin script on its edge read: *Non nobis, Domine, non nobis sed nomini tuo da gloriam*—"Not to us, Lord, not to us but to Thy Name give the glory."

Still wary, de Charney produced from around his neck a similar medallion, laying it next to the first.

"Where did you get that?" he asked softly.

"I am a lay brother in the same Order as you. I swear before God that what I am about to tell you is the truth."

De Charney stared at the man called Constantine for a long time. There was something about him that he found believable, so he slid the dagger back into its sheath and drew the stool up to the table.

"Speak, then, Drake Constantine. I don't know if I will believe you, but I will listen with an open mind."

"That is all I ask. Very well, then, can you tell me where we are?"

De Charney was more than a little taken aback by the question. He wasn't sure what he had expected Constantine to say, but that had not been it. So before he spoke, he looked around him.

Instead of the library of the Temple in Normandy, he was . . . somewhere else. In place of the empty library shelves were walls carved with bas-reliefs, figures, and symbols, all strangely familiar. A blue, ankle-deep mist hugged the floor.

"Am I caught up in a dream or a nightmare?" he asked.

"Neither," Constantine said quietly. "I suspect you know this place—or at least have heard of it."

"We are *Elsewhere*, aren't we?" de Charney said. "In Outremer, I spoke with a number of savants, sorcerers, holy men. The majority were as insane as the heat had driven them, but a few were wiser than I ever dreamed possible. They spoke of a place where our souls could walk, for a time, away from our bodies. Some of the Temple have mastered the skills needed to walk these paths."

"I know. Such skills have provided the means for us to meet here. I called you to this place so that we could speak of matters that will affect you and all those who have sworn their lives to the Temple. Not only physical distance separates us."

"I don't understand," de Charney said. "Where are you, then?"

"I am in the London Temple, in England. But it is not the London that you know. By my calendar, it is more than six hundred years in your future, in 1940."

De Charney stared at the man.

"As you said, a considerable distance."

"Indeed. And I have come to beg help of you, my brother in the Temple."

"How can I help you?"

"Know you that in only a few weeks the King of France will persuade Pope Clement to let him move against the Temple. All over France, officers of the crown will move simultaneously in an attempt to arrest all Templars—on Friday, October thirteenth. It will largely succeed."

"Can we not rally Pope Clement behind us?"

"No, you know as well as I that Pope Clement is a tool of Philip. Many, many Templars will be arrested, tortured, tried and executed."

De Charney closed his eyes, swallowing on a suddenly dry throat. *God, if it be Thy will, let this cup pass from me.*

"There is a way to help some of your Order escape—if a few of them are willing to risk one of the most dangerous things they have ever done."

"How?"

"The Templar fleet. Philip will also move to seize *it*. Have the treasury loaded aboard it, along with other things of value. Then, on the night of October twelfth, the fleet must be gone before Philip's soldiers can take it."

"Gone?"

"Yes. In my time, a great conflagration is raging between

Germany, France, and England. The army of England, along with the army of France, is being destroyed, driven into the sea at the beach called Dunkirk. Ships will come to lift off most of the men, but there will not be enough to remove everyone. The Templar fleet can make a vast difference in those few hours."

"But, you said yourself that they are more than six hundred years away from your battle."

"With your agreement, we can bring those ships forward to our time, for the one night, to carry these men to safety. The Temple can summon powers to open the gates between your time and this, for a few hours."

"This is the price of the information you have given me?"

"No, that information is a gift. This is the service I beg of you. Many will die who do not need to. But many will live to fight for the light, against evil, if you help."

"What must I do?"

"Send messages to each of your captains. Tell them only that something is going to happen that night, after they set sail. Small boats manned by Templars of my time will come alongside and guide them, act as translators."

"And when they have done?"

"When they have accomplished this task they will be returned to their proper time. But instead of the coast of France, the ships will be sailing on the waters off Scotland. There they will find allies to befriend them. Many still will die, but the Temple will live on."

Nodding, de Charney reached across the table, picking up the medallion that Constantine had placed there. He slipped it around his neck and stood up.

"There is something else," Constantine said. "Something that I could not live with myself if I did not tell you."

More than six centuries in the future, on a drizzly night in May of 1940, Constantine stood staring down at a work glove that floated on the water near one of the dock pilings. Farther along the dock, amid the ordered chaos of disembarking men, he could see two troop transports, bracketed by several small fishing craft, barges, packet steamers, and what looked like a pleasure boat.

Ambulances, coaches, lorries, cars, and anything else that might be used to transport the returning members of the British Expeditionary Force were lined up along the docks. As swiftly as one ship was emptied of its living cargo, it was pulled away to be refueled and sent back into the darkness. Lights from the ships and the ambulances and buses that lined the pier all cut through the drizzling rain that held the port in its grip.

Constantine pulled out a small pocket watch from his vest pocket. Sunrise would be in just under three hours. Constantine knew that out in the fog, beyond the breakwater, dozens more ships, both large and small, were inching their way toward Dover.

"Hello, Drake."

Constantine turned at the sound of the familiar voice. Standing near him was the thin scarecrow figure of Harley Gaiman. At twenty-two, Gaiman hardly looked like a veteran RAF fighter pilot, but he had already flown more missions than many men years older. The empty left uniform sleeve marked the mission that had taken him out of the air, but his loss had not made him any less a warrior.

"I had a feeling that you might be here—or at Admiralty Pier."

Constantine sighed. "Am I that predictable?"

"Occasionally," Gaiman said with a smile.

"I'm glad I can still confuse you."

Constantine knew where he should have been tonight: in the command center tunneled deep into the heart of the Dover cliffs, where Vice Admiral Ramsay was overseeing the evacuation. But he also knew where he needed to be, not just for the Temple but for himself.

The two men stood together for a long time, watching the ships. The sounds blended together into a confusing murmur around them.

"Is it done?" Constantine finally asked.

Gaiman nodded. "What's left of the Templar fleet has been delivered back to 1307, to the waters off Scotland."

"How many?"

"We lost half a dozen ships, some to shore battery bombardment, the others to U-boats. I have no idea how many wounded. Our men reported that they had no trouble with our 'senior brothers.' The language barrier was a little difficult at times, but it did not prove to be an insurmountable problem."

Constantine nodded. He knew that within a few hours of his conversation with de Charney, letters had been dispatched to the Grand Master, and soon enough word had gone to the Templar captains.

"And what of our other efforts?"

"As successful as could be expected. Just as we feared, the Nazis drew on a considerable array of dark magic. Our own magisters—and our allies among the Druids, the hunting lodges, those of the Old Religion—were hard pressed at times to stop them. We were able to divert some of their effort; not all, but a significant amount, I believe. But at a cost, to us and to them."

"Everything has a cost. I pray that it was enough to buy us the time we need."

Constantine looked down at the water near the pier. The glove had disappeared, drifted out of sight into the shadows.

"Our agents will remain in place, to help on a more physical level, as well," said Gaiman. "But there is one thing I'm still worried about."

"Only one?" Constantine said. "Offhand, I can think of a dozen things that are worrying me right now."

Gaiman smiled. "It's the ships, the fleet."

"What about them?"

"Won't there be reports by the soldiers we saved? I can imagine the headlines in *The Times.*"

"Oh, there will be reports—many of them." Constantine laughed. "The survivors have already begun to talk about the strange ships and men that carried them to safety. We have highly placed friends in the government, so they will be told that what they saw was something that 'officially' did not happen: the ships were simply part of Ramsay's 'cockleshell navy.' Any of the survivors who insist on writing reports will see those documents buried under the weight of the war."

Constantine extracted a pack of cigarettes from his coat and offered one to Gaiman, who shook his head "no."

"Harley, was de Charney aboard any of the ships?"

"Not that I know of," said the younger man. "Did you expect him to be?"

Constantine wasn't sure how he felt. "Not really. Though I would have understood, had he been on board."

"I wondered if you would tell him," Gaiman said. "It must have taken guts to stay, knowing he was to be executed, burned at the stake along with de Molay, professing their innocence and proclaiming that it was—how do the Americans say it?— a frame-up."

"A frame-up, indeed. I told him he could come with the ships and stay here, or go back with them to Scotland," said Constantine.

"Yet he chose neither. He chose to stay in Paris and be taken. Maybe he hoped to change things, to bring about peace between the Temple and Philip."

"Perhaps. But the oath he swore, that we all swore, would not let him leave his brothers to save his own life. Not to mention, if de Charney had lived out the rest of his span here in the twentieth century, it might have created some problems."

"Problems, indeed," Gaiman murmured.

Constantine nodded, gazing at the cigarette in his hand, seeing the fire smoldering at its tip.

"Indeed. His soul has had other lives to live since that day in 1307. Including its present incarnation."

Gaiman looked at his friend and nodded, faintly smiling.

"Yes, Preceptor."

INTERLUDE SEVEN

If, indeed, some inner circle of the Order of the Temple has continued to survive into contemporary times, it seems certain that, from time to time, the work of practitioners in other esoteric disciplines will occasionally overlap—and, if one posits the possibility of reincarnation, it follows that a soul having Templar associations in the past might well have similar connections in the present, especially if there was unfinished business in that past life.

Such a notion was part of the premise driving *The Templar Treasure,* mentioned in conjunction with the previous story. Sir Adam Sinclair, the protagonist of that novel and of the Adept series, has just such a connection—and, as a result of information that surfaced in the course of that book, was led to explore some of the further implications of his death as one of the scores of Knights Templar burned at the stake in the immediate aftermath of the suppression of the Order.

That story is told in "Obligations," which appeared in the first anthology of this series, and ended not only with a closure of this part of Adam's past but on a note of hope for another character: one Henri Gerard, now a mental patient under Adam's care, whose misdeeds in several lifetimes had brought him to his confrontation with Adam Sinclair's Hunting Lodge. It seemed about time to resolve Gerard's situation, one way or another—and, indeed, the working title of the story that follows was "Loose Ends." But a more apt title is "Restitution."

Restitution

Katherine Kurtz

Lying supine in the dappled sunshine beneath a young beech tree, with the remains of a cold lunch neatly stowed in a wicker picnic hamper and an empty wine glass in his hand, Sir Adam Sinclair reflected that he had rarely experienced such contentment. Behind him, he could hear his bride of four months crooning to the horses they had ridden up from Strathmourne House on this glorious June Sunday, feeding them apple cores and crusts of bread. Beyond his booted feet, if he squinted against the glare, he could see the crow-stepped gables and turrets of Templemor Tower and imagine it as it once had been, and soon would be again; could ignore the cluttered construction site that, on the morrow, would return to bustling life.

"All right, you'll have to settle for grass now," he heard Ximena say to the horses, before coming back to join him. As she entered his field of vision, dusting her hands against already-dirt-streaked riding breeches, he turned his head to gaze at her. Whether kitted out in riding togs or green-clad in surgical scrubs or radiant in a tartan ball gown, Ximena filled him with a joy he had feared he might never find in this life.

"She walks in beauty, like the night of cloudless climes and starry skies," he murmured, smiling up at her against the golden sunlight.

"She reeks of horses, but she loves her husband very much," she replied with an impish grin, sinking down cross-legged beside him to pick up an open Chardonnay bottle by the neck. "There's just a few swallows left," she noted, swirling the contents. "Shall we polish it off?"

"Shouldn't let it go to waste." He held up his glass and let her pour. "Come and lie down beside me," he said, patting the tartan blanket beside him. "On a perfect afternoon like this, I want you in my arms."

She discarded the empty bottle, took the glass from him and drank a swallow, then held the glass to his lips, tilting it so he could finish the rest. She kissed him as she took away the glass and laid it aside with the bottle, uttering a contented sigh as she reclined in the circle of his left arm to snuggle her dark head against his shoulder.

"Hmmm, I love it out here, especially on a day like today," she said. "Tell me again about Templemor. It's going to be wonderful when it's finished and we can run away here on the weekends. Must we have a telephone?"

"Well, I suppose we could turn the telephones off and leave your beeper back at the house," Adam said easily.

"And why do you think we haven't been interrupted today?" she replied. "I'm not on call this weekend, and I've told them not even to *try* to call me!"

"That's one of the things I like about psychiatry," he said. "We don't often get called out on emergencies."

"Not medical emergencies, anyway," she retorted, alluding to his other vocation, that sometimes required intervention of a more esoteric nature, and at decidedly odd hours. "But I don't want to talk about any kind of work today. Tell me what Templemor was like in the old days, back when the Knights Templar were here."

"Well, they never actually owned Templemor," Adam said, "though, as the name suggests, there was certainly a Templar connection. The man who built it, a very distant ancestor of mine, had a younger son who joined the Order of the Temple in the mid-thirteenth century, as did a nephew. His grandson, one Aubrey de St. Clair, also joined the Order—though as a lay knight, only committed to a set term of service. Family tradition suggests that Aubrey was in the entourage brought to Paris by Jacques de Molay, the last Grand Master, early in 1307. We believe that he made his escape with the Templar fleet, when King Philip ordered the arrest of all the Templars in France later that year. And of course, it's said that many Templars found refuge with Robert the Bruce after the suppression of the Order, and in 1314 fought for Scotland's independence in the Battle of Bannochburn."

"Do you think Aubrey was in that battle?" Ximena asked sleepily.

"Mmmm, I shouldn't be at all surprised—and survived it. We know that he sired several children after that date, and that eventually he lived here."

He went on to remark on the state of the fortified tower house before restoration had begun, telling her of the young trees previously growing from the vaulting on the upper levels, and how the ivy had been encroaching on the walls. After a while, when her breathing told him that she had dozed off, he fell silent and lifted his head to pillow it on his doubled right arm, adjusting his gaze to take in as much as he could of the tower, its newly whitewashed harling softly a-shimmer in the afternoon sun. Above the door, he could almost read the heraldic crest carved and touched out in bright paint: a red Maltese cross surrounded by seven stars. Running across the lintel beneath it, neatly chiseled into the stone, was a Sinclair motto: *Mort nunquam reget*—"Death shall have no dominion." For an Adept such as himself, who had lived many lives, both the motto and the crest were apt, as was the more recent Sinclair crest he bore above his own coat of arms: a phoenix rising from the flames.

Closing his eyes, he let himself drift on the warm, lazy tide of contentment, dipping in and out of sleep. Speaking of Aubrey de St. Clair had made him recall the psychic glimpses he sometimes had caught of his distant ancestor here amid the ruins. Once, he had even sought out Aubrey's shade, to inquire regarding a lost artifact that had connections with the Order of the Temple—for Adam himself had lived and died as a Knight Templar in a previous life.

As he floated in reverie, lulled by the warmth of the summer afternoon and the hum of honey-laden bees, the gentle whuffling of the horses contentedly cropping grass behind him and the sleeping Ximena, he found himself reflecting on that particular encounter with Aubrey, and where it had led him—and thinking of another man whose past also had been inextricably intertwined with the Order of the Temple, now a mental patient at the Edinburgh hospital where Adam had his medical practice.

He was not aware when his rumination turned to summons, as he drifted in that twilight state, so like and yet so different from sleep. Only that, all at once, he found himself standing in spirit before Templemor as it had been more than six centuries before—not the crisply pristine edifice presently being restored by workmen of Adam Sinclair's time, but as it must have appeared as a working building, with evidence of dogs and horses in the yard before it, though all was preternaturally still. As was usual during such episodes of soul-flight, Adam had the sense that he stood apart from his physical body, robed in the celestial blue that he wore in fact when working formally on the physical plane, with a blue-glowing star upon his right hand echoing the sapphire he carried always with him.

Careful not to disrupt what was taking shape—for he sensed that important inner work was about to commence—Adam drew in his focus and lifted his astral hands both in supplication and receptivity. A part of him was still aware of the dappled sunlight, warm on his closed eyelids; the weight of

Ximena's dark head on his left shoulder. But as he concentrated on Aubrey de St. Clair—and on the patient who needed the help of both Aubrey and himself—he sensed a brightening of the shadows in the doorway beneath the Sinclair crest.

He held his summons, and the brightening gradually sharpened to the image of a Templar knight, bearded and white-garbed, with the red cross of the Order vivid against the chest of his surcoat and a greatsword slung along his back, with just the pommel visible over his right shoulder.

"Brother Aubrey de St. Clair," Adam said, stepping forward in spirit—and in that moment, his own likeness shifted to that of the Templar knight he once had been.

The eyes of the other knight met his, and the head jerked in a curt nod, close-shorn above the untrimmed beard.

"Brother Jauffre," he acknowledged, greeting Adam in his Templar aspect. "Or is it Adam Sinclair, Master of the Hunt?"

"I come not as hunter but as healer," Adam replied, inclining his head, "and I thank you for previous counsel given. My prior mission did, indeed, lead to our preceptory at Balantrodoch. Three treasures did I find there—and one curse, which I was given grace to resolve. But he who unleashed the curse was witness to soul-crippling horrors. His body I was able to save, but his mind is deranged—and his soul remains in peril, if he cannot break free of what he has called upon himself by his own choices, both in this life and in at least one past that links him to the Temple."

"Acquaint me with the details," Aubrey said.

Faster than thought itself, in that not-space between worlds, where time did not exist, Adam laid out what he had learned of one Henri Gerard, erstwhile student of archaeology and less reputable pursuits: a soul fastened on the procurement of dangerous knowledge and, by the using of it, the acquisition of illicit power and wealth. Pursuing dark obsessions shaped by a past extending over several lifetimes, Gerard had purloined certain treasures long guarded by the Temple, esoteric implements by which King Solomon himself had bound away an ancient evil—the twin demons Gog and Magog, which Gerard and an accomplice had unwittingly unleashed.

Only barely had the intervention of Adam and his associates recontained the demons—and not before they ripped apart and devoured Gerard's accomplice. Gerard himself, witness to that terrible spectacle, had paid the price of madness for his dabbling; the ultimate price might yet be his soul.

"I see," the other Templar said. "Much is now clearer. You should know that I, too, have dealt with this man . . . for, in that other life, I compassed his death—as he compassed yours, I think."

Far memories of that death flashed briefly before Adam's inner sight, though disconnected from its sensory anguish— burned at the stake like so many of their brethren, his body writhing in the flames that slowly roasted his flesh from his bones—and the gloating face of Guillaume de Nogaret, the king's chancellor, who had masterminded the persecution and destruction of the Order of the Temple.

"You have a link with Nogaret?" Adam asked, shaken nonetheless, though he had long since come to grips with that death, and long since ceased to be surprised at such "coincidences" when dealing with affairs of the inner planes.

"It was Nogaret who urged the king to act against the Temple," Aubrey said sharply. "And it was one of the brethren martyred with you at Senlis who prefigured the Grand Master's curse on king and pope by summoning Nogaret to join him before the throne of heaven to answer for his crimes. And it was I who assisted him to keep that appointment."

"*You* killed Nogaret?" Adam asked.

Aubrey de St. Clair looked away. "I was not then what I am now. Had I then known what I later learned, I would have spared him to perish by his own folly—for it is clear that, even then, he was courting the glamours of Darkness. A reckoning then might have spared the innocent in later times."

"Or not," Adam replied. "Every soul must work out its own destiny, its own salvation—and it is not our place to judge."

"But you would heal him," Aubrey said.

"It is the Creator who heals," Adam replied. "But if I can, I would bring Henri Gerard into that healing Light."

"He will face a terrible judgment," Aubrey warned.

"I know that. But Mercy may yet temper Justice, if he truly repents."

Aubrey bowed deeply from the waist, a profound gesture of respect from a lesser Adept to a greater.

"Then, go with the Light, my brother. I have not the grace to assist you in this work, but such intercession as I can make for your intentions, I offer freely. *Adieu.*"

Just so quickly, he was gone, leaving Adam with much to ponder. A while longer Adam lingered in trance, contemplating Aubrey's words, then surfaced with a sigh, opening his eyes. His right arm was cramped from being folded behind his head, and his left had gone numb from the weight of Ximena's head. He winced as he shifted both arms, straightening the right one. The movement roused Ximena, who had slept through the entire episode.

"Who moved my pillow?" she murmured, turning her head to smile at him sleepily.

"Sorry, darling, my arm got cramped."

"A likely story," she replied, snuggling closer against his side. "My first Sunday off in two weeks, and my horrible husband is determined to sabotage my nap!"

"No, he's determined not to have his arms fall off from lack of circulation," Adam replied with a chuckle, easing his arm from under her shoulders and sitting up. "But we probably ought to consider heading back to the house. I'd like to do a bit of research."

Ximena sighed, stretching cat-like, then reluctantly rolled onto her side and also sat up, indulging a yawn.

"You do look preoccupied," she said, eyeing him as she

pulled the picnic hamper closer to stash the remaining debris from lunch. "Did you have one of your dreams?"

"Not exactly," he said truthfully. "But I did find myself thinking about one of my patients. I think I might have come up with a few new insights into his case."

"Nothing alarming, I hope."

"Not at all. He and I have a past—and with any luck at all, he may now have a future."

"A past—as in, past lives?" she asked, her face clouding.

He shrugged and gave her a wry smile. "I can't blame you for being dubious about the notion. Sometimes, so am I. But sometimes therapy does move forward when one treats so-called past-life information 'as if' it were real."

"I know. You've told me that before," she said, getting to her feet and tugging at the blanket to get him to rise as well. "I'm ready to believe many strange things, Adam Sinclair—especially after living with you for the past six months—but past lives . . ."

Smiling, he rose and helped her fold the blanket for stowing behind one of the saddles.

"I don't ask you to believe it," he said easily. "What matters is whether or not it works. This case is one of my more interesting ones—and more challenging. I'll let you know what happens when I've next worked with him."

The encounter with Aubrey de St. Clair continued to occupy Adam's thoughts as he and Ximena rode home. Later that evening, he consulted the history references he had available at the house, looking for information that might corroborate Aubrey's claim to have caused the death of Nogaret. Other than a vague reference that Nogaret had died by the spring of 1313, he could find nothing more specific. But whether or not Henri Gerard had been Guillaume de Nogaret in a previous life—and Adam had good reason to believe that he had been—Gerard was, beyond question, a deeply disturbed individual in this life.

He dreamed about Gerard that night but could remember little of substance upon awakening. On arriving Monday morning at Edinburgh Royal Hospital, he confirmed that Gerard's next appointment was scheduled for Wednesday afternoon. Then, after completing teaching rounds, he settled down with a sandwich and a cup of tea to review Gerard's case notes.

The official accounting was stark, as was the prognosis at present. Formally diagnosed as a catatonic schizophrenic, Gerard had been taken into psychiatric care some eighteen months before, when police found him cowering in a culvert near an Edinburgh golf course, dazed and incoherent, unable even to give them his name. Unrecorded was the fact that Adam and his associates had left Gerard there to be found.

In the next few weeks, monitoring from afar in his capacity as a special consultant to the Lothian and Borders Police, Adam had quietly tracked Gerard's progress through the medicolegal system—for outside discovery of the true nature of Gerard's crimes would lead only to questions about later developments that were best left unasked. Though soon identified, and briefly considered in connection with a fatal robbery-assault in Yorkshire—of which he was guilty, though it was likely never to be proven—his condition made it abundantly clear that Henri Gerard was in no fit state to answer questions about anything. Eventually, Adam had pulled professional strings to have Gerard assigned to his public caseload.

But they had made little progress, thus far. Gerard steadfastly denied having any conscious memory of the incident that had pushed him over the edge into madness—and, indeed, had hardly spoken for nearly six months after being taken into care, though his selective amnesia was punctuated by episodes of raving, wild-eyed hysteria, when he had to be restrained and sedated. Only rarely would he make fleeting reference to the terrible things he had seen and done, even in this life, much less in any previous ones. Though he had proven a relatively responsive hypnotic subject when dealing with minor issues, he would not allow himself to be taken deep enough to go beyond his fears and actually confront any part of his past.

Over the next two days, Gerard's case was never long out of Adam's mind. He dreamed about Gerard again on Monday and Tuesday nights, again with uncharacteristic inability to remember the content. Vaguely troubled, he skimmed over Gerard's case notes again on Wednesday morning, in preparation for their afternoon session, and had formulated a tentative game plan by the time a ward nurse brought Gerard to a consulting room near Adam's office.

Slight of stature and painfully thin, the Frenchman looked far worse than he had at their session the week before. Long gone was the dapper pencil mustache he had sported when first taken into care; and his once-dark hair had gone almost completely white in the past year. Hollow-eyed and nervous, his furtive manner suggested that he was wary of imminent assault by personal demons—and, indeed, his experience of very real demons, and in Adam's presence, had given him cause for such fears.

"Bonjour, Henri," Adam said, as Gerard silently shuffled to the upholstered chair opposite the desk and sat, huddling down in his hospital-issue dressing gown. *"Bonjour,"* he repeated, when Gerard did not speak. "Would you rather speak English today?"

Gerard heaved a heavy sigh and buried his head in his hands.

"I am not sleeping well, *Docteur,*" he murmured. "The dreams have come back. The demons are waiting."

"Shall I order you a stronger sedative?" Adam said quietly, though he knew what Gerard's answer would be.

The Frenchman shook his head. "I am a doomed man. I shall perish utterly."

"I have told you, the demons may not pursue you here," Adam said. "Even in your dreams, they may not harm you."

Biting back a sob, Gerard lifted his head to scan the room nervously, giving little indication that he even saw Adam. "What would you know of any of it?"

"I know far more than you realize," Adam replied. "Shall we begin again, Henri?"

The question was a posthypnotic trigger for Gerard to go into trance. As if a switch had been pulled, the dark eyes glazed over, Gerard's tension draining away as he exhaled with a pathetic little sigh, head lolling against the back of the chair. Adam spent several minutes deepening his patient's trance, lulling and reassuring, taking note of every flicker of external reaction, then carefully began leading Gerard yet again toward a guarded confrontation with the guilt and fears that haunted him.

"Henri, despite past errors, you have within yourself the resources to relieve your distress. At least on some level, you are aware of actions and inactions in your past life that you regret—not so much because of fear of punishment, but because you have grown in wisdom. Release requires an honest acknowledgment of past errors. It requires remorse, and restitution—atonement, or *at-one-ment,* a coming back into the cleansing light of—"

"I have killed," Gerard said suddenly, though his voice was flat and toneless.

"I know that," Adam said, after a beat.

"Not directly," Gerard went on. "It was never my hand that did the deed. Well, once—but I never meant the old man to die. And all those Templars . . ."

His eyes popped open and he slowly focused on Adam, though he was still in trance.

"I know you," he whispered. "I watched you burn. And all

those other Templars—dozens, scores . . . They were no better and no worse than any other men, but I coveted their treasures—the gold and the knowledge. *Mon Dieu,* what I have done?—and all for empty promises, for greed . . ."

He began breathing rapidly, eyes darting around the consulting room in alarm, hyperventilating. Adam only watched, ready to intervene if necessary, but knowing that important inner work was taking place. Finally, Gerard shook his head and looked again at Adam, still hard in the grip of whatever was in progress.

"Please—I need paper, and pen," he pleaded, reaching out to Adam. "I must write it. . . . *Il faut que j'ecrive . . . je vous prie . . .*"

Wordlessly Adam pushed a yellow legal pad across the desk to him and handed him a pen. Wild-eyed, faintly whimpering, Gerard seized on the items as if they represented his only lifeline, hunching over the pad with a fevered intensity, his fingers gripped white-knuckled on the pen as he began laboriously to write.

Watching him, moving quietly lest he interrupt what finally had begun, Adam delved into the pocket of his starched white lab coat and found the ring that symbolized his esoteric office, for he sensed that Gerard had reached a breakthrough on many levels. Slipping the ring onto his right hand, he leaned back in his chair and propped his elbows on the chair arms, cupping his left hand over the ring's bright sapphire. Though his own greater work had aspects both of healer and enforcer of a higher Law, his optimum focus in the present unfolding remained unclear.

For several seconds, Adam simply watched Gerard laboring over his yellow pad, single-mindedly pouring out at least a portion of his inner anguish. After a few seconds more, as Gerard continued to write, tears now streaming down his face, Adam let himself slip into his own working trance, seeking guidance of the mentor to whom he answered on the inner planes.

The shift into trance brought with it that familiar, faintly giddy instant akin to vertigo, as his higher self settled into a level of consciousness not normally accessible amid the psychic buzz of the workaday world. A slowly drawn breath, exhaled on a silent prayer for wisdom and discernment, took him yet another level deeper toward the center-point, to immerse him in an all-permeating sense of benison.

All at once, overlaying the commonplace of the consulting room and Gerard's bent head, the vista before Adam seemed to unfold upon a broad plateau, silvery in the moonlight. Ranged beneath a canopy of stars were twelve bearded and white-robed Templar knights seated in a horseshoe shape, with the opening toward Adam and a thirteenth chair set like a throne within the horseshoe's curve. Hovering within the confines of that throne was a shining spindle of golden-white light that slowly began to coalesce into the seated form of a thirteenth figure, robed in the chapel garb of a Templar Grand Master and with gauntleted hands clasped to the hilt of a greatsword grounded between his sandaled feet.

While a part of Adam continued to observe Gerard, ready to react when he stopped writing, that inner core of him that was Adept and vassal of the seated Master moved forward on the inner planes, himself now clad in the white robes and mantle of the Templar knight he once had been.

Bide warily, Master of the Hunt, came the Master's warning, before Adam could make his petition. *Another has spoken on behalf of this troubled soul, and insight has been offered. Your charge has redemption within his reach, if he will but grasp it. The balance can be restored, but he must be strong.*

"I have prayed that he might be brought into the Light," Adam replied. "Is there aught I can do to assist him?"

He must be strong, and you must be strong, came the reply. *Temporal balance must precede the higher Balance. Restitution must be offered. Remember a healer's first instruction: First, do no harm. But what is to be must be permitted to run its course.*

Grounded and solid before the spectral figure of the Master and his knights, Henri Gerard finished a determined flourish at the end of the page, stared for a long moment at what he had written, lips moving silently, then leaned forward abruptly to lay the pen back on Adam's desk. His hands were trembling as he picked up the yellow pad and again gazed at his written words, then briefly bowed to touch the pad to his forehead, murmuring something unintelligible under his breath. He seemed to crumple just a little as he turned his gaze to Adam once more—still anxious-looking, but now totally without fear as, in the presence of the Master and the assembled Templar court, he leaned forward to extend the yellow pad to Adam.

"Forgive me," he whispered, in a tone that bespoke utter clarity of focus.

Still maintaining his vision on the inner planes, Adam reached out his physical hand to take the pad, casting Gerard a quizzical glance as he turned it to read what the Frenchman had written.

"Avant le Dieu de la pitié, je confesse . . ."

The scrawled French was a confession, acknowledging utter culpability for the two deaths he had caused as Henri Gerard—and for the scores of Knights Templar who had died protesting their innocence more than six centuries before: more than a hundred burned at the stake, and scores more dead from torture or even suicide to escape it. He further renounced the dark Forces he had courted in his quest for wealth and power, repenting his blind foolishness and throwing himself on the mercy of Heaven. At the bottom, he had inscribed two signatures: Henri Marcel Gerard and Guillaume de Nogaret.

It was an extraordinary document. But even as Adam grasped its import, Gerard began to babble rapidly in French.

"Mon Dieu, je me repents de tous mes péchés . . ."

Adam looked up sharply, for Gerard was reciting an act of

contrition, hands clasped before his breast, face upturned and eyes clenched shut. Beyond him, the Master and the twelve Templars now were standing. The very air in the room had become charged with expectation.

"Aidez-moi, Seigneur!" Gerard prayed, tears streaming down his cheeks. *"Donnez-moi de grâce. . . ."*

As if in response to that plea, wisps of smoke began to curl upward from behind Gerard's clasped hands, flames suddenly bursting from his chest in a terrible blossoming of supernal fire. Adam sprang to his feet with a swiftness that overturned his chair as Gerard stifled an anguished cry and thrust his hands heavenward in a gesture of oblation—and the hands became torches, exploding into flame.

"Pardonnez, Bon Seigneur!" Gerard cried, on a wailing sob.

As sheets of flame enfolded the Frenchman in a raging winding sheet of flame, his supplication choked to a faint mewling that wrenched at Adam's heart. Backing off from the intense heat, his hands thrown up both in warding and in orison, Adam found himself torn between yearning to save Gerard's body—though he knew that was futile—and pleading for the soul surely about to leave that body, now writhing in an agony that Adam himself had experienced firsthand, and by the connivance of this very man.

But mitigating his very human revulsion at this terrible suffering was an ever clearer certainty that, on some level, Henri Gerard had chosen this fate as partial expiation for crimes committed in this life and in the past, as a measure of his remorse for having fallen so short of the mark—which was, in the final reckoning, the true dimension of sin. Buoyed by his own faith—and by hope that the divine Mercy would be extended even to Henri Gerard—Adam hardened himself to the physical agony Gerard was suffering and wrenched his psychic focus back to the watchers on the inner planes: to the Master, now a vague, fire-limned figure with only vague semblance of mortal form, whose fiery hands rested on the cross-hilt of a flaming sword akin to that which guarded the gates of Eden; to the twelve knights of Gerard's jury, who had turned, as one, to regard the roaring inferno that now contained the plaintiff.

In that instant, Adam knew beyond doubt that it was not his place to intervene in any way, that it was Henri Gerard who had brought himself to this state to offer amends—and in giving up his life amid remorse for his past sins, he would, by grace and mercy, be permitted to pass into the healing Light.

Enlightenment came to Gerard in that same instant. From out of the heart of the physical conflagration came a psychic cry of wondering discovery as a dark form sparkling with a net-like tracery of golden light rose phoenix-like from the physical fire and stepped away from it. As it lifted its arms in thanksgiving, blackened shards began to flake away like fragments of a shattered shell, revealing a newly cleansed and shining spirit, as innocent as a child's. With a child's trust, the soul that, most recently, had been Henri Gerard moved with halting steps toward the Master, who was agent of a far higher Grace, there to humbly kneel in gratefulness. Simultaneously, the twelve Templar knights moved in to cluster close around him, stretching out their right hands to touch his shoulders in benison and pardon.

Then the light from all the thirteen converged and merged with Gerard's kneeling form, shrinking to a single point that vanished with a hollow *pop,* leaving Adam staring dumbstruck at the grisly, reeking remains that once had been Henri Gerard, still seated in an upholstered chair untouched by the fire that had all but consumed mortal flesh.

Later—when Adam had made the obligatory stunned and agitated calls for help, lending a hand with the fire extinguisher that an orderly brought on the run, though not before he pocketed Gerard's confession; when he had made the requisite statement to the shaken young police constable who first

Katherine Kurtz ✠ 181

came in response to the emergency call; when the body had been taken away—Adam stripped off the starched white lab coat that now reeked of burnt human flesh, stuffed it into a hospital laundry basket, and retreated to his office with the young constable's supervisor, who was also his closest colleague in the esoteric work of which this was one of the more startling examples.

"Well, that's a first for me, at least," said Detective Chief Inspector Noel McLeod, as he flopped into a chair beside Adam's desk. "Spontaneous human combustion, like something out of Charles Fort. I'd read about it, of course—and you and I have even seen forms of it, on the astral level—but this is the first honest-to-God civilian instance I've ever encountered. I read P.C. MacAlister's report. Do you want to tell me what really happened?"

"Something rather wonderful, actually," Adam said, smiling faintly, which produced a look of disbelief on the part of his Second.

But by the time he had finished relating his impressions of the working on the inner planes, handing over Gerard's confession and translating the gist of it, McLeod, too, was smiling.

"It does sound as if our Mr. Gerard achieved some kind of personal epiphany," the inspector said. "Remorse, repentance, confession, a kind of restitution—and forgiveness. A hell of a way to go, though. Do you think he caused the combustion himself, or was it visited upon him?"

Adam shook his head. "I couldn't say. The others were watching him expectantly, but I didn't have the impression they actually did anything in that regard. He had come to grips with what he had done, in this life and in the past, had reached an honest contrition, and it was up to him to choose a suitable punishment—or, not a punishment, but a purification, I think. A refinement by fire—rather fitting, I suppose, given the fate of all those Templars. And while he may have wished it upon himself, I certainly wouldn't regard it as a suicide."

"Well, I'm sure the postmortem and the official report won't reflect any of this," McLeod said, handing back the confession. "Just one more odd case I'm going to have to try to explain to the press."

"Aye, and made more difficult by the fact that this is one of those cases that I'd almost like to be able to report openly: that, even for someone like Henri Gerard, there is hope of redemption."

McLeod nodded. "That's certainly what most of the churches teach. I suppose it takes a higher wisdom than ours to determine when the balance has been redressed. As ye sow, so shall ye reap, the Bible says."

"Yes, and an eye for an eye, and the wheat separated from the chaff, and the tares thrown into the fire," Adam agreed. "But in some cases, as I believe I've witnessed today, the divine Mercy can redeem life from death, and new hope can be reborn. Henri Gerard may yet have to make further reparations—perhaps the cosmic equivalent of community service, as we all must answer for our failings, in kind—but I think he laid his demons to rest. Restitution has been made."

INTERLUDE EIGHT

Many modern practitioners of esoteric disciplines continue to assert that the Templars are still among us, carrying on the hidden work of the ancient Order, policing the astral planes, that Second Road—as they once policed the pilgrim routes around Jerusalem . . . and took up the mantle of their destiny. One of the more satisfying speculations about modern esoteric involvement of some ongoing facet of the Order's secret work was introduced in "Stealing God," in the first volume of this series. Peter Crossman is a modern secret agent of the Inner Temple, and his sometime working partner is Sister Mary Magdalene of the Special Action Executive of the Poor Clares, a stunning redhead who—

But, read on. One can wistfully wish that there *were* such secret agents, to take appropriate action when misguided folk embark upon "Selling the Devil."

Selling the Devil

Debra Doyle
and James D. Macdonald

J'd come to New York on business, switching out fabric samples from the Shroud of Turin so that the scientists who were doing the tests would declare it a fake and give it a rest. Once the job was done I stayed in town. I took a room at the Waldorf-Astoria under the name Peter Crossman—it isn't my real name, but I've got papers that say it is—and caught up on my sleep.

After a couple of days, time began hanging heavy, and I felt the need to get back into the scene. I called Chatillon on a secure line and asked for an assignment, something easy and local.

We're the Knights Templar. I'm in the Inner Temple. You won't have heard of the Inner Temple, but that's okay; most of the Order hasn't either. We're out there just the same—three and thirty of us, all priests and all warriors—doing the work we've done since the beginning, protecting the holy things and the holy places, guarding pilgrims of all kinds. The times change, the tools change, the mission doesn't. *Non nobis, Domine, non nobis sed nomine tuo da gloriam*—"Not to us, O Lord, not to us, but to Thy Name give the glory."

The briefing book came over a little after 3 P.M. It contained a surveillance report and a homemade advertising flyer. The report had the details on a character whose nom-de-magick was "Black Eric," a supplier of amulets and other working gear to well-heeled, left-hand-path types. He had his shop up in Newburgh, in the shadow of the I-84 bridge. He'd recently taken a contract to provide a sword-and-chalice rig to a person or persons unknown.

The advertising flyer wasn't much different from the ones you see tacked up on telephone posts and grocery-store bulletin boards all over the world, put there by people holding yard sales and giving away free kittens to good homes. But this one offered something else.

HAIL SATAN! it read, in sprawling capitals. THE MASTER WILL ARISE IN THE FLESH THAT ALL MAY SEE AND BELIEVE!

A block of smaller lettering in the bottom half of the sheet gave a street address up the Hudson in Poughkeepsie, the date —today—and the time—11:30 P.M.—plus a twenty-bucks-a-head "initiation fee." It ended with SATAN COMMANDS! in more block capitals.

Someone thought the two items were important. I agreed. The address on the flyer was the one to which Black Eric had delivered his latest commission.

Black Eric worked in precious metals and jewels, not sharp iron. I put in a call for a list of all reports dealing with swords, worldwide, over the last month. When it arrived I folded the sheet of paper into quarters, slipped it into my pocket, and made ready for my night's excursion.

I'd go in as a civilian, playing earnest but not too bright—the sort of gullible failure who'd show up to watch somebody conjure a living Lord of Darkness into the mortal sphere. I slid a .45 Colt into a shoulder rig, dropped a crucifix into my right coat pocket and a flashlight into my left, and headed out to rent a car.

By eleven I was in Po-town. The address on the flyer belonged to a run-down Victorian Gothic mansion in a seedy neighborhood full of potholed streets and weed-choked vacant lots. The house had a FOR SALE sign out front. The windows were boarded up and the yard was overgrown with tall grass. I showed the flyer to the door guard—a young man trying to look tougher and more world-weary than he really was—and he took my twenty bucks without looking at my face.

Inside, the house was dark; nothing came in through the boarded-up windows, and nothing would get out, either. Candle glow and the murmur of voices led me to what must have been the ballroom back when this was the rich side of town.

The light came from a dozen or so candles stuck into empty bottles. Down front, one end of the hall had been partly curtained off, turning that portion into a makeshift proscenium stage. Through the gap, I could see a pentagram six feet across chalked on the floor by the back wall, with an unlit candle in each of the five corners.

The audience was sitting on the floor in front of the curtains. I counted maybe seventy, seventy-five people; at twenty a head, that meant the evening's take stood at about fifteen hundred clams. Not bad for a night's work. I put my back against a wall and waited for events to unfold.

I didn't have to wait long. Somebody behind the curtain lit off a chunk of incense, mixing a thick churchy odor with the smells of rot and mildew, then started beating on a drum—a low note, pulse-beat slow.

A man came out to stand in the center of the pentagram. A black hood shadowed his face, and his black robe had an upside-down cross in white sewn on the front. He raised his hands, palm-up, and started chanting in a mixture of bad Latin and worse Hebrew—any demon he raised would have to be not only low-ranking but illiterate. Pretty soon he had the whole crowd chanting *"Veni veni Satanas, veni veni Satanas,"* and swaying in time to the beat.

The chanting went on for quite a while. I had to admire the guy's technique, if not his theology; he was doing a good job of getting everybody hyperventilated and into an autohypnotic state. Then, without warning, he clapped his hands and all the candles in the pentacle lit themselves at once. Candles like that have been part of stage magicians' gear since the nineteenth century, but the audience didn't care. They gasped in near unison, and the unseen drum speeded up like a racing heartbeat.

The robed man stepped outside the pentagram. He turned to face center stage, and shouted "Come, Satan!"—in English, for the benefit of anybody who hadn't figured out yet what was going down. A flash of white light went off in the center of the circle. A thick column of smoke rose up above the chalk pentagram, and the smell of sulphur filled the room.

The drum stopped and a demon eight feet tall, all horns and red scales, appeared in the smoke.

It looked good from out front, but I'd already spotted the flashpot—and it was obvious where they'd hidden the slide projector. No reason to have curtains hung up otherwise. The illusion wouldn't last long, so the guy in the black robe didn't milk it. He spoke a few words in a low voice to the fake demon and pretended to listen in return. Then his offstage assistant hit a dimmer and faded the beast.

The guy in the robes faced the crowd and announced, "Satan desires a bride!" He was reading body language and expressions from the front, and I was trying to do it from the rear, but I still figured out who he was going to pick a moment before he did. He pointed at a young woman about three rows back and said, "Satan commands!"

She stood and came forward, moving like a sleepwalker. Not a bad figure, and when she got up to where Black Robe was standing and he turned her around so everyone could look, her face wasn't bad either. Fair-haired, twenty-something, with the wide-eyed look of a true believer desperate for something to truly believe in.

The assistant showed up from the side where the slide projector must have been. He wore a set of black robes like the first guy's and carried a sword and a chalice: Black Eric's merchandise. All I could see at this distance was that the chalice was new and ornate, and the sword was old and plain. The two Priests of Satan went through some buffoonery with the props—nothing complex, because they had to keep the girl from thinking twice and bolting for the door—while I did some thinking of my own.

Until now, I'd figured avarice for the prime element in their scam, but it looked as if the real motivator was lust, with the cash-per-head merely a handy extra. Pretty soon the magician and his assistant had the girl's clothes off, and her on her back. Black Robe never took off his vestments, just opened the front and went to work.

He was still screwing Satan's Bride right there on the floor when the assistant pulled the curtains all the way closed and ushered everyone out. Less embarrassing for the boss that way, I suppose. What was in it for the assistant I couldn't tell. Half the gate and sloppy seconds, maybe. Two bits of stage magic, and there's the door.

It still lacked a couple of minutes of midnight. I was near the back of the crowd on the way out. I wondered if I should wait around to see the cleanup and listen in on what Robe One and Robe Two had to say to each other—maybe find out whether they thought they were real or knew they were fakes. Then I decided it would be only a near occasion of sin for me, and kept on moving.

Out on the street, the audience dispersed quickly. No telling how many of them thought they'd met Satan in the incorporeal flesh, or if any of them realized that they'd traveled a couple of hours and paid twenty bucks to see the same kind of show they could have gotten on Forty-second Street for a buck and a half.

I chalked this job up as a negative report, and headed to my motel, about a mile away. Sleep didn't come easy: The show was still nagging at my subconscious. Something was going on, and I'd missed it.

I don't like missing things—it can be fatal. I got up and stood beside the window, looking out into the night. The darkness echoed the feeling in the back of my head. A traffic light changed from red to green beyond a fringe of trees, and the distant headlights started moving. Time for me to be moving, too. I dressed, then got in my car and drove back to the abandoned mansion where Satan was promised and a sleazy magic show delivered.

I circled the block. One car parked on the road, on the side closest to the back of the building. Out-of-state plates. I continued on, then parked around the next corner. I sat a moment in the dark and quiet, wondering why I was there. This job had been a flat bust, a time-waster. But something wasn't right. Death is the daughter of Sin and Hell, and I was pretty sure I was hearing her wings.

I shook my head to clear it. This was no time to get poetic. I got out of the car before my better judgment could talk me back to the motel, climbed the fence onto the grounds, and commenced sneaking up to the house.

No lights ahead, no movement. Silence. The house loomed up out of the night, dark against the city glow. The grass was crisp with frost, and the wind rustled in the bare trees. I risked a pencil-beam with my red-lens flashlight and did a quick reconnoiter around the back.

The rear porch had a door that had been boarded up. Now the boards were pulled away, and tool marks showed on the jamb near the knob. That would be where Black Robe and his pal had gained entry. A couple of days ago at the latest—before their flyers had been printed and distributed, and before somebody showed up at this address to take delivery of Black Eric's commission. I continued circling the house.

All normal so far. I came to the front door and saw that it stood open about two inches, a darker line against the darkness.

"Sloppy, sloppy," I said to myself. I waited, not moving, for a hundred heartbeats. Then I put out my hand and swung the door in. No shouts or sounds of feet, even though the hinges squeaked. Nobody home, it looked like. I stepped inside and waited again.

The house was quiet—the empty, unmoving quiet of a deserted place. A nasty smell, worse than rot, underlay the mustiness.

I had the flashlight in my left hand. I eased out my Colt with my other hand and held it beside my body at waist level while I retraced the route I'd taken earlier that evening. In the ballroom the makeshift curtains were still up. An archway beside the stairs led farther back into the house. The dust in that direction was disturbed. The dust at the top of the stairs wasn't.

I went over to the curtains. They were drawn shut, the way I'd seen them last. I found the opening and stepped on through.

Black Robe was lying stretched out on his back in the center of his pentagram, the chalice in his hand. His hood had fallen away so I could see his face: mid-twenties and blond. His eyes were fixed and dilated, his mouth open, with a trickle of congealed blood running down from one corner.

There wasn't any need for me to check for a pulse. He'd been cut open from top to bottom—I could see his heart, and it wasn't moving. The smell of blood mixed with dung was coming from him.

More blood formed a big pool around the corpse, but I could get close enough to reach out and touch his forehead. Still warm, but cooling fast. I took out my crucifix and sketched a quick cross in the air above him.

"For the sins of thy past life, I grant thee absolution," I said. Not that it would do much good, since he'd most likely had his particular judgment while I was tossing in the No-Tell Motel, but it couldn't hurt. His career as a fraudulent raiser of demons had been small stuff by this world's standards—there were men in the corporate towers of Wall Street who worshipped Mammon and Lilith with a singleness of purpose that would have made this boy look like he made First Friday every month.

The faint scuff of a footstep on the other side of the curtains told me that I wasn't alone. I snapped out my light and blended into the shadows on the wall. A white light was moving out in the main part of the room, coming closer.

Keep calm, I told myself. Keep your breathing normal. If this is Jack the Ripper returning to the scene of his crime, then the case is solved and you can get back to bed.

The red lens of my flashlight had left me with some night vision. The curtains bellied a bit, black against black, then pushed open to let through a tall woman with flame-red hair and an overtime body. Flashlight in one hand, pistol in the other, just like me. I knew her—we'd worked together on a couple of cases in the past.

"Hiya, Maggie," I said. "I was wondering when you'd show up."

She didn't shoot me, which was good.

"Hello, Pete," she said, shining her flash at the mess on the floor. Under white light the guy looked even worse than he had before. His appearance didn't seem to faze Maggie any. I wasn't surprised; it takes more than a little carving job to upset Sister Mary Magdalene of the Special Action Executive of the Poor Clares.

"What brings you out here?" I asked.

"I thought a drive in the country would do me good. How about you?"

I gave her a quick summary of the evening so far and gestured at the body. "What do you think? Partner got tired of playing second banana, took out the boss, and ran away with the loot?"

"Nope," she said. "Partner's inside the back door. Something took his head clean off."

"Not looking good. Think they really managed to raise Satan?"

"That doesn't look like demons," Maggie said, gesturing at the corpse. "No signs of predation."

She flashed the light around the curtained alcove. The drum, the slide projector, the flashpot, the candles, a set of girl's clothing . . .

"Wait a minute," I said. "We've got either one corpse too few or one too many. Where's the girl who fits those threads?"

Maggie picked up the top item, a flower-print skirt. "Little Miss Bride of Satan," she said. "Let's see if we can find her."

We went over the house from top to bottom. Other than the paths from the back door and the front door to the ball-room, the dust hadn't been disturbed in maybe twenty years. The assistant was lying where Maggie had said he would be, dressed in jeans and a shirt, and decapitated with something sharp. The head had rolled against the wall, where it lay staring at the ceiling with a startled expression. Judging by the spatter, he'd been running when he got hit, and made a couple more steps before his body realized it was dead.

Wherever the girl was, she wasn't inside. We finished up back in the ballroom at the first murder scene. The dead man in the pentacle wasn't looking any healthier.

"Seems like this is all we've got," I said. "Two known dead, whereabouts of the Bride of Satan unknown. Either the perp took her away with him, or she did it herself."

"Which leaves a stark naked girl running around the streets of Poughkeepsie soaked in somebody else's blood." Maggie shook her head. "I don't see it. She'd get picked up before she made three blocks, and this place would have been crawling with cops when we got here. Think she's a succubus?"

I poked at the pile of clothes. "Succubi don't leave their panties behind."

Maggie cocked an eyebrow at me. "Have a lot of experience with 'em, do you?"

"More than I like." I shone my light around the room again. "Something else is missing. The sword."

"So it is. Looks good for the weapon on both of our dear departed."

"That rules out the Princes of Hell—mortal weapons aren't their style. For now, I'm going to call this a double murder and a kidnapping. Are your fingerprints anywhere around here?"

Maggie held up a gloved hand, gave me a disgusted glance, and went back to poking around the scene.

"Right. I'm going to leave, find a phone booth, and call the local constabulary. Let 'em earn their pay. If this is mundane, they're equipped to handle it."

"And if it isn't?"

"I'm handling that end," I said. "If that girl is still in the hands of whoever did this . . ."

"Oh, Pete, you're such a true knight."

I gave her my own disgusted glance and left.

Twenty minutes in the Hudson Valley will take you from skyscrapers out to rural roads where the houses don't have numbers. Twenty minutes out of Poughkeepsie took me to a café that opened its doors at sunset and shut them at dawn. I bought a cup of coffee, took it to a booth down back, and nursed it with a single-mindedness that would have won me a medal from the Red Cross if anyone was watching.

Someone was. Pretty soon a young man sat down across from me. Black clothes, silver dragon-head ring on his left little finger.

"Rudi knows me," I said.

"I'm Rudi, and I don't know you from Adam."

"We met last year in Prague."

He sat back and laced his fingers. "Yeah?"

"I need a reading. Got somewhere private?"

"This is as private as it gets," he said, hauling a tarot deck out of his pocket. "Any preferences as to style?"

"As long as it isn't a Crowley, what you like suits me fine."

"Great." He had an eastern European accent. Possibly

Czech. Maybe someone really had met him a year ago in Prague. Who knows? His name might even have been Rudi.

He shuffled the deck for a bit, and I could see him doing relaxations as he went. "This for you or someone else?" he asked after a minute.

I finished my cold coffee at a gulp. "Someone else."

"Got a significator in mind, or are you going to make me guess?"

"Try Page of Pentacles," I said, thinking of a young man, and money, and things of the earth—I know the deck as well as anyone, even if I don't use it myself.

"Page it is," he said, running the cards face up between his hands, flipping out the desired pasteboard and putting it on the table between us. He handed the deck across to me. "Think about your guy. Shuffle three times, cut three times. Hand it back."

I did, then he did the same and started laying out the cards. He got done and put the deck aside. Then he looked at the layout, turned back to the deck, checked the undealt top card without showing it to me, and looked up.

"Sure are a lot of swords, man," he said.

There sure were.

"I think if you're looking for this dude, you're out of luck, because he's dead."

"Exhaust your knowledge."

Rudi tapped the card above the Page of Pentacles. It showed a young woman sitting up in bed, crying and covering her face. Nine swords floated above her. "There's a girl mixed up in this." He tapped the High Priestess, at the bottom of another row of cards. "That confirms it."

"Where is the girl?" I asked.

"She's nothing," Rudi said. "Forget the girl. Follow the sword. A dead man will tell you where to go next. And watch yourself." He picked up the top card from the deck—the one that he'd peeked at before—and turned it over. The Four of

Swords; it showed a knight lying on his tomb, his hands folded in prayer. "Here's where the old gypsy lady hands you your money back. That's you, big guy."

"I'll keep it in mind. Tell me more about the sword."

"The girl has it."

"Anything else?"

"You want her birthday and home phone number? You'll have to ask someone else. I have a friend who gazes crystals."

"Funny," I said. "The cards. What else do they tell you?"

He tapped the King of Swords, standing by itself at the top of the row where the High Priestess was at the bottom.

"Justice is done at the end," he said. "Three more words: sisterhood, Scotland, clarity. Keep 'em in mind."

"Thanks," I said, and left.

I drove back toward Poughkeepsie until I came to a lighted phone booth outside an all-night donut stand. I put a thin-film enciphering adapter over the handset and got a secure line to the Temple's New York phone drop. The crypto double-beeped as it synced, and I was in.

"I checked out that midnight fund-raiser you asked about," I said. We spoke Latin, and maybe that would slow down someone with a parabolic mike.

"Anything going on?"

"Double murder is all."

There was a pause on the far end. "Then this should be right up your alley. Got it from a bug on the Knights of Malta. One of the pro outfits reported losing two of their deep-cover guys. They called the Kilo Mikes for assistance."

"Who's 'they'?"

"We're working on that. But we got the details on the missing people."

"Don't tell me—they misplaced 'em in Poughkeepsie. One of them's a skinny blond in his twenties, five-ten, hundred and twenty, the other one is dark, not much older, a little shorter, a little heavier."

"You're psychic."

"Yeah."

I went inside and grabbed a donut.

Following the sword meant looking up Black Eric at his digs in Newburgh. I got there at what would have been sunrise if this were midsummer, which it wasn't—the early morning had at least an hour of darkness yet to go. One of the doors on the street was open when I showed up. I'd seen something like that before. Recently. I went up to the door, pushed it open a bit farther, and walked in.

Black Eric had better taste than his customers; the air inside was heavy with genuine frankincense. He had a workshop on the first floor—drill press, lathe, tabletop kiln. An ingot of pure silver sat untouched on the bench, with a spill of diamonds on a wooden plate beside it.

That got me to wondering about Eric's late customers back up the river in Poughkeepsie. Despite appearances, they hadn't been a cheap-ass magic act: They had expensive props from this place made to order, and backers with enough pull to call on the Knights of Malta if things went wrong. I had to be looking at one of the big outfits that had money to burn, no scruples about where they got it or how they spent it, and lots of connections. I wondered what my two unknowns had really been working on.

The bedroom was upstairs. Usual thing—black candles, black sheets, black walls. The unusual bit was on the floor, where the person I guessed was Black Eric lay on his back in the middle of the room. He had his torso sliced open and his guts sitting in a pile beside him, just like my robe-wearing buddy back in Po-town.

Black Eric had been an older man, if the wrinkled face and the white hair were anything to go by. Sixty, maybe. My guess was that he took his dive after the guys at the Haunted Mansion bought their part of the farm. The sword started with them, came here, and went—where?

I thought about Rudi and his prediction that a dead man would tell me where to go next, and moved on to the study, across the upstairs hall from the bedroom. Black Eric may not have feared God or the Devil, but sometime during his career as a freelance craftsman he'd picked up a healthy respect for the Internal Revenue Service. I found a couple of shelves' worth of notebooks, journals, and sales receipts, all tab-indexed and neatly filed. I pulled down a fat black ring-binder with a section labeled "chalices," and started looking.

Each page had a photo of the finished chalice on it. They were arranged in reverse chronological order, the most recent on the top. Third down was a bingo. When I looked at the return address on the matching correspondence, I recognized that as well: a drop box that I knew eventually led to the Knights of Saint John. Which made it an easy twelve to seven that the Johnnies were the ones who'd asked the Malta Mounties for help.

I figured, why stop when I was on a roll, and flipped through the tabs looking for one labeled "swords." I found the correspondence I was looking for filed under "expenses."

Black Eric had gotten the sword half of the Johnnies' ritual gear through a Scottish import-export firm. The firm was real vague about where it had picked the sword up in the first place.

I pulled out my list of missing swords and checked it, eliminating all the blades that were too short, too long, or too ornate to be the one I'd seen. That left me with three possibles, one of them from Scotland. An old but noncataloged sword had gone walkabout from the storage vaults of the Scottish United Services Museum in Edinburgh Castle. The interesting part was that—give or take fifty vertical feet of rock—the missing blade had been kept directly beneath the altar of Saint Margaret's Chapel.

The hair stood up on the back of my neck. Swords don't get stashed beneath altars by accident.

Scotland, Rudi had said. And *clarity.* It had to be; there was a sword once that went by the name of Clarent.

Most people don't know about Clarent—but knights of the Temple aren't most people. I knew that King Arthur had owned two swords, not one. Excalibur was the famous one, his sword of war. Clarent was his sword of justice. Some people say it's the sword that killed him.

Clarent was also supposed to be either mythical or permanently lost. Maybe the Knights of Saint John had found out something different; maybe the sword had gotten lost for a reason, in what should have been a nice safe place. And I could understand why. Perfect justice isn't something you want running around loose.

If the Johnnies were so deep in this mess that they'd started yelling for assistance, maybe I ought to volunteer to give them some.

I beat the rush-hour traffic back into the city. An all-news-all-the-time station was reporting a murder/suicide in Poughkeepsie. One young man blew his partner's guts out with a shotgun, then put the barrel in his mouth and blasted his own head off. If that's what the scene looked like when the cops got there, that meant a cleaner had worked over the dead men after I left and before the law arrived. A shotgun at close range made a good choice; there wouldn't be any sword marks left on the bodies afterward.

I dropped off the rental car and hoofed it over to the local business offices of the Knights of Saint John. I was hoping that no one there knew my face. The Johnnies and the Temple have a history, and it isn't all sweet-cakes and tea.

The office I was looking for was on the second floor of an art-deco office building, midtown on Madison. Glass outer doors, wood inner doors. I rang the bell and stood holding my hands in one of the Maltese recognition signals. It wasn't exactly lying. My hands could have just happened to hang that way.

The inner door opened, and a guy who looked like he'd gotten about as much sleep as I had opened it. He was wearing a blue blazer and gray slacks, with a little Cross of Saint John lapel pin. He looked at me, saw the hands, and came over to open the deadbolt on the outer door.

"You wanted a knight?" I asked.

"Yeah," he said. "Glad you could make it so quickly. Come on in."

Things would get interesting in a hurry if the genuine Malt showed up anytime soon. I followed the guy inside. The outer door he locked behind us. The inner door took us to a passageway paneled in wood and decorated with gold-framed paintings interspersed among assorted crosses, crossed swords, and crucifixes. They'd been burning incense here, too. Maybe Consolidated Incense was going to be a growth stock.

The inner office had a leather couch, a big desk, and drawn shades. The guy sitting behind the desk was bald and fat, but the kind of fat that said he'd been plenty strong when he was younger. I didn't know him.

Over on the couch was someone I did know. Maggie.

I marched over to the man at the desk and stuck out my hand. "John Ryan," I said.

Baldie stood, shook my fist, and said, "Simon Stock. The fellow who brought you in is Fred Weber."

"Pleased," I said.

He nodded toward the couch. "Have you met Lynda?"

Maggie shook her head side to side, just a trifle. "That's Lynda with a *y*," she said.

"No, can't say I have." My guess was that not one true baptismal name had been given so far. *Sisterhood,* Rudi had said. Whatever Maggie's game was, I'd back her play and hope that she'd back mine.

"Come with me," Simon said. He stood, indicated the door, and headed down the hall. Maggie, Fred, and I trailed after him. We took a side corridor to the left while he kept talking. "There was an event last night. The police are calling it a murder/suicide. A pair of young drifters—very sad."

"What's our angle on it?"

"It was not a suicide. And those were not drifters. They were Knights of Saint John."

It's always nice to have your theories confirmed. "What were they working on?"

"There is a very real possibility that we can end Satan's reign on earth," Simon said. "I am told that certain members of your group have experience with demons . . ."

"That's never been proven," I replied, while I wondered how much of my cover he was seeing through. Just because he was a Johnny didn't mean he was stupid. The story was a slander anyway, no matter what the King of France thought.

". . . and that you are one of them," Simon continued, as if I hadn't spoken. "Our men were attempting to raise Satan and, on his arrival, kill him."

The plan came clear to me, and I didn't know whether to laugh or start praying. The charade at the deserted house had never been meant to do anything except find a willing sacrifice. The two Johnnies had deliberately made their act look cheesy, the better to give everyone else the bum's rush as soon as they found a girl who truly wanted to be sacrificed to the devil. The real action wasn't scheduled to start until midnight, after everyone but the sacrifice had left. A slick bit of psychology— and I'd fallen for it along with the rest.

Of course, I hadn't had any reason to suspect Black Robe and his pal of being involved in such a damned-fool plan as the one Stock was talking about. You can call up the devil, but you can't kill him—not with the weapons of this world, anyway. Better men than the Johnnies had tried.

"Didn't work, eh?" I said.

"No. But we believe that our brothers did in fact raise Satan. The theory holds. We lack, however, the weapon that can vanquish the Adversary."

"Perfect faith in Christ isn't good enough for you?" I muttered, but I don't think he caught it.

Meanwhile, I had a new worry. Their cleaner might have been watching the house while I was inside, and might be able to ID me when he showed up.

Then it hit me. *Maggie* was the cleaner. The Johnnies had probably made the arrangement in advance—whatever they'd planned, they wouldn't want any traces left in the morning. Maggie must have gotten a surprise when she showed up and found a pair of dead Johnnies and a live Templar, but she got lucky, too; the Templar was a professional acquaintance and sometime partner, and she'd played the connection for all it was worth.

Peter the Perfect Knight. I wanted to kick myself. I'd been made a sap of by a dame, and me celibate to boot.

We'd come to the end of the second passageway, and a closed door. I was starting to get a real bad feeling about what I might find on the other side. The holstered Colt in my left armpit gave me some comfort, but not much. The principle of evil doesn't pay a lot of attention to .45-caliber slugs.

"We're counting on the assistance of your organization in recovering the sword," Simon said.

"We're interested in finding it," I said, and I wasn't lying even a little this time.

Simon's assistant opened the door for us, and we filed in. The place had mood lighting—blue track lights shining on a polished marble altar. I didn't like what I saw carved there. Not the Alpha and Omega, not the Chi Rho, not the Nazarene Cross; this one had the Baphomet Pentacle.

Behind us the door swung shut.

Then a sword came whirling out of the dark, from the blind zone behind the door. It hit Fred-the-assistant-Weber in his side. He went "Ooof!" and collapsed in a heap, made heapier by having his spine sliced in two.

I spun, took a step to put my back against a wall, and hauled iron. Before I could get a round down-range, Maggie punched me in the biceps. My arm went numb and my shot went wild, zinging once before it buried itself in the paneling.

Maggie didn't wait. She chopped down on my wrist with the edge of her hand and caught the Colt before it hit the floor. Then she stepped backward, a pistol in each hand. Mine she had pointed at me, and her own H&K 9mm was pointed at Stock's gizzard.

"Lynda!" Simon said. "What is the meaning of this?"

I stood there and said nothing, and tried to make sense of everything I was seeing. The Johnnies had been looking for a sword, and so had I. Well, now we'd found one. Three and a half feet of gleaming steel, straight-bladed and double-edged, held two-handed by a young woman who had it pointed at Simon's head. She was approaching him one slow step at a time.

And I recognized her. She was skinny and blond, with patches of dried and flaking blood on her face and arms, and she was wearing a flower-print skirt and blouse. The last time I'd seen her, she'd had her heels in the air in an abandoned ballroom, with a quondam Priest of Satan in the saddle.

Simon backed up as she approached. He kept on backing until he rammed into the altar and stopped. The point of the lady's pig-sticker was an inch in front of his nose.

"You're looking for Satan?" she asked all of a sudden. "Tell him I sent you."

She pulled the blade back in a windup for a killing stroke.

Whatever else happened, I couldn't allow a death on that altar. I glanced over at Maggie—she was watching the blade with eyes as shiny as the sword. I figured I wouldn't get a better chance. If she hadn't shot me already, maybe she'd decided not to. It might take her a split second to change gears.

I thought of Rudi flashing me the dead knight on the Four of Swords, did a dive-and-roll, and caught Maggie in the knees. She went down hard, and I was all over her, grabbing for her wrists, slamming her head down, trying to get her weapons before someone—namely me—got shot. Maggie fought back, and she fought dirty. For an innocent nun she knew entirely too much about male anatomy. But I outweighed her by a hundred pounds, I had surprise working for me, and, way down deep, I don't think she really wanted to kill me.

The noise of our scuffle distracted the sword-swinging Bride of Satan. She looked over at me and Maggie in a tangle on the floor, and Simon took his own opportunity. He reached over the top of the blade, grabbed the girl's shoulder, and pulled, spinning her around so that her shoulders were against his chest. His right hand gripped her right arm at the wrist and pulled the blade, still in her hand, back toward her throat. His left hand pinned her other arm down at her side.

By this time I'd gotten hold of both handguns and was trying to cover everyone at once. Maggie was rubbing her wrist the same way I'd been rubbing my arm a minute ago.

"Thank you," Simon said to me. He still hadn't figured out that I wasn't on his side. "All has come together. The altar, the weapon, and the sacrifice."

I stood up, and lifted my right-hand weapon so that the post stood in the vee on the sights, and post and vee were both centered on Simon Stock's right eye. He'd be staring straight down the barrel, and the muzzle would look about a yard wide to him.

"Let the bimbo go," I said. "There isn't going to be any demonolatry in here. Not while I'm holding the aces."

"Who are you?" he asked.

"A Knight of the Temple," I said.

"Then go to Hell with the Master you worship!" He side-stepped and yanked back against the girl's arm, trying to make her slice her own throat.

The girl ducked under the blade. I don't know how she managed it without dislocating her own shoulder, but she still had the sword. It hit Simon on the side of his face, opening a long, bloody gash, and he let go of her arm. She turned, holding the sword two-handed again, and slashed upward in a long arc.

The tip of the sword entered his belly and cut up, severing bone and cartilage, cracking his chest in half right along the sternum. Arterial blood spurted out, and he fell back, arms wide on top of the altar, crimson staining the white marble. He lay there a second, while everyone else in the room froze. Then a mist seemed to form over him, black with sparkling bits inside of it, twisting like a living thing.

It *was* a living thing. It grew, took shape and form, and stood on the altar, a creature of horns and scales, looking as real as the thing up in Poughkeepsie had looked fake. It reached down, picked up Simon Stock's body, casually turned it inside out, and slipped it on like a man putting on a set of coveralls.

I let my rods do my talking, pumping out rounds as fast as I could pull the triggers. It didn't take long to empty both magazines.

I tossed Maggie's empty H&K back to her, dropped my expended magazine, and reloaded—more out of habit than out of hope that it would do any good, because the demon hadn't even noticed the gunplay. It got down off the altar and made a step toward the girl with the sword. Ropes of intestine hung in loops around its feet.

The Bride of Satan took an instinctive step backward as the demon advanced. She'd forgotten about the late Fred Weber—we all had—until she tripped over his body and fell sprawling on the floor, dropping the blade when she hit.

Clarent was lying on the floor, and the demon had taken human shape. The next move was obvious. I sprinted forward, grabbed the hilt, and came up to guard.

"Run!" I shouted at Maggie. "Take the girl and bug out!"

The demon swiped at me with a roundhouse right, Stock's finger bones showing on the outside of its hand like talons. I'd trained in kendo, but even so it felt like Clarent itself was taking over, rising high and left to block. The impact took chips of bone off the demon's radius and ulna, and staggered the creature back.

I swung low toward the demon's all-too-obvious guts with the blade. The walking corpse bent almost double with the impact, and I used the rebound to loop over and strike down at its bony shoulder. The clavicle broke, and I had to yank hard to pull the blade back out of the meat beneath.

Then I had to get into guard, because after that the demon straightened up and quit playing. It tried a one-two combination, and I blocked first left, then right—but my second block was slow, and the demon put a slice across my side, over the ribs. I could feel the blood running down under my shirt.

The demon-corpse kicked low, and I had to jump back to avoid being kneecapped. I heard the sound of a pistol shot nearby and realized that Maggie hadn't left. She'd reloaded and was plinking away with her handgun every time she could get a clear shot past me—not that it was doing much good. Clarent was leading me around, guiding me through blocks and attacks that were way beyond my level of training, but even so I was barely holding my own.

The demon was fast, and it hit hard. I was bleeding from half a dozen cuts. My right arm was starting to cramp up where Maggie had smacked it, and a sense of unreality was settling in, like my head was stuffed with cotton—the first symptom of fatigue. Even with Clarent doing most of the work, there was only one place this could end, and I didn't like that place at all.

I blocked outside, then had to retreat as the demon charged. On the way in, it tore a chunk out of its exposed liver and threw the dripping gobbet into my face.

The handful of slimy organ meat spattered across my eyes, blinding me with goo. In the same moment the demon-corpse was all over me, attacking with fangs and claws and sharp bony protrusions I could feel but not see. I heard the sword hit the ground with a clang. The aches in my side and in my injured arm were intense and getting worse. I fought back bare-handed as best I could, but there aren't a lot of pain pressure points on a corpse.

Then the thing pulled off, and I heard a woman's voice yelling, *"Avaunt!"*

I shook my head and raised my hand to scrape Stock's liver off my face. One of my eyes wasn't focusing too well, but I saw the Bride of Satan with that sword back in her hands, doing a pretty good imitation of all seven of the Seven Samurai. Clarent was doing the talking, and she was listening better than I ever had.

Maggie was kneeling on the floor beside me. "Peter," she said. "I'm a true virgin."

"I'm proud of you."

"I didn't mess around, not even once in high school," she said. "I want you to hear my confession."

"Maggie, you aren't going to die in here. Get out while you can."

"Dying isn't part of the plan."

Somebody had a plan. That was good. "Okay," I said.

"Bless me, Father, for I have sinned. It has been three days since my last confession." And she went on from there, talking fast. Apparently she'd been a busy girl for those three days. Somewhere along the fifth iteration of uncharitable thoughts, I got an inkling of what she was up to. A sinless virgin is something no demon can stand against. She wrapped up with, "For these and all the sins of my past life I am heartily sorry."

"*Absolvo te,*" I said. "For your penance, send this demon back to Hell."

Maggie stood in one fluid motion and went to work.

The girl with the sword had been pressed to the wall. "Look behind thee, Satan," she yelled, just as Maggie slammed into the corporate spirit of evil, took it by the left hand, yanked down on its flayed arm, and twisted the arm up behind. She put her right arm under the corpse's right armpit, nestled her hand on the back of the exposed cranium, and pushed the head forward and down. The demon went to its knees. She pushed, it folded. She slipped her grip from the half nelson to a full hammerlock. After that she got nasty, whispering the Credo into its ear.

All at once she wasn't wrestling with a demon. She was holding an empty skin. She left it lying on the floor in front of the altar.

"Let's get out of here," she said.

We got. Maggie and the Bride cleaned me up as best they could, stowed our assorted weapons out of sight, and kept me from falling over as we left. The sidewalk was full of people heading to work. You'd think that two good-looking women helping a bloodstained guy out of an office building would attract some attention, but this was New York, where how you make your fun is your own business.

As we were going out the revolving door, a man wearing a blazer with a Maltese Cross worked in crimson and gold on the breast pocket went in. He'd find some interesting things on the second floor. I hoped for his sake that he knew what to do about them.

I got myself patched up by a Knight Hospitaller at a subrosa emergency room in Hell's Kitchen. The Hospitaller didn't ask any questions—he's seen a lot of folks come and go, and he's tended stranger wounds than mine—so I took the opportunity to get everything straight in my head. Maggie was long gone by that time, of course, and the onetime Bride of Satan along with her. I suspected that the Clares would keep the girl under wraps until she got back however much of her own mind she'd had to start with.

Maggie and I talked for a bit in private before we split up, long enough for her to supply some of the details I was lacking. The way she told it, after I left the murder scene she went back to her car—

"For the shotgun?" I asked.

She nodded. "You weren't going to give me time for a job that would fool Interpol, but a quick-and-messy might baffle the local cops. But when I got out to the car, there *she* was in the backseat, curled up stark naked with a bloody sword. I don't mind telling you, Pete, I was surprised. I said, 'What in God's name are you doing here?' and she started babbling. Something about how the sword wanted her to do it."

"Uh-huh." It sounded like Clarent hadn't liked the idea of being used as the tool in a blood sacrifice. So the sword came into the Bride's hand—by accident or as part of the ritual, who could say any longer?—and it dispensed justice.

Maggie looked at me curiously. "You don't sound particularly startled by the revelation."

"Let me tell you about that sword someday."

"I'm not planning to hold my breath waiting," she said. "Anyhow, I still had business to take care of. I told her to stay put while I went back into the house, and when I'd finished up in there, I brought her clothes and the chalice out to the car with me. As soon as she got dressed, she made a break for it. I dissuaded her."

"Right." I'd seen Maggie's idea of dissuasion once or twice before; it could get vigorous.

"After a bit I let her up for air and asked her what she thought she was doing. She told me she was following the sword."

"And you decided to go along for the ride."

"Seemed like a good idea at the time," Maggie said. "Something funny was going on, and I wanted to find out what. So we drove down to Newburgh—"

"That must have been cozy," I said.

"I've had times I enjoyed more. It didn't surprise me all that much to find out that Black Eric was involved—his maker's mark was underneath the foot of that fancy goblet. So it all worked out."

And Black Eric wound up with his guts on the carpet—probably the sword's idea, though it didn't sound like Maggie had protested much. She'd found out from Eric the identity of his recent customers, and of the organization that had hired the Clares' Special Action Executive for the cleanup. Her superiors would have known which group was involved when they gave her the assignment, but a field operative like Maggie didn't have a need to know. Once she had the names, she headed straight into Manhattan with the Bride of Satan, and the sword, in tow.

I never did learn what story Maggie told the Johnnies. With their carefully laid plans falling to pieces around them, they must have been scared enough to believe almost anything. She managed to break away long enough to let in the Bride and stow her in the chapel—along with Clarent, still hot to do justice.

I think the sword was running both of them by then. Maybe it was running me, too. The oldest magics have a way of making things look like they happened by accident, through natural causes and coincidences. That kind of magic could have influenced the Johnnies to hire the Clares, and persuaded me to call headquarters for an assignment, all for the sake of bringing me and Maggie and Clarent together in time to fight Stock's demon. Time and space and causality are nonbeing to anything that Arthur touched.

I still had Clarent with me when I left the emergency room, but not for long. I wrapped up Arthur's other sword in clean white silk and about ten layers of bubble-pack and shipped it off to Chatillon for safekeeping. Doing justice is all very well if you're Arthur, King of the Britons, but I'm not and neither is anybody else anymore, and justice without mercy is a fearful thing.

While I was at the post office, I sent a back-channel note to the international headquarters of the Knights of Saint John, letting them know that their New York cell had gone bad on them. Then I made an interim report to the Temple:

"Stayed up all night with two women, raising the devil. All secure. Details to follow. Crossman sends."

INTERLUDE NINE

Our final story brings forward into the near future the theme of the Knights Templar as guardians of the Holy Grail. Aside from its most common connection with the Cup of the Last Supper, with which Christ instituted the sacrament of the Eucharist, the concept of *a* Grail—or of Grails—embraces far more than Christianity. Grails take many forms besides a cup, from cauldron of plenty to floating platter to secret gospel to carved head of Jesus—perhaps akin to the head the Templars were accused of worshipping—to Lapsit Excillis, the stone with which God banished the angels who failed to support him against Lucifer, to the great emerald struck from the crown of Lucifer as he was flung from heaven. But the common thread linking all Grails is the notion of the Grail as a symbol of or link with Divinity. Common, too, is the idea that certain individuals, for varying reasons, are designated by higher authorities as their Keepers.

Keepers

David and Julie Spangler

It was 4 A.M. when she awakened, the dream dark and troubling like the local sky when it threatened to calve tornadoes. It was the third night in a row she had had it. At first it had been a curiosity, for she normally did not have nightmares. But now she worried about what unknown shadowy thing was stirring in her subconscious or what message she was missing.

Still, the dream had not seemed personal. It had been vaguely threatening, but the threat did not seem aimed at her, at least not directly. Each time had been basically the same. She was in a dark room filled with swirling vapor like crimson fog. There were shapes in the darkness, reminding her of the kind of simple stick figures that children drew, but she could not see any of them clearly. What she could see in the middle of this room was simply a blob that heaved and pulsed, covered with what looked like fuzz.

Whatever it meant, it had occurred three times in a row, which for her was a sure sign something was up. Perhaps it was time to do some investigating? She made a mental note to prepare during the upcoming day for some special work that night.

She swung her feet over the side of the bed, groping for the slippers that invariably never stayed where she put them when she slipped them off to climb under the covers. Her feet found them and slid happily into the warm fur. She stood up, stretched, and went into the bathroom. A few minutes later, now robed, she emerged. On impulse, she went out a set of French doors onto a small balcony outside her bedroom and looked up.

Out here in the country, there were no lights to dim the glory of the stars. As always, she felt a tug in her heart when she looked up into the river of light that was the Milky Way. Once, she had planned to be one of those who went out there, and had even graduated with a degree in astrophysics. But life had intervened, as it always did, and other responsibilities that she could not refuse had come to the fore.

The balcony faced the east, and as she watched, she saw a bright new star appear over the horizon as if fleeing from the sun that was soon to follow. It was The Ship. A visitor from the stars, here after traveling God knew how many millions of miles, arriving fittingly just as humanity celebrated the first year of a new millennium.

She watched as the light moved across the sky. Who were they, she wondered, and where did they come from? What did they want? No one knew. They had been in orbit for a week, but as far as anyone knew, no contact had been made yet. Or if there had been messages, they had not been made public— which, she thought cynically, was more likely. As always, the government would try to keep people in the dark for their own good, as if truth were a virus that had to be isolated and contained. But no one could deny the truth of that new light, and from what she saw and heard the few times she turned the television on, the citizens of the world were getting restless.

Oddly, though, there had been no panic, as some had feared there would be if first contact ever occurred. As if some part of the collective unconscious had been expecting this, most everyone was reacting with a strange calmness, in spite of the spate of alien invasion movies that had recently made the rounds of the Cineplexes throughout the nation.

That was certainly true for her. Given that once she had wanted to be an astronaut, the appearance of The Ship had had remarkably little effect on her. She had consulted her own sources of information, but, aside from assuring her that all was well, they had been strangely unforthcoming. She had no choice but to respect that. So each day, she worked at her potter's wheel, tended her garden, and played her music as if nothing unusual were going on in the world.

A sudden gust of wind made her shiver. She turned and went back in. Time for some coffee, she thought, and then there was that new glazing she was working on. There was plenty to do; and thinking about The Ship would not get it done.

By mid-afternoon, shadows were already lengthening on the ground as she adjourned to her garden. She was bending over a patch of carrots, trying to decide which ones to pick for her dinner, when she heard the distant sound of an automobile. It could, she knew, be heading to the village down the road in the valley, but, instead, she felt it would go past the turnoff and up the hill to her house. It was part of a game she often played with herself, predicting outcomes and flexing her psychic muscles. *If I'm right,* she thought, *I'll soon hear it when they leave the paved part of the road, and in the meantime I've got carrots and beets to pick.*

She continued examining and picking, putting the chosen vegetables in a basket next to her, but when she heard the crunch of tires on gravel, she gave a small smile and stood up. *Score one for the intuition,* she thought.

As she picked up her basket and headed toward the house, she saw the black car turn into her driveway and park. Two men, dressed in identical dark suits and wearing dark glasses, got out. They looked so much like stereotypical government agents from some television drama—or the legendary Men in Black—that she almost burst out laughing until something about their demeanor triggered a painful memory.

She stopped, time shifting around her, and she was newly

home from college, unpacking in her bedroom upstairs in the house where she had been raised, watching out the window as a dark car parked at the curb and two men in dark uniforms got out, coming onto the porch and speaking in hushed tones to her father, who had opened the door to them. She could not hear what they were saying, but a sudden premonition filled her with foreboding. She turned and ran to the stairs, but when she got to the first floor and into the living room, she saw her father was closing the door, an envelope in his hand.

He turned to her then, and his eyes were filled with a grief and loss so great that she was frozen in place and involuntarily dropped her own gaze to his feet, watching as the envelope fluttered to the floor. She then ran to her father, but he raised his hand, forbidding her to come any closer. Without a word, he walked past her into his study, closing the door behind him.

She picked up the envelope and opened it, already knowing what the letter inside said. The words didn't matter; whatever the phrases, the meaning was simple. Her brother was dead.

She took in a few fragments, ". . . killed in action . . . plane shot down over Iraq . . . a hero's death . . . the President's sorrow . . ." Then she sat down on the couch and wept—for herself, for her brother, for her father. She knew he would not open the door for her, so she curled up in the chair by herself and cried till she had no more tears. Then, to her surprise, her father had come out and taken her in his arms, the first time he had done that since her mother had died, her first year in college, and they had wept on each other's shoulders. It was his last gift to her, that he shared his grief and opened himself to hers.

Later that evening, he had tried to tell her his secret, not knowing that she already knew and had known since she was a girl. But in the midst of his story, as he had taken a worn jewelry case from his pocket and opened it, showing the obviously old and beautifully crafted red cross within, he had suddenly complained of fatigue. He had laid down on the couch, then, without warning, he shuddered and died.

All this flashed before her eyes as she stood just outside her garden. Then the sound of a voice calling her name brought her back to the present, ten years later. One of the figures had taken off his glasses and was walking up the slight hill toward her while his partner stayed by the car.

But whose death could this be? she thought illogically, the foreboding of her earlier experience staying with her even as she struggled out of the sudden onrush of memory.

"Christina Bartlett?" the man called again. As he came closer, she saw that he had that fresh Midwestern look that seemed so archetypically all-American.

"You're FBI," she said, knowing it was true even as the thought jumped from an intuition to a statement.

He paused, momentarily surprised. Then he grinned. "Yes. Is it that obvious?" With that, he pulled out his wallet and showed her his identification. "I'm Special Agent Jonathan Patrick. And you are Christina Bartlett?" She could see in his eyes that he already knew the answer.

"Yes." Suddenly, looking at him, she was struck with a sense of familiarity, as if she had known this man most of her life instead of just meeting him for the first time. The feeling was momentarily so intense that she blurted out, "Have we met before?"

Her response took him by surprise. For a moment a flash of recognition passed across his face as well, quickly being replaced by confusion.

"I don't believe so," he replied, and she detected a note of hesitancy in his voice. He seemed about to say something else, something personal perhaps, but instead he shifted back into his official persona. "Miss Bartlett, I've been trying to reach you most of the day, but your phone line has been busy."

As quickly as it had surfaced, the sense of familiarity receded into the background. *Where had that come from?* she thought; but out loud she said, "I disconnect it when I'm working in my studio and don't want to be bothered. I'm afraid I forgot to plug it back in when I went out to garden. But why has the FBI been trying to reach me?"

"It's not the FBI, ma'am, but the White House. The President wishes to talk with you."

"The President?" Now it was her turn to be confused. She flashed momentarily on the object in her kitchen. Could they know? She didn't know how, but if they did, whoever they might be, they surely wouldn't send an FBI agent to confront her. Nor could she imagine the White House being interested.

"What on earth would the President want with me? Are you sure you have the right Christina Bartlett?"

"I do, if you're the Christina Bartlett who graduated with honors from Stanford University with a doctorate in astrophysics—which, by the way, you never used professionally. Instead, for the past ten years you've been working as a potter and a musician. Your father was General Stewart Bartlett, U.S. Army, and your brother was Lee Bartlett, a Navy lieutenant killed in action when his fighter was shot down during the Gulf War ten years ago. Is this correct?"

"Yes." She had a sudden thought. "Do you have a file on me?"

"Everything I mentioned is simply in the public record. As far as I know, there is no file on you."

But I bet there will be now, she thought. Aloud, she said, "You have the right Bartlett, but as I said, I've no idea why."

"I couldn't say either, ma'am. All I know is that the President is waiting to speak with you right at this moment."

"Well, come on up to the house and I'll plug in the phone. Then we can both find out what this is about."

"Actually, Miss Bartlett, I've brought a special secure phone for you to use. I would have done that anyway, even if the White House had reached you earlier. They just wanted to alert you to the fact that I was coming."

"I see. In that case, get your phone. I'll go put some water on for coffee or tea, or get something cold ready for you and your partner there to drink."

"That's not necessary, ma'am," he said, starting to turn away. Then he paused and turned back, some inner conflict or puzzlement briefly showing in his eyes, which, she noticed, were a warm and inviting blue. Abruptly he grinned, his serious FBI persona set aside.

"Actually, something cold would be appreciated."

She grinned back. "OK, then. I'll get the ice cubes going."

She walked on to her house, going through the back door into the kitchen, where she set her basket of vegetables on the counter. Suddenly she realized she felt lighthearted and a little nervous, like a schoolgirl with her first crush.

How strange! she thought. *Surely I haven't been missing male companionship* that *much, that I'd flip for the first FBI agent who comes along!* She smiled. *He does have nice eyes, though.*

Then she remembered that there was nothing social about this visit, and pushed her sudden, strange feelings into the background as she concentrated on her tasks. She went to the pantry to fetch a handful of lemons. A sudden thought took her back outside, where she cut several sprigs from the mint growing under the kitchen window. She had just returned to the kitchen when the front doorbell rang.

"Come on in," she shouted, taking a knife down from its holder and cutting the lemons and the mint.

The front door opened, and a moment later the two FBI men walked into the kitchen. Agent Patrick was carrying a portable phone, and his partner had a black box under one arm.

"Make yourselves at home," she said. "I'm going to fix us some fresh mint lemonade."

"That sounds wonderful, ma'am," Patrick said, as he set the phone on the kitchen table. "By the way, this is my partner, Special Agent Matthews." The other man nodded at her.

"Miss Bartlett," he said by way of acknowledgment. Then he went to the kitchen phone, unplugged it from the wall, and plugged his black box in instead.

"Hi," she responded, then went back to making the lemonade, focusing on what she was doing in order to quiet her suddenly churning emotions. She was feeling apprehension, relief, bewilderment, excitement, and peacefulness all at once.

Why? she asked herself. *What's going on?* Then, as she reached up to a top shelf above a cupboard to take down a large pitcher, her eye caught one of the objects sitting on the shelf and she said inwardly, *Help me. Whatever is transpiring, let it reflect Your Will.*

The two agents were ignoring her, going about their business of setting up the secure phone line and testing it. Then, when all seemed in order, Special Agent Patrick turned to her and said, "We're ready to make the call, Miss Bartlett."

"Good." She handed them each a tall glass in which ice cubes tinkled like small bells. "So am I."

She took a sip of her drink while the connection was made. Then Matthews, who seemed to be acting as the technician, handed her the phone.

"Hello?" she said tentatively.

"One moment, please," said a man's voice at the other end. There was a silence, then the crisp, clipped tones of the President's voice sounded in her ear.

"Miss Bartlett?" Her voice sounded just as it did on television. "Thank you for responding to my call."

Did I have a choice? she asked herself. "It's a pleasure, Madame President."

"I'm sure you have many questions, foremost of which is why I'm calling you. The fact is, I don't know myself—at least, I don't know the reasons behind it."

"It's the aliens, isn't it?" she asked, struck by a sudden intuition so powerful that she knew it must be true.

There was silence on the other end for a moment. Then the President replied, "Either you are very perceptive, or very lucky, or you know something I need to know. Why did you say that?"

"I don't know. It just flashed into my mind."

"Ah, woman's intuition." There was a pause. "All right. I'll accept that. I've used that myself many a time on my way to this office. It can be damned useful. And you're right. It *is* the aliens."

There was a pause on the other end, then the President continued. "They contacted me three days ago. Not just me. All the world governments who have representatives at the UN. It seems they want to have a meeting, speak to the world, that sort of thing."

"That sounds like a good thing, Madame President. At least they're not invading us."

"Yes, I suppose it is, though it poses several challenges that have my advisors running around six ways from Sunday. I can only imagine what's happening in the other governments. In fact, I've been on the phone with so many world leaders in the past forty-eight hours that I don't have to imagine. I know." The President sighed. "And you're right, they're not invading us. They claim to be peaceful, but they do have a technology that is way ahead of ours, so we're taking no chances.

"The funny thing is, Miss Bartlett, that after speculating about alien contact for so many decades now, and after all the books and movies about warlike invaders or alien scientists coming to study us, no one ever thought that the first visitors from outer space would be monks!"

"Monks?" Puzzled, Christina had a momentary image of a space ship crewed by chimpanzees and gorillas. Then she realized just what the President had said. "You mean, someone who lives in a monastery?"

"Yes, that's what they say. Of course, something may have been lost in the translation, but they claim they are spiritual seekers who are exploring religious traditions and mystical practices throughout the galaxy."

"That's . . . amazing!" she said, her mind trying to grasp the concept.

"Yes. Yes, it is. And a number of my advisors do not believe them, though for myself, I see no reason not to do so. At any rate, in addition to the usual human representatives from science, governments, and so on, they also want to meet with religious and spiritual leaders from around the world."

"But what does that have to do with me?" she asked, though she was suddenly afraid she might know the answer.

To her relief, though, the President replied, "Well, that's where I can't help you. I don't know. You see, in addition to asking us to set up this public meeting, the aliens also asked if one of them could come to meet you, specifically, in your home."

"Me? Here? In my home?" She was so taken aback by this revelation that for a moment she could not think clearly. "When? Why?"

Stop it! she told herself. *I'm rambling like a crazy woman. Next thing, I'll be asking the President what I should wear! But then, this is crazy, isn't it? Aliens here, in my home?*

The President was speaking, and Christina forced her mind to concentrate. ". . . hoping you could tell me. I know you're not involved with SETI, but with your background in astrophysics, are you part of some private research project that deals with the search for extraterrestrial life or communication with outer space?" There was a pause. "My God! You're not one of those . . . you're not . . . what is it called . . . a channel?"

"A channel?"

The President sounded sheepish. "You know, one of those people who claim to talk to dead people and aliens."

Christina swallowed a chuckle. "Madame President, I assure you, I am not a channel, nor have I ever been in contact with aliens. Nor am I associated with any research projects, private or otherwise. I'm just what your people must have told you I am—an artist. Once I thought I wanted to be an astronaut . . . but things change."

"I see. Well, whatever the reason for it, the alien representative wants to see you as soon as possible—tonight, even, if you can arrange it."

"Tonight?" She looked around to see the state of her house, then she caught herself and began to chuckle.

"Miss Bartlett?" asked the President.

"I'm sorry, Madame President. It's just that I suddenly found myself looking around to see if my house was presentable—but then, how would an alien know if it were messy or not?"

The President laughed, a warm and friendly sound. "I like you, Miss Bartlett. I think you are my kind of woman. I'm going to enjoy meeting you tonight myself."

"You . . . tonight, Madame President?"

"Yes, I said I needed to come, too. I told them that you were my responsibility as President, and that it was my job to ensure your safety. I'm not sure they liked it or wanted it, or even believed me, but they agreed in the end. They seem to appreciate strong leadership and courage. Something about them reminds me more of warriors than monks. Very few of my advisors think it's a good idea. They want to send another observer, but this is one occasion I must see for myself. I want . . . no, I need to know what is going on."

Christina thought about the President coming to her home, a place where she had treasured her anonymity and her privacy for nearly a decade. She thought about aliens descending upon the valley and the effect it would have on her neighbors. She pictured hordes of Secret Service people, military people, aides of various kinds, all tramping about her yard, investigating her studio, invading her life. And she thought about the thing she guarded and treasured. She began to feel the dark, troubled spirit of her nightmare coming back upon her.

The President obviously had her own brand of intuition, for she said quietly, "Miss Bartlett, I know you're a private person. I don't know your reasons for living alone since your father died, but I'm sure they are good and sufficient, and I respect them. I can just imagine what you're thinking, but I assure you, I will come with a minimum of people. I can hardly do otherwise. The aliens themselves have requested that their meeting with you be very private and very discreet. I don't know why, but I agree with them. It would cause an international incident if it were discovered I was having a clandestine rendezvous with our visitors before the official meeting. So I assure you, this will be a very private meeting. We will come and go with minimum fuss, and no one will be the wiser."

"I appreciate that, Madame President. You're right, I was worrying about all the notoriety, not to mention all the bodies coming here to my small home. Thank you for your consideration. But I do have another question."

"If I can answer it, I will."

"What if I say no to this meeting?"

She could hear the President take a deep breath before saying in a quiet voice, "We have reason to believe that the aliens intend to give us certain technologies—which, as you can imagine, would be invaluable to humanity. Though they have not put it so bluntly, my advisors also believe that this generosity is, for whatever reason, contingent upon their meeting with you. Understand, therefore, I must do all in my power, short of letting you be harmed in any way, to bring this meeting about. The rewards are too incalculable to do otherwise."

"So you would force me to comply?"

"Miss Bartlett, you come from a military family. You know what it means to feel an obligation to your country and to fulfill it. Shall I appeal to your patriotism? This is one of those moments Kennedy talked about, when you must ask what you can do for your country . . . and," she added, "in this case, for humanity."

Christina smiled to herself. "I understand. Of course I'll do it. Besides, if you know my background, you know I once wanted to be an astronaut. The chance of meeting a visitor from the stars is something I've always dreamed of. I simply wanted to know just how far you were prepared to go."

"Miss Bartlett, you want to know how much I value one individual's freedom and well-being. Well, I value it a great deal. It is what I've based my entire political career upon. If you said no, I would use every skill and resource I have to persuade you otherwise, but, failing that, I'm not sure now what I would do. I'm glad you're not putting me to the test. I want to believe that I would respect your decision, and would tell the aliens that you had declined the visit. But, believe me, I want very much to be the President who made a peaceful first contact with alien visitors and brought new benefits to humanity. That's a powerful temptation. You're not the only one, Miss Bartlett, who has had dreams of the stars."

"I understand, Madame President. I will do whatever I can."

"Thank you, Miss Bartlett. I wish I could advise you further. Believe me, there are a host of men here who are itching to come out to your home and tell you what to do. One or two will come with me, but they have promised to keep their mouths shut, unless asked. For tonight, at least, you will be humanity's representative to an alien species. From our little talk, I believe you have the wisdom to handle whatever happens. And if you need it, you will have help on hand."

"Thank you for your confidence."

"All right. We've got a lot to do, and very little time in which to do it. I need to leave immediately if I'm to arrive on time. The meeting is set for eleven P.M. I will be there before then. Now, let me talk to Special Agent Patrick again."

Christina handed the phone to the FBI man. "The President wishes to talk with you," she said, as he took the receiver. As he listened intently, she turned and walked away into her living room.

In six hours, she thought, *the stars will come to visit me here! Who would have believed it? I gave up the stars for something greater, but perhaps the stars are being given back to me.*

Suddenly, the image of the pulsing blob popped into her mind, and she shuddered, shifting her gaze out the front window to two ancient oaks that grew in her front lawn.

"Give me the wisdom the President thinks I have," she prayed in a whisper, "and give me courage and strength, so I may carry out all my responsibilities successfully in the hours that are ahead."

The FBI agents left, saying they had to prepare things for the President's arrival later that evening. She assured them she would be all right, and stood on her front porch as they drove off. Then she went inside and began to prepare herself a light dinner. She was too excited to be hungry, but she knew she needed to eat something so her strength would not flag later.

She was sitting in her kitchen eating, the lights off as she looked through the window at the sun setting behind the rolling hills to the west, when she became aware of a glow suffusing the room. Involuntarily, she glanced up at the shelf that ran the length of the kitchen above the cupboards. Along it, various examples of her pottery stood like sentinels, but nothing seemed unusual there.

She realized the glow was coming through the open doorway into the living room beyond, but by the time she turned around, it was already fading. A sudden tingle of anticipation coursed through her, and she stood up.

Walking into the living room, she was not surprised when there came a knock at the door. She went to the door and opened it. Outside, on her porch, a tall figure stood. It was wearing a large overcoat that hung loosely about it, and a wide-brimmed hat was on its head, casting shadow over its features. For a moment, she thought she was being visited by the Shadow, a fictional detective with psychic powers whose adventures she had enjoyed as a teenager; then her breath caught as she looked more closely and realized that the round orange eyes with the black X at their centers had not evolved under the same sun as had her own.

Involuntarily, she stepped back.

The figure made no movement, but a surprisingly deep voice came from the shadow under the hat.

"May I come in, Christina Bartlett?"

"Of course," she said, stepping back still farther into her living room as a preternatural calm descended upon her. "You're early." *And the President will be very put out when she discovers it,* she thought amusedly.

The being seemed to float in, rather than walk. "We will still meet when your leader comes," it said, its tone seeming to reflect and share her amusement, as if the two of them shared a secret. "But we must have a private talk first, yes?"

"You can read my mind as well as speak my language?"

"Yes, but only a little bit. It is not easy. Reading your mind, that is. Your language is very easy. You can understand me all right, yes?"

"Yes, you speak English very well." The ordinariness of the conversation struck her as funny. *What about news from a galaxy far, far away?* she thought.

The being moved into the living room and floated—yes, she realized it was floating, about six inches above her floor—toward the kitchen. She hurried to intercept it.

"You must treat me as you would treat one of your neighbors," it said. "Invite me in, ask me to sit down, offer me coffee or tea, talk about the weather, yes? Very ordinary, yes?"

"Yes, if my neighbors ordinarily came from God knows how many light-years away," she replied. "I don't know how many alien worlds you have visited, but this is *not* ordinary for me." She reached the kitchen door and stood in it, blocking the alien's progress from the living room.

"But that is not really true, yes?" the being said. "You are very familiar with the not-ordinary. You are in touch with what is beyond the ordinary. Visiting other worlds is strange to you but ordinary to me. Yet, what you do is extraordinary to me."

"I'm sorry, but I don't understand you." Yet, even as she protested, part of her knew exactly what he was talking about.

"I am sorry if I am confusing you. But you are a Keeper, are you not? Surely you cannot be a Keeper and not know it?"

With a sudden thrill of fear that slashed through her calm

like lightning through a clear sky, she knew what the being was talking about. It was her secret, and it had been her father's secret before her, and would have been her brother's, had he lived. It was the secret that had been guarded by the men in her family for over seven hundred years. *That's why they're here!* she thought in horror. *They want to steal it!*

"No! No!" the alien suddenly shouted, as if sharing her horror. It stepped back from her, its thin, twiggy arms outstretched, two hands with six long fingers protruding from the loose sleeves of the overcoat. "No! You misunderstand! I would never take that which you guard! I am here to honor it and you. I simply wish to see it."

The alien's reaction was so genuine that the fear left her as quickly as it had come. *Of course!* she thought. *So many have sought it through the centuries. Why not some seekers from the stars? With the Sacred, all things are possible.*

"I'm sorry," she said softly. "I misunderstood and was afraid. Of course you can see it. But how did you know about it? How did you know about me?" She turned and walked into the kitchen, the alien floating behind her.

"We have a Keeper, too, on our ship. He knew. He had a dream that revealed it to him. Then he visited you in a dream. He discovered you and told us about you. That is why we came to your world, yes? That is why we tried to find you. Our Keeper knew your name and something about your past, about the other Keepers who preceded you. We knew from his dream the land you were in. But we did not know how to find you. So, we simply told your President what we knew, and told her she had to find you and set up a meeting between us, yes? It is very important. We have offered in return certain of our knowledge that may help your planet and prepare it for others who may come later."

"Your Keeper," she said, remembering the blob she had seen in her dream. "He is different from you, isn't he?"

The alien laughed, and the sound was startlingly deep and

rhythmic, like great bass drums being played in a marching band. "He will laugh when I tell him how you saw him in your dream. He is different, yes, but he is not a 'blob.' "

"Well, I can't apologize for my dreams." She picked up a chair and took it over to put it under the cupboards. She suddenly remembered what the alien had said and turned back to him. "You said I should ask you to sit down and offer you coffee or tea. Were you serious? I'm happy to fix you anything you want."

The alien laughed again. "No, Christina Bartlett. I cannot sit down. See." And it opened its overcoat, revealing a stick-thin, sharp, angular body supporting an overlarge head. Immediately, she thought of the shadowy figures she had glimpsed in her nightmare. Then she saw that the angles and sharpness were not part of its body but were some kind of frame or exoskeleton it was wearing.

"Your gravity is much more than I am used to," it explained, covering itself up, "so this device I wear compensates and makes me light. It is one of the things we would give to you. And I cannot drink your beverages. They would harm me."

"So, why did you ask me for them?"

The being sighed, a very human sound. "I was making—what do you call it?—tiny speech?"

"Small talk?"

"Yes, small talk. To make you comfortable. And, to be truthful, to make me comfortable, yes? Being around a Keeper always makes me inwardly turbulent."

Christina laughed. "Being a Keeper sometimes makes me nervous." She stood on the chair and reached up. From the high shelf, she reverently and carefully took down a small, plain cup from the midst of other cups and goblets that she had made in her pottery studio. She got down and took it over to the alien.

"In our legends this is called by many names, and it has had different shapes, but for two thousand years, it has looked like this and has been known as the Grail. Would you like to hold it?" She held it out to him.

The alien reached out with his long fingers and touched the cup. It seemed to glow under his caress, but he made no effort to take it from her.

"Ah," the being said, "I do not know its story, but I feel the universe around and in it. And it is happy with you, yes? It sings. That is what I wanted to know. That is what our Keeper wanted to know." He looked up at her, his strange cross-like pupils widening. "You have kept it well."

"Thank you. A lot of the time I believe it keeps me! Also, I think at times my forebears are turning over in their graves at how I have kept it, as you say, but different times require different approaches." She set the Grail down on the table, next to her dinner dishes.

"It is a very precious thing. I can see that. How did it come to you?"

"I inherited it. It was to have gone to my brother, but he died." She sighed and sat down. "It's a long story, but basically, the Grail was protected, along with other sacred relics, by a military and spiritual order known as the Order of the Temple of Jerusalem, or more commonly as the Knights Templar. They were Keepers, but they made enemies because of the secrets they possessed and the wealth they managed. One of these enemies happened to be the king of the country they were in, which was not a good situation for them. He destroyed their Order, arresting hundreds of their members in an attempt to seize their wealth and sacred relics."

She got up. "You may not drink tea, but I do, and I'm going to make myself a cup, if you don't mind. . . ." The alien nodded.

She began gathering the tea fixings. "Anyway, legend has it that a fleet of Templar ships escaped with many of these relics aboard, but no one knows what happened to them. Except for one, the one that bore the Holy Grail.

"That one was shipwrecked near the coast of a country called England. As it happened, my ancestor had a vision, so family legend says, to go to the beach—and knowing how the

Grail works, I can believe it—where he found one of the Templars dying of his injuries but clutching an ornate box containing this cup. When he saw my ancestor, he had some kind of revelation that he was to give the Grail to him, which he did, making him swear many oaths. He also gave him his Templar cross and in some way initiated him into that Order, though not as a celibate priest. Otherwise, I wouldn't be here."

She smiled and brought her steaming cup of tea back to the table. "Since then, the Grail has been passed down from father to son in my family for nearly seven hundred years, until me. My only brother, who would have become the Keeper, died in a war. That left only me to carry on the tradition, the first woman to do so."

She sipped her tea, remembering. "The Grail did not come to me by default, though. It had been talking to me in dreams and visions all the time I was growing up. Sometimes I saw it as a cup, sometimes as a beautiful, radiant Lady, and sometimes as a fiery youth. I knew I was to be the next Keeper even when I was a teenager."

"A remarkable story! But given its power and value, I am amazed you keep this cup out so openly. Should it not be hidden away and protected? Are you not afraid it might be harmed or stolen, displayed so openly?"

She laughed. "Who would recognize it? As you can see, in its present form, it's just a plain cup, much as a beginner at pottery might make. So I put it in plain view and surrounded it with other cups I made. Who would ever suspect that the Holy Grail sat openly on a shelf in a kitchen among other cups and pots and dishes? So it's there for those who can see it, but it's truly hidden from those who are expecting something else."

She finished her tea and put the cup down. "My father and all his ancestors before him believed that the Grail should be hidden away, so that no one could steal it or harm it. My father even kept his possession of the Grail a secret from me because I was a woman, and I kept my attunement to the Grail a secret from him. This secret caused us much pain, and, I think, it may have contributed to his death.

"So when I moved here a year after he died, I promised myself no more secrets. I took the Grail from its hiding place and put it out in the open. I felt that it was never meant to be hidden away. In fact, by making it a secret, I believe the Templars brought their own doom upon themselves, for those in power detest those who have secrets they do not themselves possess.

"But those were different times, so who am I to judge? Still, I felt now was the time to bring the Grail out into the open, to let it feel the sun and breathe the air and to let its radiance flow freely into the world. I put it in my kitchen because it is such an everyday place, an ordinary place, and it's time for the spirit of the Grail to be part of our everyday lives again. Actually, it's a step toward a time when everyone will know where the Grail is, but, at that time, we will know it is not a cup but a spirit in our hearts."

The alien was silent as she finished her tea. Then it said, "Do you use it?"

"Use it?" She laughed. "I assume you don't mean do I drink tea in it? Yes, I use it—or rather, we use each other. When needs arise in our world, there is an energy that flows to bring aid. Sometimes I initiate it, sometimes it does, and sometimes we both serve a higher power."

The alien nodded in understanding. "Keeper, we also are a spiritual order, one that includes beings from several worlds, and one of our tasks is also to protect sacred relics, yes? And to use them in service. Or to be used by them, as you said. However, the government that rules most of the planets from which we all come has decided that it, too, wants our wealth and our relics. It sees them as objects of power that it could use on its own behalf." What sounded like a very human sigh came from the shadows masking its face. "Like your Templars, we were attacked, but many of us fled to the stars in ships like the one that brought us here."

The being began to float about the room, as if pacing. "We have one relic on board our ship that is very precious. It is like your Grail. We think of it as a shard from the One Who Made Us All. It is a musical instrument once used by a Peacemaker to bring all the warring worlds together and create the civilization we now have.

"Unfortunately, a faction has seized the government of our collection of worlds. You would say it wishes to feed on power, yes? It is not favored by most people, so it will not last unless it can show that it possesses the sacred relics, including most particularly the instrument of the Peacemaker. To prevent this, we fled, as I have said."

"Just like the Templar fleet," she whispered.

"Yes. But our Keeper says that we will soon be found and overtaken. If so, our pursuers will surely find this relic and seize it. That is why we have come to you."

"To me? But what can I do?"

"Why, you are a Keeper. You can keep our relic for us until a time when we can reclaim it."

Her mind whirled. "You mean, you want to leave it here with me?"

"That is what our Keeper proposed. It came to him in a dream in which he was shown your face as a fellow Keeper. He has had many dreams since then that helped us find you. At first, many argued against him. How could we protect this relic if we let it go? But he said our enemies would think this, too. They would not believe we would leave the most precious object on all our worlds in the hands of what, you will excuse me for saying so, is a backward and undeveloped civilization, yes? I hope I give no offense?"

"No, none taken, at least not by me."

"I must confess, I was one of those who argued against his idea, which I think is why he sent me to meet you. But having met you and seen how you keep your Grail, I understand what our Keeper is saying. That which is in the open is often the most difficult to find, especially by those whose minds thrive by possessing secrets."

"What an astonishing day." She got up, too excited and restless to continue sitting, and began to pace. "First I am told that the President of the United States wishes to talk with me, then I am told aliens have asked to visit me, and now I'm told these same aliens want me to take care of their equivalent of our Holy Grail! What more can happen today?"

"You will do it?"

"What if I say no?"

"Why, then we will give our gifts to your world as a gesture of friendship, and we will depart. We cannot force a Keeper to Keep, yes? But you are the only Keeper we have found or are likely to find before we are discovered."

She turned away from him and looked at the Grail, still sitting on her kitchen table. It seemed so small and nondescript, yet she knew it was only a portal between this world and a larger realm of spirit. It was a living thing, not really an object at all, but the barest fragment of a Being whose love encompassed the world.

Looking back, she said, "It may not be either my decision or your Keeper's. If your relic is like mine, it chooses its own way. It picks its Keepers. I may agree, but I cannot speak for your holy thing."

"I understand, but our Keeper feels you are the one to guard it, so I would assume it has already spoken to him."

She nodded. "So what do we do now? Do you have the relic with you?"

"No, we thought that too dangerous until we could meet you and truly see what kind of Keeper you are. Now, I am satisfied you are the one, yes? The next step is for you to meet our Keeper."

"Do you mean I must travel to your ship?"

"No, Christina Bartlett, that is not necessary at this time. I have a device that will set up a link between you and our Keeper, so that you may see and talk to each other."

"Like on television?"

"No, more direct. It is a telepathic link. It will be for you as if you are on our ship. Then, when he is satisfied, we will teleport the relic to you here." The alien looked around. "There is one question I have, though. Where is your partner?"

"My partner? What do you mean?"

"Your, how do you put it, your mate, your life-joining? Our Keeper said you would have a partner."

Oh Lady! she breathed silently. *Now what do you have up your sleeve? Please, no more surprises!*

To her visitor, she said, "I don't have a partner. I live alone here. Your Keeper must be mistaken."

Except for its eyes, she could not see the alien's face, and probably couldn't have read any emotions from it if she did, but it seemed bewildered to her.

"I do not know. It is something to ask him about. But he was so certain, and he is rarely wrong."

"Well, even Keepers are wrong sometime," she said wryly. "I know from experience."

The being seemed to shrug. "All right. I have a device that is linked to the Keeper's mind. I will point it at you and it will project a link into your mind and body. It will not hurt. Are you prepared?"

"Yes. As much as I ever will be, I suppose!"

From deep within its overcoat, her visitor pulled out a tube that was curved on one end and bulbous on the other, looking like a cartoon blaster she had once seen in a drawing. It pointed it at her.

Suddenly, the world exploded into light and sound and motion.

The sound was that of her kitchen door bursting open, slamming against the wall. A voice, a human voice, cried out, "Down! Down, Christina! Down!"

Everything seemed to shift into slow motion as she turned toward the sound of the voice. She saw motion by the door, a black figure flying into the room, landing and rolling, coming up, an object in its hand.

A gun.

Abruptly, her mind shifted and she flashed on a scene from *The Day the Earth Stood Still,* an old science fiction movie that had been a favorite while she was growing up—a scene in which an alien visitor, come to present a gift to the President, was shot as he pulled the object from a pocket. She realized in an instant what was happening, and she screamed, "No! Don't shoot!"

But it was too late. Light flashed twice. There was a sound like twinned thunder. There was a cry.

And everything speeded up again.

She saw Special Agent Patrick kneeling on her kitchen floor, dressed in a black, skintight suit, pulling a black mask from his face, a gun in his hand. She looked where the gun was pointing. On the other side of the table, the alien lay prostrate on the floor with a red stain on the front of its overcoat that looked very human in its implications. Its hat had flown off, and she saw a large, round, bare head, with large eyes—now closed in pain or death—and that was all. No nose. No mouth. Nothing.

And on the ground by its feet lay the tube. The connection to the alien Keeper. Broken in two.

A feeling of horror and grief washed over her, and she felt faint. She grabbed the edge of her kitchen counter to keep from collapsing. Then, fury ran like fire through her body, bringing a tsunami of adrenaline with it, and she whirled upon the FBI man, angry words springing to her lips.

They were never spoken.

At that same moment, the Grail began to glow, filling the room with a radiance that turned everything soft and dream-like, as if the hard edges of reality had melted. There was a deep sound that she could not identify but that pulsed through every part of her, striking her dumb.

As she watched, the FBI man changed. His dark stealth outfit faded away, to be replaced with a brown tunic and trousers, overlaid with chain mail and a long surcoat of white on which shone the Templar cross in blazing red.

She then looked down at herself and saw that she was similarly garbed.

Movement caught her eye and she raised her head. Agent Patrick was moving wonderingly toward the Grail, which shone like a small star on the kitchen table. She tried to move as well, but she couldn't. She could only watch as he reached out to touch the radiant cup, then fell to his knees, his head bowed, saying simply, "At last!"

He stayed that way for a moment in adoration of the mystery before him, then he looked up at her. As their eyes met, she saw their future together: long life, children, and a strange and wondrous work as Keepers together, for this man, she knew in that instant, was her partner, her "life-joining," as the alien had called it. And she knew he saw it as well.

The Voice came, entwining both of them in remembrance and grace. *"Templars once, Guardians now, partners always. Blessings."*

Then, beyond the table, she saw that the alien was slowly getting to its feet, its eyes bright and wide with what she knew was wonder. The blood on its overcoat was gone. Whatever damage it had suffered, wherever its soul had been prepared to go, it was now healed.

The glow intensified. Before them, in the middle of the room, a shape appeared, and she realized it was the other Keeper, the one whom she had seen in her dreams. But the alien was right. It was not a blob. If anything, it looked like a ball of fur, a hedgehog rolled up tight, but as beautiful and natural as anything she had ever seen.

Then its intelligence touched hers and Patrick's, and she was transported by its clarity and depth into a new place within herself, a place of seemingly infinite spaciousness.

What passed among the three of them at that moment she was never able to put in words, but she knew that they were forever joined in a kinship that no one planet could circumscribe. And into her mind flowed knowledge and information that she realized would take the rest of her life to decipher and unpack.

The alien Keeper faded away, yet still they all were held in a stasis of wonderment and mystery, for a heartbeat later another glow joined that of the Grail upon the table. It was a shining circle, a round tube with holes spaced along its surface.

No sooner had it appeared upon the table than its light and that of the Grail merged into each other with a brightness that forced all of them to look away. She fell to her knees with a cry that was part awe, part fear, part joy. The floor seemed to disappear, and she was suspended in deepest space, looking out upon the galaxy, knowing that what she was seeing, Jonathan—*my partner, my beloved*—and her alien friend were seeing as well.

What she saw was a figure of light, spanning the galaxy, its life touching millions of worlds—and everywhere it touched, there was a Grail. A universe of Grails shining more brightly than the stars, all reaching toward one another, all seeking to touch and become one. And where they had touched, this figure sprang into being at least a little bit.

Then she heard the Voice again. *"You are called to begin a new Order, a new lineage. You are called to serve an inner temple that lives in all things, whatever their shape, wherever their world. You are called as Keepers and Mediators not only of the Grail of your world, but the Grail of the cosmos, in which all life will discover a new unity and give birth to the Light which I represent."* Simultaneously, the Templar apparel that she and Patrick wore was transformed, supplanted by simple trousers and a tunic on which was emblazoned a circle surrounding the spiral swirl of the galaxy.

She bowed her head before the enormity of the vision and closed her eyes. When she opened them a moment later, the glow was gone, and her kitchen was back to normal. Except that the alien relic was gone and the cup of the Grail now had a handle, looking for all the world like a coffee mug. Deep within, she felt more than heard a rich and cosmic chuckle.

A coffee mug? she thought. *Well, why not? It's certainly a symbol of friendship and getting together. Who would suspect it was the new Grail?*

And she began to giggle, and then to laugh. As she did so, her two companions began to laugh as well. Over and over they howled, the laughter releasing their tension, bringing them back to earth, bringing them closer to one another.

And when the spasm was over and they lay on the floor or floated in air, spent and happy with the wonder of what had happened, Agent Patrick looked at the alien and said, "I'm sorry I shot you. The President asked me to keep guard on Christina because she doesn't trust you, I'm afraid. And when I saw you pull that thing, and it looked like you were going to blast her with some ray gun or something, I just reacted. I felt I had to protect her at all costs."

"You needn't explain," the alien replied. "I understand. Though you didn't realize it, you were protecting your partner and your Keeper. You could not have done otherwise."

Christina sprang to her feet. "Oh, good gracious!" she said. "The President! She'll be here in an hour. What are we going to do?"

Agent Patrick, glancing at his wristwatch, said, "It may seem like forever, but only a few minutes have passed since I jumped in here. I'm supposed to radio the Secret Service every twenty minutes to let them know if all is well. My next check-in is just about due. I'll go and give them the OK." He started to leave the room, then turned to Christina and added, "But I won't be far." He took her hand and kissed it. "I'll never be far again."

"I know." She smiled at him. "Go make your report."

With that he left. She turned to the alien. "But what about me? By involving me with the President, you've involved me with national affairs. The President now wonders who I am and why you have singled me out. My anonymity is compromised and probably lost. I'm no longer ordinary in the eyes of my government, and my ordinariness was my protection."

"We thought of that, but we did not know how else to find you quickly, for we dare not stay around your planet any longer than necessary lest we make our pursuers suspicious. However, at this moment, two of my companions are just meeting your President at the spot where they agreed to rendezvous. They will come here as arranged and they will speak to you about inconsequential things, about your life, your work, your country, yes? Then your President will be informed that our meeting with you was simply to talk to an ordinary citizen, and that we had chosen you randomly using our own methods. We will also let her know that she has passed a test of her integrity as a leader, for if she had tried to manipulate or control you, we would have known it and would have used that as a reason not to share our technology. She will also be told that other teams from our ship are visiting other ordinary citizens around the world—which is true, for even now as we speak, my companions are setting this up."

"So, having singled me out, you will now make me part of a . . . a random test group."

"That is correct. Your President will accept what we say, for even if she suspects something else is involved, she will have no way of proving it, yes? And we will insist that all those citizens whom we contact be kept anonymous for their own protection. It is not a perfect solution, but we feel it will allow you in time to settle back into the privacy and ordinariness you require."

She thought about it. Knowing the craziness that could occur in government circles, she was not sure it would work.

But then, she realized, so many miracles and wonders had already occurred today, what was one more to add to the list? After all, if the Keepers were to protect the Grail, surely in this instance the Grail would protect the Keepers?

Her visitor intruded on her thoughts. "I must go now. I have much to contemplate and much to report. I am filled with much wonder, yes? I must take time now to empty."

"How do you get back? Do you have transport nearby?"

"The Keeper is very powerful in manipulating time and space. He will teleport me back to our ship, even as he teleported our Grail to you."

"You mean, you're going to beam up?" She giggled. "I think I'm going to call your Keeper 'Scotty'!"

She saw puzzlement in the alien's eyes. "Scotty? I do not understand. Is that a good thing?"

"Oh, yes!" she said with a grin. "That is a very good thing!"

"Then I will say good-bye now, Keeper. I go knowing that one day we will meet again." He began to glow softly; then, with a pop of inrushing air to the spot where he had stood, he was gone.

Christina Bartlett stood for a while, her mind wandering out to where a ship of alien monks floated in orbit about the world. Then she heard Agent Patrick—*Jonathan*—speaking into his phone, assuring the Secret Service that everything was still quiet and well.

With that she sprang into action, first putting the Grail with its graceful new handle back into its place on the high shelf, then getting out her finest china cups and saucers. She carried them into the dining room and laid them out on the table, but, looking them over, she shook her head, gathered them all up again, and returned them to their cupboard in the kitchen.

Then she took down a set of her own hand-thrown mugs and a pot and took those to the dining room instead.

After all, she thought, *the President is coming, and I want her to have the best.*

Epilogue

Are the Templars still among us? In many respects, one would like to think so. From monkish Military Order (and more, perhaps) to international banking institution to kick-ass medieval police force (perhaps on other roads besides the pilgrim ways at Jerusalem)—whatever their full nature, the Knights Templar became and remain a potent symbol of mystical guardianship and protection, and have found an enduring place in the mist-veiled corners of our Western mythos. Perhaps we shall never know the full extent of what they were and what they became.

But we can speculate . . . which is what the world of fantasy is all about. Readers hungry for further food for speculation may wish to avail themselves of the books in the partial bibliography that follows—and to dream their own dreams about the Knights Templar. . . .

—Katherine Kurtz

Partial Templar Bibliography

Baigent, Michael, and Richard Leigh. *The Temple and the Lodge.* London: Jonathan Cape, 1989.

Barber, Malcolm. *The Trial of the Templars.* Cambridge, England: Cambridge University Press, 1978.

Barber, Malcolm. *The New Knighthood.* Cambridge, England: Cambridge University Press, 1994.

Burman, Edward. *The Templars: Knights of God.* Wellingborough, England: Aquarian Press, 1986.

Hancock, Graham. *The Sign and the Seal: A Quest for the Lost Ark of the Covenant.* London: William Heinemann Ltd., 1992.

Knight, Christopher, and Robert Lomas. *The Second Messiah: Templars, the Turin Shroud, and the Great Secret of Freemasonry.* London: Century Books, 1997.

Kurtz, Katherine, ed. *Tales of the Knights Templar.* New York: Warner, 1995.

Partner, Peter. *The Murdered Magicians.* [Also published as *The Knights Templar and Their Myth.*] Oxford, England: Oxford University Press, 1981.

Robinson, John J. *Born in Blood.* New York: M. Evans, 1989.

Robinson, John J. *Dungeon, Fire, and Sword.* New York: M. Evans, 1991.

Simon, Edith. *The Piebald Standard: A Biography of the Knights Templar.* Boston: Little, Brown, 1959.

Upton-Ward, J. M. *The Rule of the Templars.* (Translated from the French of Henri de Curzon's 1886 edition of the French Rule, derived from the three extant medieval manuscripts.) New York: Boydell Press, 1992.

About the Authors

Debra Doyle was born in Florida and educated in Florida, Texas, Arkansas, and Pennsylvania—the last at the University of Pennsylvania, where she earned her doctorate in English literature, concentrating on Old English poetry. While living and studying in Philadelphia, she met and married her collaborator, James D. Macdonald, and subsequently traveled with him to Virginia, California, and the Republic of Panamá. Various children, cats, and computers joined the household along the way.

James Douglas Macdonald was born in White Plains, New York, on February 22, 1954, the second of three children of W. Douglas Macdonald, a chemical engineer, and Margaret E. Macdonald, a professional artist. After leaving the University of Rochester, where he majored in medieval studies, he served in the U.S. Navy. From 1991 through 1993, as Yog Sysop, he ran the Science Fiction and Fantasy RoundTable on the GEnie computer network; these days—once again as Yog Sysop—he manages SFF-Net on the Internet/World Wide Web.

Doyle and Macdonald left the Navy and Panamá in 1988 in order to pursue writing full-time. They now live—still with various children, cats, and computers—in a big nineteenth-century house in Colebrook, New Hampshire, where they write science fiction and fantasy for children, teenagers, and adults.

Diane Duane was born in Manhattan in 1952. She spent her childhood and adolescence on Long Island, her early adulthood back in Manhattan again, and her later adulthood in Los Angeles, Philadelphia, and (rather to her surprise) Ireland, where she now lives, married to fellow writer Peter Morwood.

She began writing professionally in 1980, both novels and screenplays, and is presently working on her twenty-eighth novel, along with various projects for television. The rest of her time she spends feeding cats, and being grateful that her husband can feed himself.

Deborah Turner Harris was raised in Florida and earned a doctorate in English literature from Florida State University. Author of the Mages of Garillon and Caledon trilogies, she has also collaborated with Katherine Kurtz on the Adept series of novels; the pair are presently at work on another novel involving the Knights Templar, entitled *The Temple and the Stone*. At home in St. Andrews, Scotland, where she lives with her husband, Robert, and their three sons, she plays the guitar and Celtic harp and enjoys riding.

Robert J. Harris has, in his time, been a classics scholar and a bartender, but is perhaps best known as the inventor of the world's best-selling fantasy board game, *Talisman*. His hobbies include gaming, fencing, and always backing the losing team in the Super Bowl.

Alexandra Elizabeth Honigsberg is known for her darkly numinous, romantic-gothic poetry and fiction. Anthologies such as White Wolf's Dark Destiny series, *Dante's Disciples,* and *Pawn of Chaos,* as well as *New Altars, Blood Muse,* and *Angels of Darkness,* are its typical literary homes. She is a professional musician and a scholar of comparative religions, and lives with her husband and cats in Upper Manhattan, land of forests, fjords, and the Unicorn Tapestries.

David M. Honigsberg lives, works, and writes in New York City. His short stories have appeared in numerous anthologies, including *Elric: Tales of the White Wolf* and *Magic: The Gathering: Tapestries*. He has also written the *Chaosworld Campaign Book* for Hero Games, in collaboration with Michael A. Stackpole, and a role-playing supplement for Atlas Games that incorporates aspects of Kabbalah into the *Ars Magica* role-playing system. A guitarist and songwriter, he has performed on stages from New York to Seattle both as a solo artist and with the Don't Quit Your Day Job Players. Lastly, David is enrolled in the Modern Rabbi program at the New Seminary in New York City and hopes to be ordained sometime in 1998.

Katherine Kurtz is the author of more than a score of mostly fantasy novels, including the well-known Deryni Chronicles, the Adept series (coauthored with Deborah Turner Harris), and several stand-alone novels, not to mention the occasional short story. Born during a hurricane in southern Florida, and educated at the University of Miami and UCLA, she has made her home for the last decade in County Wicklow, Ireland, in a Gothic Revival house that she shares with husband, Scott, son Cameron, four cats, and at least two resident ghosts.

Andre Norton published her first novel in 1934, her first science fiction novel in the early 1950s, and has more than 150 books to her credit, in a distinguished career that spans more than half a century and is still going strong. Born in Cleveland, Ohio, of a family that came to the United States in 1634, she had intended to teach history, but while still in high school got sidetracked into writing instead—and, in doing so, became a part of the reading history of probably everyone reading this anthology. A background of twenty-two years as a librarian, coupled with her astounding success in the field of fantasy and science fiction, has given her both the background and determination to establish a specialty library and retreat center in Murfreesboro, Tennessee, for the use of genre writers of fantasy and science fiction.

Robert Reginald was born at Fukuoka, Kyushu, Japan, and spent his idle youth living in Izmir, Turkey, and other such places. His first book, *Stella Nova*, which was also the first who's who of science fiction and fantasy literature, was published in 1970; his ninetieth volume, *Codex Derynianus* (with Katherine Kurtz), appeared in 1997. He lives with his wife and friend and frequent collaborator, Mary, and their ever-changing menagerie (presently two dogs, one cat) in an old, two-story house in San Bernardino, California. In his spare time, he writes.

Bradley H. Sinor was born and raised in Oklahoma. He still lives there, with his wife, Sue, three weird cats, and an odd number of computers. His short stories have appeared in a number of anthologies such as the Merovingen Nights series, *Time of the Vampires, A Horror a Day,* and *Roger's Friends.* A few years ago he encountered a friend who he had not seen in some time. The friend asked if Brad was still writing. Sue replied, "Brad still has a pulse, he's still writing."

David Spangler is a writer and educator whose work deals with the Western Mystery tradition and personal and cultural transformation. A former codirector and spokesperson for the Findhorn Foundation community in northern Scotland (1970–3), he has also designed and taught classes in future studies for the University of Wisconsin in Milwaukee, and in 1990 began designing and teaching classes on-line using computer telecommunications. He has also worked as a professional designer of both science fiction and fantasy board games and computer games. David's books include *Reimagination of the World,* coauthored with cultural historian William Irwin Thompson, *Everyday Miracles, A Pilgrim in Aquarius,* and *The Call.* His first short story, "An Adventure of the Grail," appeared in *Within the Hollow Hills,* an anthology of new Celtic writing edited by John Matthews.

Julie Spangler is a human-relations counselor and teacher, a homemaker and mom. An avid science fiction and fantasy fan, her collaboration on "Keepers" represents her first foray into professional storytelling and writing. The Spanglers live near Seattle, Washington, with two sons, two daughters, and a ferret named Pixie.

Richard J. Woods was born and reared in New Mexico, works in Chicago, where he is on the graduate faculty of Loyola University, tutors and lectures at Blackfriars Hall, Oxford University, and revives in Ireland. A Dominican friar with a particular interest in Meister Eckhart and the medieval mystics, he has published eight original nonfiction books, edited three anthologies, and authored a number of articles in spirituality, sexuality, and Celtic studies. He dabbles in watercolors, makes Celtic harps, sometimes fiddles, and sings in chapel and the shower. Close friends include two elderly cats and one young dog who still tolerates his efforts in art and music.